Red Clark Rides Alone

Center Point
Large Print

Also by Gordon Young and available from
Center Point Large Print:

Fighting Blood
Red Clark o' Tulluco

**This Large Print Book carries the
Seal of Approval of N.A.V.H.**

Red Clark Rides Alone

GORDON YOUNG

CENTER POINT LARGE PRINT
THORNDIKE, MAINE

This Center Point Large Print edition
is published in the year 2018 by arrangement with
Golden West Literary Agency.

First US edition: Doubleday, Doran

The text of this Large Print edition is unabridged.
In other aspects, this book may vary
from the original edition.
Printed in the United States of America
on permanent paper.
Set in 16-point Times New Roman type.

ISBN: 978-1-68324-726-5 (hardcover)
ISBN: 978-1-68324-730-2 (paperback)

Library of Congress Cataloging-in-Publication Data

Names: Young, Gordon, 1886-1948, author.
Title: Red Clark rides alone / Gordon Young.
Description: Center Point Large Print edition. | Thorndike, Maine :
    Center Point Large Print, 2018.
Identifiers: LCCN 2017056285| ISBN 9781683247265
    (hardcover : alk. paper) | ISBN 9781683247302 (pbk. : alk. paper)
Subjects: LCSH: Large type books. | GSAFD: Western stories.
Classification: LCC PS3547.O4756 R435 2018 | DDC 813/.6—dc23
LC record available at https://lccn.loc.gov/2017056285

TO
LYNA

Who, if she had not been born a girl,
would have been a cowboy.

CONTENTS

Red Clark Rides Alone

CHAPTER I

SINGIN' IN A COWTOWN JAIL

Unmusical sound came from the calaboose. A plaintive high-pitched wail about a certain unnamed maiden who appeared to have slightly violent views on courtship:

> "An' she said, 'Sir, if you jus' dare
> To put yore hand on my yaller hair,
> I'll kick you plum' right in the snoot,
> F'r I'm a lady, you dang galoot!'
> Oo—oo—toot-toot—yip-ee-eye—oh!"

A young gentle-faced Mexican, with his broken straw-bottomed chair propped back against the sunny side of the adobe wall, stirred in his dozing, cocked an ear, waggled his head in sorrow, and looked pained. Tony, being musical, knew how song ought to sound.

He hooked his heels over the bottom rung of the chair, felt about with the back of his head for a soft spot on the wall, brought down the brim of his wide hat over his face.

The song went on and on. An uncountable number of stanzas dealing with the remarks and antics of the unnamed maiden were clearly

11

remembered by the young redheaded cowboy who, contrary to the usual custom of Tahzo, had been locked overnight in the calaboose.

For one reason, he was a stranger, so there were no friends to whom he could have been turned over. And it wouldn't have done to let him roam about by himself longer. Both the marshal and the sheriff had had to argue with him at some length. They did it with unusual gentleness for them. Nobody had lost his temper. The sheriff and the marshal had shown much tolerance. The grinning redhead had cut many capers that amused some people and annoyed others, but he had good manners and hadn't really busted proper cow-town etiquette until, with great obstinacy though entire good nature, he had tried to take his horse upstairs to bed with him over at the hotel.

So he had been taken to the calaboose to sleep it off. He slept well, and, having awakened shortly after noon, was plaintively recalling, at the top of his voice, the sad experiences of a gallant puncher with the unnamed yellow-haired lady.

The gentle-faced Tony was irritated. He arose with purposeful air, straightened his hat, and put his face against the iron bars of a small window. Tony swore beseechingly in rippling Spanish.

To Tony's surprise, Spanish words came back at him, unmusical but fluent and good-natured. "Glad to see you," said the redhead. "Sorta lonesome here."

"*Señor*, it is the hour of the siesta!" said Tony, with all the expostulation of one gentleman appealing to another.

"Fine. Just you curl up and I'll sing you to sleep."

"*Por Dios*! It is why I cannot sleep! The noise you make—!"

"I ain't wept f'r a long time over folks not likin' my singin'. Most folks are egotistic-like. They sing to please other folks. Me, to comfort myself. When do I get outa here?"

Tony shook his head, denying all knowledge of the future.

Redhead grinned and mused. "I couldn't have done anything much wrong. Didn't have money enough. An' give my guns to some owl-eyed bartender, somewhere along the line. My instinks are all peac'ble. What'd I do besides sing, h'm?"

Tony too grinned, then put up his hands in amazement and rolled his eyes, shaking his head. He couldn't begin to tell it all. Tony's smile had much pardon and some admiration. This redhead was the maddest of all gringoes, none of whom are quite sane. Even the hard old sheriff of Tahzo had bottled up official wrath and gazed with interest and not entire disapproval at the drunken young devil, now under lock and key.

"I insult some ladies?" asked Redhead cautiously.

"No, no, *señor*. But you are skillful with the *reata*!"

"Yeah? So that's it, h'm? I do some monkey-shines with a rope?"

"*Sí, señor.* Much monkeyshine."

"Who'd I rope?"

"The padre, *señor*!"

"No! Gosh, I must-a been pie-eyed." Redhead meditated, scratched an ear, shook his head. "Wonder why I done that?" He looked inquiringly, but Tony said nothing. Then, with threatening air: "Want me to sing some more?"

"No, no, please, no!"

"Then help me get outa here!"

"But ah, *señor*! I am helpless!"

"Well, I ain't! It's hot in here and stuffy. Lonesome too. I'll just show you why I been singin' so loud!"

"*Señor*!" Tony shouted, anxious and protesting as he saw what was coming.

Redhead crossed to the opposite window, and, with what seemed to Tony amazing strength, jerked two of those bars free at the lower ends, bent them upwards, and began to wriggle through.

The calaboose was old. It had been built years before for some obscure reason connected with an excuse for spending ten times as much money as it ought to have cost.

Redhead, with the bail taken from a bucket, had amused himself in loosening the adobe under the bars of the window, and now squirmed on his belly, half in, half out, going through.

Tony ran round the calaboose, invoking saints.

Redhead, having come through head first, arose from the ground and dusted his clothes with his hat.

Tony did not know what to do. The few prisoners that the sheriff really wanted to keep for future use were snapped into handcuffs, with a deputy sitting by, not in the calaboose but in the sheriff's back office. Those stowed away in the calaboose were usually permitted to sleep it off and go; or, if they had any money left over, go back up town and get drunk again.

Tony was young, gentle, and did not carry a gun. He lived rent free at the calaboose and was therefore the jailor, but didn't have the key. He looked at Red in puzzled displeasure.

"Here," said Redhead, holding out his hat, one that had once been very fine, much used, still not frayed. "Brush me off at the back, please."

Tony could not refuse such a courteous request, but he bargained. "Please, *señor*, you will not run away?"

"Me? *Run!* Hell. 'Sall I can do to walk. I want to wash my face an' get some funny tastes out of my mouth. I'd like some coffee, and I want a cigarette." Tony brushed away at Redhead's back. Redhead said, "Be guided by the experiences of yore wisers, son." There wasn't more than two or three years' difference in their ages. "Don't never start drinkin' till you've et. You wake up empty as a rain barrel in the desert. You promise me?"

Tony smiled and promised.

"Then let's go eat, an' I'll just show you how much a full-growed empty belly can hold!"

Redhead had such an air of friendly assurance that there was no resisting him. Tony took him into his own room and began to make coffee.

Redhead stripped to the waist to wash, using much soap, of which there was but little. He splashed water, dipping his head deep into the basin. Tony's water had to be dry-sledded from a pump up in town, and he used it sparingly.

Redhead made gleeful spluttery noises, said, "Whew, I feel better," and, as he combed his hair, whistled.

CHAPTER II

"THEY HUNG THE WRONG MAN!"

In the cool of the evening Sheriff Martin rode toward the calaboose, which sat like a squat box off beyond the edge of the town. Tahzo had once been proud of its monument to law and order. It looked nice sitting out there. Sometimes men tried the range of their revolvers on it.

As the sheriff drew near he heard the tinkling of a guitar and something else that sounded not unlike the plaintive squeak of coyote pups learning to yelp.

The sheriff pricked up his ears but did not smile. He had a grim leather-tough face, deeply wrinkled. Walking his horse slowly, he came round to the front of the calaboose, drew rein, looked down, forearm on the horn.

Tony and Red sat together on a blanket before the doorway. They had played monte until Tony won Red's two dollars, which all he had; and now they were having music. The two dollars helped Tony to endure Red's singing. Red lay on his back, knee up, one leg crossed over the knee, and waved his foot, perhaps under the impression that he was keeping time. His arms

17

were folded back under his head for a cushion.

As the sheriff drew rein, Tony's fingers left the guitar quite as if the strings were red hot. He arose, smiling nervously. Red raised up, took a look, then stood up, grinning.

The sheriff frowned. His was a stern face. He had lived dangerously all of his life; and now, with gray hairs on his head, the dangers had not lessened. Against little horse thieves or big cattle rustlers, he enforced the code of the range. Nobody thought about trying to buy him off. From time to time some people had thought about killing him off. He was an honest man and, though in an aloof rebuking way, had much tolerance toward other honest men who happened to make fools of themselves.

"Tony," said Sheriff Martin coldly, "why did you let him out!"

Tony invoked a few of the saints and used much gringo blasphemy in protesting. Redhead had simply pulled the bars from the window and crawled out, demanded food, water, tobacco, and music. But see! He had not run away. Tony begged Sheriff Martin to take notice that the prisoner was present! But, oh, the beans and bacon this gringo had eaten!

Sheriff Martin looked from one boy to the other. Both mere kids as far as years went. Tony's face was soft, gentle, almost girlish. The other had a wind-whipped, sunburnt face, a good-natured mouth, but eyes that had looked at trouble—straight at it, and lost something of their mildness. The sheriff got off his horse, dropping the reins. He came forward slowly, limping. An old rifle bullet was embedded near the knee of his right leg.

He towered above Red and looked down. There was something about Redhead's respectful but somehow impudent grin that made the sheriff want to smile too. But he set his jaws and asked ominously:

"Do you know what-all you done last night?"

Red's lips twitched with deepening smile. "No, sir. But if I didn't steal no horses, insult no lady, shoot nobody, then I reckon I'm guilty as hell! But can't a fellow celebrate a little?"

The sheriff cleared his throat. "You roped the parson out in front of the Horse Shoe and rode your horse in, with him followin'."

Red shook his head, said simply, "I sure ain't proud of that. Nozir."

The sheriff again cleared his throat, looked away, said calmly and without approval: "Yet it wasn't so bad as might've been, seein' it wasn't pure cussedness. You argued gentle at first in tryin' for to persuade him that ever'body there would donate for a little church he's tryin' for to build. Then you jus' up and brought him in to prove it. You made quite some speech!" The sheriff's eyes swung back straight at Red's face.

19

"He went out with a hatful o' money. He's new from the East and didn't know gamblers was generous. You learned him a lot. He told me so this mornin'."

Red sighed, seemed relieved. "What else did I do?"

"Where'd you learn to use a rope?"

"No place special. Only I sort o' growed into it."

The sheriff said, "Um," and waited.

"Y'see, when my mother died, Dad got an ol' Mexican for to nurse me. Before I was outa the cradle, old José put a string in my hand and made me rope my bottle o' milk or go hungry. Least, so folks say. Nobody'd rope against old José. Jus' so much of what you call lost motion to try it. So I growed up with a rope in one hand an' bridle reins in the other."

"Your name is Red Clark?"

"That's me."

"Um." The sheriff frowned down into Red's face as if looking for something. "You said last night that was it, an' your father was once sheriff of Tulluco. That right?"

"Yessir."

"You don't look like him much an' don't act like him a-tall."

"He was a man," said Red simply.

"I know it. I knowed him well. We were friends. I don't reckon he'd have been very proud of your capers here in town last night."

Red said nothing but did not drop his eyes, did not look sullen or resentful; and yet did not look ashamed.

The sheriff glanced toward Red's waist, looked again into his face, pointed: "Now, son, when a youngster comes to town an' leaves his guns with the first barkeep, it means one of two things: he's either afraid because he can't shoot fast and straight, or he's afraid because he can. Which was it with you?"

Red said evasively, "My dad, he allus thought that takin' off his guns was good manners in a stranger that come to town. Besides, when you want to be soc'able, like me, what's the good in making folks suspicious?"

"Why two guns?"

"They're a sort of a pair. That's all."

"One is enough for most folks unless they come from over Lelargo way." The sheriff said "Lelargo" as though he did not like the sound of it.

Red was not looking at the sheriff now, but at the horse. A beautiful horse, long-limbed, deep-chested, with intelligent flick of ear and swing of head. Red had much the same look of admiration as if the horse were a pretty girl.

"What about them two guns?" the sheriff insisted.

"Shucks. None is enough for me."

"Then why you been wearin' 'em?"

"Oh, I won 'em onct at a little Fourth o' July doin's. Just habit, packin' 'em. Sorta proud maybe. Made me look full-growed—'r so I thought." Red grinned, as if hopeful that the sheriff would understand.

"What sort of doin's?"

"H'm?"

"You heard me!" The sheriff sounded as if more than merely curious.

"Well, sir, you see, ol' José made me rope an' ride. That's a mighty purty horse of yorn, Sheriff!"

"I'm listenin'."

"Well, an' my dad, he was sort o' pernickity about shootin'. He said it was all wrong, this thing of havin' to shoot twict at something. Didn't approve of that a-tall! But the main thing was to do her quick. Not be slow-poky about it. So he learned me a lot. Said there wouldn't be near so many bad men if good men was better shots. It's practice as does it—so he said. I reckon so. Anyhow, come that Fourth o' July when there was some quick shootin' from horseback, I was plum' lucky."

"Lucky for to have Sheriff Clark for a dad, son."

Red's grin spread all over his face. "I'm an awful fool some ways, but I never made no mistake about that."

The sheriff nodded, somehow seeming to agree

merely with the first part of Red's statement. "Last night when you started upstairs to bed, you started for it on horseback—"

"Oh my gosh!" said Red, but not very sorrowfully.

"Yeah. An' you broke up some furniture and stairs, the which'll have to be paid for. Wonder you didn't kill yourself. And break the horse's leg. How can you be such a fool, bein' Sheriff Clark's boy?"

"I was jus' celebratin' a little," said Red, humbled.

"Celebratin' what?"

"Some good luck that come unexpected."

"What?"

"Well, sir, I'm allus lucky—'cept at cards. An' purty girls. If they's a purty girl around they's sure to be a handsomer feller than me somewhere around, too. Otherwise, I sorta got a habit o' being lucky."

"Why don't you get the habit of stickin' clost to what you're asked? What was you celebratin'?"

Red cleared his throat, moved his feet, was a little uncomfortable, but looked straight at the sheriff. "Purt-near got hung an' didn't!"

The sheriff made a very soft sound in his throat, waited.

"A while back up north at Clayville," Red went on, "a couple of fellows told some folks I answered the description of the man who'd killed an ol' nester and stole some money he had in a sack. They said they'd seen me ridin' off from the nester's!

"Some friends, they come an' told me what was bein' said before the posse rode out. Y'know, it sort o' made me peevish-like. 'F I stayed around and got caught, I was most sure to get hung. 'F I cut an' run, ever'body'd say, 'Shore, he done it!' So I set around in the brush, meditatin'. My dad, he had a way of sayin' that when somebody accuses an innocent man of somethin', it's more'n most likely the liar hisself done it."

The sheriff nodded, murmured softly, "Yes."

"Well, one day I just saddled up and rode right square into town and went to the saloon where them two fellers was. We had some argyment, and when it was all over one o' them fellows thought he was dyin' too, so he up and said him and his pardner killed the nester and poked some stuff in my saddle bags to put the blame on me.

"Well, sir, the feller, he didn't die like he figgered he was a-goin' to. But I just heard yesterday that up to Clayville they had decided that he was well enough to be hung, an' they done it. So I rode along down here for to celebrate. Now I'm broke, so ever'thing'll be all right again."

The sheriff eyed him grimly. "Yes. I heard about that case. So you are the boy? Sort o' peculiar, seein' what I had in mind. We had a

24

case similar. And about the same time. You ought to be interested. They hung the—"

The sheriff checked himself and with slow, stiff-legged movements turned, looking about in the starlight, not nervously, but with caution. Sage and cactus blotched the ground like things asleep in the darkness. He said something in Spanish which Red understood as well as Tony. Tony put down his guitar and started around the calaboose.

The sheriff reached out an arm, dropped his hand on Red's shoulder, spoke solemnly:

"You ought to be interested, boy, because down here they hung the wrong man!"

Red swore, used hard cuss words, but somehow they had the sound of quick prayer. A kind of sickening feeling hit him right in the pit of the stomach. He couldn't have explained, he wouldn't have tried; but, like most range-born men, he had a sort of unworded, unwordable, faith in hemp—in the hands of honest men. He had ridden on man hunts, and with cowboys that came down on rustlers. And hanged them. If honest men hanged a man, he deserved it; and innocent men, however much suspected, would somehow have their innocence known before they swung. That feeling, that range-bred faith in the right of being guiltless, had carried him through up in Clayville.

"I trust Tony," the sheriff explained, "but I

didn't want him to hear that. A lot o' people hereabouts are beginnin' to think the wrong man got hung. There is some as know I know. Right here, now, they may be somebody doggin' me. Tryin' for to listen as well as"—he glanced over his shoulder—"as shoot. Twice in two weeks. But with a rifle. They don't want to get up close," said the sheriff calmly, with pride.

Red swore some more and in a kind of hushed tone.

"How much of a stranger are you to this part of the country, boy?"

"Me, Sheriff? Why, teetotal!"

"Want work?"

Red grinned. He waved a hand toward the Mexican boy who had just returned. "Tony here, he took my last bean for some lessons in monte. They was worth it. I learnt a lot that I ought've knowed before. Mexicans is better monte players than 'Mericans."

"Are you willing to try something, something pretty hard?" asked the sheriff.

"Yezir. I like to eat. 'Less you feed your prisoner better'n so far, he's willin' for to fight a bobcat for his supper."

The sheriff gave no answering smile to Red's flippancy, but gazed at him with frowning scrutiny, trying to weigh him, judge him, see how much good iron was down under that happy-go-lucky good-natured impudence. It wasn't an easy

26

scrutiny. The sheriff's was a grim face, and he was a cautious man. Red's antics and jokes didn't fit in well with the sheriff's mood nor seem to suit the kind of man he wanted.

He asked, rebukingly, "Aren't you ever serious?"

"Not if I can help it, I ain't!" said Red with feeling. "When I'm ser'ous I'm sick, just like a calf or colt when he's ser'ous, too."

"But there are times when—"

"I reckon," Red admitted. "Like that story you jus' told me. 'F I was a brother to that boy they hung I'd be so gosh-danged ser'ous I reckon a lot o' people would get hurt." Red's voice was earnest enough then, not loud, but it had a sound that struck response in the sheriff's feelings.

"H'm. Suppose you just come along up to my office. Your guns are there. The barkeep brought them in this morning. He said you was a nice kid and wouldn't hurt a fly. For a barkeep, I think maybe he didn't look no deeper than that grin. Usual, barkeeps do. And"—another lingering hard look at Red's face—"I ain't yet quite sure, but I think maybe I know how you can make some wages—if you live long enough to earn 'em!"

"Yezir," said Red, with a hopeful sound.

"Come along. We'll walk and talk a little more."

27

CHAPTER III

"I'D LIE LIKE HELL!"

The sheriff walked with slow stiff-legged stride, leading the horse that came along with swing of head and inquiring forward flip of ears. Sure a mighty fine horse, Red thought.

He, a watchful boy, noted that the reins were over the left arm and that the sheriff had the thumb of his right hand hooked in the belt over his hip. His hand wouldn't have far to go if he wanted to set about making some noise. Yet there was nothing skittish about this tall, hard-faced grim sheriff who had the earmarks of the sort of men Red had known from babyhood. The sheriff, casual-like, glanced this way and that; and Red, knowing the signs, found himself also looking to the right and left and now and then back across his shoulder. When a man like the sheriff showed caution, it was time to keep an eye peeled.

Sheriff Martin asked questions about his old friend, Sheriff Clark of Tulluco, most of them in an offhand way. He learned that Red knew only as much as any son would about his father, but had a deeper and more frank respect than most reckless range fellows would acknowledge for fear of seeming a bit soft.

It was also evident that Red had been about the country much more than most boys. The wander-fever had driven him; he had worked here, there, somewhere else, and liked to drift into new places, see new country, have things happen.

Sheriff Martin meditated even as he talked. Then he said, "Now see here, boy, I've got to know about you. What do you think is the bravest thing you ever did? Come, be truthful. Don't try to be modest. Just up and tell me what are you the proudest of as a piece of downright courage?"

It was a question the sheriff often asked men. He probably had never heard the word "psychology," but he understood about it and could judge men mighty well by the way they talked of themselves.

Red said, "Gee-gosh. Me? Hell! You mean where I sort o' had to take my heart in both hands and hold on tight to keep from backin' down? Not goin' through with what I started?"

"Well, yes, something like that, I suppose. What have you done that you think shows the coolest, steadiest nerve of anything you ever did do?"

"Well, sir, I'll jus' up an' tell you something. I've sort o' experimented around with a lot of damn-fool craziness, but onct—and I was plum' scairt ever' step o' the way!—I walked right square up to a little feller as was settin' there waitin'—me, movin' slow and cautious, you can just better bet! I got up to 'im and I reached

29

down mighty slow at first, then grabbed. An' was I scairt! But I'd heard it could be done, an' me bein' cur'ous, I experimented. She worked! Sheriff, I cross my heart an' hope to die if I ain't tellin' the truth that I onct picked a polecat up by the tail—an' nothin' didn't happen!" Red seemed serious. "You don't need for to snicker. You just go try it. That's all. You ain't easy scairt, I know. But just you try that onct. You'll know what I mean. Yezir!"

The grim sheriff grinned. Even chuckled a little. "I've heard it could be done, but wondered how anybody ever knew, 'cause I never knew anybody that tried it. You're the first. As I figure it, a skunk just stands and faces you. Don't startle him and you are all right. I'm afraid if I tried it I'd scare my skunk a little. But, boy, how about the times you've stood in smoke, peering through to see who was on their feet and who wasn't? How'd you feel about that?"

"Why, Sheriff, you're an old-timer. You know that don't take no what you call cold nerve. No more'n swimmin' after you fall into some cold water. 'Fore you know it, you're in. Then they's nothin' to do but keep movin'. But I allus feel a little shaky after the doin's is over. Sort o'—you know. Like I'd et something that lay heavy on my stummick."

The sheriff nodded understandingly. "Ever been hit?"

"Me? Say! Sheriff, I been shot fourteen times. All to onct! With a scattergun. I was stealin' a watermelon. The feller that owned the watermelon had a close choke an' a danged good eye f'r distance. Old José, he picked out fourteen o' them pellets—an' I et standin' f'r two weeks, and slep' on my belly. My dad, he was away from home for some time, 'r I'd-a been paddled before them wounds o' mine got healed. But I didn't drop that watermelon. It's mighty seldom I get in so much of a hurry that I turn loose of anything you can eat!"

The sheriff began to feel that light-heartedness was just as much a part of the boy as the color of his hair or the shape of his face. But the sheriff wanted to get down inside of him, find out whether or not he could feel safe in trusting Red with a pretty dangerous piece of work. The boy was reckless, but could he be cautious? Use judgment? He had courage and a sound heart, but did he have plain horse sense?

"Tell me, son. Did your father ever talk to you about his—well, not troubles exactly; but about his work? Tell you things he didn't want other folks to know?"

"Well, sir, I knowed for more'n a year before any of the deputies did that my dad thought a certain rancher down in our county was a hoss thief. Is that sort o' what you mean?"

"Yes," said the sheriff.

"An' when I was home," Red went on, "the which wasn't much after I could reach up high enough to put a saddle on a horse, Dad an' me was twins. He was a great one to ride alone, my dad was."

"I know that, son."

"An' folks used to wonder why he'd go out lone-handed after fellers. He took me along and showed me why. You don't have to blame nobody but yoreself if things happen the way you don't want. Now 'f you'd asked me a while ago what made me happiest and *feel* proudest, I'd have said, 'Ridin' out, just me an' my dad, on a man hunt!' "

At that the stern sheriff's arm fell on Red's shoulder, and, turning the boy about, he looked down steadily.

"Then, son, why do you ever go and get fool drunk?"

"It ain't a habit I've got. Honest!"

"Um-m-m." The sheriff sounded a little skeptical.

"When you was my age, didn't you ever act the fool some?"

The sheriff, being honest, had to nod, even if reluctantly.

"Sometimes, these days, I near forget that I ever was young!"

"I hope I don't never," said Red.

"You won't! Now then, son, listen clost. I want

32

a man that I can trust. He has to be somebody nobody knows. 'Specially I don't want it known that he knows me, leastwise favorable."

"I can talk mad as a hornet about you throwin' me in the calaboose!"

"I want that man to go into a part of the country where, if folks find out he's come from me, they'll kill him!"

"How they goin' to know? Usual, I tell the truth. In a case like that, I'd lie like hell!"

CHAPTER IV

RATTLESNAKES!

Tahzo was what is called "right smart of a town." Cowboys and miners made it pretty lively at times, but honest folks had the upper hand. They were willing to put up with a lot of noise and monkeyshines, but Tahzo was proud of itself for law and order. Bad men usually rode out much faster than they had come in—else stayed to be buried. Tahzo, town and county, would hit saddles and join with the sheriff to chase lawbreakers. The sheriff was a stickler for a fair, square trial by jury; and most times the people let him have his way because they knew he always hurried things along.

In Tahzo, if you wanted to insult somebody, you said, "You must've rode in from over Lelargo way."

Red and the sheriff walked along slowly and came to the sheriff's office by the back way.

This office was in a long low adobe that sat by itself on a corner lot with the rear on an alleyway that ran behind the town's big stores, such as they were. The adobe had a narrow covered porch at the side where folks whittled on chairs, told stories, cracked jokes, and waited for the supper gong of the hotel across the street.

In the alleyway the sheriff dropped the reins of his horse, saying, "Wait a minute, son, till I light a lamp." Red put his fingers up behind the horse's ears, gouging and stroking gently. "You shore are purty," he said, just about as he would have said it to a girl if she could have coaxed him out of his bashfulness.

The sheriff pushed open the back door and took a step into the dark room, but he came stumbling back out of the house almost as if thrown. His stiff leg turned, and he fell hard against Red.

Red's hand instinctively clapped at his hip and he crouched. No gun was there. He said, "Shucks!" rather sheepishly.

The sheriff took hold of his shoulder. "Listen close, son."

Red bent forward, ears strained. In the utter stillness he heard the soft scratching scrape of something like a stiff rope being drawn slowly over the rough pine floor.

"What's more," said Red, "I can smell 'im. I'll just get a stick!"

The horse, too, could smell and sidled back with high nervous jerk of head. "Whoa-a-a," said the sheriff gently and pulled at the dangling reins.

Red ran off at a jog trot down the alley and came back with the piece of a packing case he had found behind the Emporium.

The sheriff struck a match and, leaning through

the doorway, held it above his head, peering through the faint flickering light.

"See 'em, Sheriff?"

"Yes. It's a rattler, son."

The match burned down to his fingers and was shaken out.

"I don't want to win me no medals fightin' rattlers in the dark," said Red. "But you just strike a couple more matches an' I'll whack 'im."

Red stood in the doorway, peering and holding his stick ready.

The sheriff put three or four matches together, struck them. The tiny flame flared. Red jumped forward and began to flail the floor. He had only a little light, and that wouldn't last long.

Then the sheriff shouted, "Look out!" and Red blindly jumped forward as if touched by a spring that threw him. The sheriff's tone carried just that sort of warning; and when Red got that sort of warning he wasn't a boy to stand and ask questions. The matches had gone out. It was pitch dark. The sheriff said solemnly, "There's another one, son. He's coiled!"

"Gosh A'mighty!" Red gasped. Then, irrepressibly, "If you want to know when I been most scairt in my life, this here is purt-near it. Maybe do me some good, though, 'cause if this is what folks have when they get D. T.'s, me, I'm through with likker, Sheriff!"

36

"Don't move. Stand quiet and you'll be all right. Snakes strike at only what moves, so—"

"Yeah, but my heart is movin' fast an' shakin' the rest of me!" said Red, cheerfully.

"I'll go round front and get a lamp."

"If these here are rattlers, Sheriff, they're awful liars! Rattlers rattle—an' these don't!"

"Be quiet. These here," said the sheriff enigmatically, "must be from over Lelargo way. They have that sort o' snakes—an' men!—over there!"

Red stood in his tracks. He knew, or at least had heard and tried hard to believe, that he was safe as long as he did not move.

He could hear the scratching scrape of one of the snakes and also the quick threshing about of the other which he had injured. He knew, for he had seen hurt snakes dying, that this fellow was probably snapping right and left, and there were plenty of stories—now easily believed!—of a rattler's fang going right through boots. But he did not move. Cold sweat stood out all over him, and he felt frozen, peering blindly at the black floor and a little sickened by the snake odor in the stale hot room.

He could dimly see the outline of a table just beyond arm's reach. The impulse to jump for it and climb up there was strong, but he stood fast. His toes squirmed about in his boots, and his muscles were tense, dreading the fang snap any moment against his leg; but he did not move.

The door opened behind him. He twisted his neck, looked over his shoulder, blinked into the lamplight. Light flooded the door. Red stepped across near the sheriff, said "Oo-whew! Now 'f you'll just hold the lamp, I'll—I'll be damned!"

Red broke off and pointed at a coiled snake about four feet from the doorway, now clearly seen. Its flattened V-shaped head was drawn back with a hairpin curve at the neck, ready to strike. Its tail stuck up an inch or two above the coils—a sharp tail, slightly blunt, that vibrated like the trembling of a bow string, yet made no sound. The rattles were gone!

"My holy gosh, Sheriff!"

"Yes," said the sheriff, low and cold of tone. "These snakes are from over Lelargo way. I'd shoot, but folks would come. I want to talk to you alone. That other fellow's rattles are gone too!"

"They're honester than the men that put 'em here!" said Red, indignant. "They're tryin' for to give warnin'!"

"Right, son." The sheriff set the lamp on the table. "Much honester!"

One snake, not dead but badly hurt, lay writhing in a tangle of coils.

Red leaned forward and poked out his stick at the other. It struck, leaping, and was hit and flailed before it could settle back again into a coil.

When the snakes were dead, Red balanced

them over the end of his stick and carried them out into the alley, pitched them off to one side. The horse shied timidly, backing off with reins dragging. Red paused to soothe the horse, led him back nearer the doorway, stroked his nose, whispered silly things in a lover's tone.

The sheriff stood silent in the doorway, looking on. From just this small incident of killing snakes he thought he had learned quite a bit about Red Clark; at least he had stronger nerves than most men.

"Y'know, Sheriff, if that feller hadn't been crawlin' when you opened the door, you'd of been bit!"

"We were lucky, son."

"Long as it ain't cards, 'r women, me, I'm allus lucky!"

"Come in and set down, son. I want to talk and talk fast."

Red came in. The sheriff closed the door, then took down belts and guns from a peg on the wall. "Here are your guns. And when you go in about twenty minutes from now, I want you to go shootin'!"

"Shootin'? Me? At what?"

"Just so I can say you got away from me. Jump my horse—he's a good one—and ride hell-for-leather south, toward Lelargo!"

Red held his guns. He looked hard at the sheriff, felt uneasy and a little suspicious. Slowly, thoughtfully, he began prodding out the shells from each chamber of the guns, eyeing them critically. That was one of the things his father had taught him: Look well to your guns if they have passed through somebody else's hands. He said nothing for a time. When the guns had been examined he strapped them on, settling them low down on his hips, tied the holsters' tip thongs about his legs, then eyed the sheriff, demanding an explanation.

The grim, wrinkled, sun-blackened sheriff said softly, "That way, son, nobody'll know I sent you!"

"Um-m-m," Red murmured, very amazed and just a wee bit suspicious. He liked this sheriff, but to be urged to steal a horse and ride off shooting—that had a smell of hocus-pocus.

"Don't you understand, son?"

Red put his hat far back on his head and rubbed at his forehead with his palm. "I allus sort o' understood that one way for to get yourself strung up quick was to steal a hoss, particular a sheriff's horse!"

The sheriff grinned, calm and reassuring, and would have said something; but Red kept on talking:

"He's a good one, that horse. An' he'll be knowed all through the country. Fellows'll ask questions. It's sometimes mighty hard to give convincin' answers when you're settin' on some other fellow's horse. I done my share o' most near ever'thing that's done on the range, but somehow I sorta ain't got around yet to much experience in hoss-stealin'. No, sir."

Red was trembling right on the edge of a flat refusal; so the sheriff said very quietly:

"That's just it, son. They ain't no other way for me to fix it so it'll be all right for you to go. Nobody ain't goin' to think me, sheriff of Tahzo, would have give up this here horse. So they'll believe your story over in Lelargo. I'll see to it that word comes from Tahzo as how you got away from me and rode off on my own horse. Some folks'll make you right welcome!"

"Nope, not my kind o' folks, they won't!"

"I know that. So now set down an' listen close. I want to tell you something."

CHAPTER V

THE STORY OF A MURDER

In the small back room of the sheriff's office, which was the hotter for having the doors shut and the dusty window closed, the sheriff leaned on the table, with the lamp at his elbow, and in a low voice, as if talking of something that hurt his throat, he told this boy—a total stranger who, some twenty hours before, had been locked up for drunkenness—a tragic story. The sheriff was a grim and silent type of man who kept many things to himself; but now he confided what he had not dared tell to another person.

The daughter of a small rancher by the name of Rand had been murdered.

She was a young school teacher, one of the prettiest and loveliest girls in the country. Everybody knew her, everybody liked her; so after her murder the country had not been in a mood to go slow and weigh evidence: that would have been too much like trying to make out that perhaps the guilty man wasn't guilty to suit the feelings of the range.

It looked, offhand, very much as if she had been killed by a cowboy that worked for her father.

This boy had been caught, badly used, and, half unconscious, lynched.

Even the sheriff at first believed the dead cowboy was guilty. Had no reason to think anything else. The unofficial hanging did not greatly trouble his conscience. Then he began to have doubts; and those doubts troubled him greatly.

Without confiding in anyone, he began to piece things together, and soon was sure that somebody had cleverly thrown the appearance of guilt on the cowboy.

It happened that the Rands had a neighbor by the name of Leon Lenard, who had once been known as a dangerous outlaw. He was an old old-timer, and his past was more or less ignored because he had settled down, lived alone, tended to his own business, and seemed honest.

When the sheriff found out that Lenard had been one of the girl's closest friends, he began to suspect the old outlaw. They had often been together, Lenard falling into the habit of riding to and from school with her. Lenard was more than twice her age and seemed really a dour, almost savagely silent man, keen and hard of eye, yet the pretty girl liked him very much. Any number of people could recall how she had spoken up for Leon Lenard, saying he wasn't at all the man he appeared!

Well, maybe he wasn't. The sheriff had rather

thought so, too. He knew old Leon had courage; and the sheriff was inclined to think well of any man who had it. But shortly after the murder and lynching, Leon Lenard left the country. Just dropped everything and bolted without a word of explanation to anybody.

It was soon learned that Lenard had shown up over in Lelargo, where, as an old-time outlaw and a man dangerous at any time, he would find friends and a welcome, particularly now when they were having a lot of range trouble over there.

In that lawless county there were two or three big cowmen and a mining company or two that had everything their own way—at least as far as little fellows were concerned. They ran everything wide open, drove out nesters and settlers; but also they fought with one another, hired gunmen and welcomed outlaws.

Shortly after Leon Lenard disappeared and was soon heard of again over in Lelargo, the dead girl's brother came home. For years he had been down in Texas, but had ridden in, bringing with him a friend by the name of Wilkins.

The sheriff had some long talks with Rand, the girl's brother, and the friend Wilkins. They had decided that Leon Lenard wanted some looking after. So the two boys had set themselves up as horse thieves on the dodge and gone over to Lelargo and nosed around in an effort to get

Lenard into a corner and ask some questions.

"Now, son," said the sheriff, "they're over there somewhere. I don't even know what names they've taken. Most likely, though, Wilkins is still usin' his own. But since they're sure to be hangin' round close to Leon Lenard, you can be sure Rand ain't callin' himself Rand."

Red nodded. He sat forward with elbows on knees, listening intently.

"I got to get word to 'em and in a hurry or another innocent man is likely to be killed! That Wilkins and the Rand boy is likely to do something hasty. I don't know what Leon Lenard cut an' run for, but he never killed that girl!"

"How you sure?" Red murmured, breathless.

"Because I know now who did! I just learned lately. An' the man who done it knows I know 'twas him! How he learned, I can't imagine, because I haven't told a living soul!"

"Gosh!" said Red.

The sheriff paused, moodily. "But now twict lately I've been shot at by somebody who knew which way I was going to be ridin'—alone. You saw yourself what was waitin' for me in here tonight. It was done by somebody that knew I'd be comin' along back in here in the dark, because—shucks!—nobody's afraid of a couple of rattlers in his room in daylight. I've pitched 'em off my blanket more'n once when I been sleeping out on the ground. Folks say they like

45

the warmth—but I'm talkin' about something else."

The sheriff meditated, rubbed his hand across his mouth, dropped the hand to Red's knee. "Listen, son. I've got a witness that saw that girl killed!"

Red swore. "And he let an innocent man get hung!"

"No. No, he never. That's why he come in to see me. After the murder he run off 'cause he knew it was much as his own life was worth to have it known he knowed. But when he heard what had happened it bothered him a heap. He's a Mexican and he's scairt. But he's honest. That's why, when he finally made up his mind, he took his life in his hands and come tearin' out of Lelargo to tell me the truth. I've got him hid away careful. Fellows are lookin' for him high an' low. They's a big reward offered for him over in Lelargo, where they claim he's wanted for murder, an' I don't know what-all else."

"I know," said Red. "That's what is called dis-credit-ting yore witness. My dad, he had some o' that, too."

"Yes. They are trying to discredit my witness in case he ever does get to court to tell his story. But folks will believe him before I'm done. An' I'm going to bring that guilty man to trial right here in my county or die tryin'! I want to show them Lelargo fellows that law can reach right in among 'em an' drag out by the ears one o' the biggest rascals they've got, set 'im down in front o' twelve good men an' true, an' hang 'im!"

"Gosh," said Red, "you talk like my dad used to!"

"Now, son, I believe there is just three people alive that know who killed Bessie Rand. The man who done it, of course. The Mexican who saw it. An' me."

"Then the man who done it must be the same party that has been takin' pot shots at you an' catchin' rattlers?"

"No. No, I think the man that has been shootin' at me is just somebody that has been hired to do the job. Somebody I know well, most likely. If he got up clost and missed, he'd have a hard time explainin'!"

"I bet he would," said Red, grinning. "Just me takin' a couple too many drinks—look how I had to talk an' explain!"

"I'm being watched. I don't know by who or how many. That fellow who killed Bessie Rand is scairt. Not scairt of ever bein' brought to trial— he thinks he is plum' too big for that. But he's scairt that I'm goin' to spread my story an' have it believed. An' there's a dozen men right here in Tahzo as would lay for 'im. His own father, as bad a man as there is in Lelargo, would make it hot for him. Oh yes, sir, that young man would be in for a lot of trouble if the story ever got

47

out. So he's havin' ever' move I make watched."

Red nodded in agreement. He saw the sheriff's point.

"That there is why you've got to go to Lelargo as if you were runnin' away from me."

"Yeah, but hell afire," said Red. "You're a real sheriff, an' who is goin' to be fool enough to think I'd ever get the best o' you?"

"That won't be hard for 'em to believe over in Lelargo. They sort o' want to think I'm a fussy old woman anyhow. An' you bein' a stranger helps a lot. I want you to find that Rand boy and Wilkins. Like I told you, they'll be somewhere clost to Leon Lenard. An' Wilkins, I'm purt-near sure, will be usin' his own name, so that ought to make it easy. I don't want them to shoot Leon, then drift back down to Texas again an' think they've settled with the man that killed Bessie Rand."

"Then you ain't yet got no idee a-tall why Leon Lenard cut an' run?"

"Not unless he was offered some big wages to get into the cattle war. Old Lenard—he's pretty old—he's a hard man yet, mighty hard. They's nothing against him over here that I know of. And my business is knowin'.

"And I want Rand and Wilkins to know the name of the man they are after; but I want 'em to promise to help me get 'im across the county line so we can bring 'im into court. Will you go?"

"You want me to make the girl's brother promise not to shoot that feller!" Red exclaimed in astonished protest. He knew what sort of luck somebody would have in trying to get him to make a promise like that. Red had a properly-brought-up sheriff's son's respect for courts—but a lot more for justice, no matter where and how it was handed out.

"Well, I think they owe that there much to me, yes," said the sheriff. "First off, when I begun to think about sendin' you over, I thought I'd just have you look up Rand and Wilkins, tell 'em they was after the wrong man and to get in touch with me. But now I trust you, son. And them snakes make me feel maybe I'd better let somebody know who did murder that poor girl, 'cause if something happened to me, then—don't you see?"

Red nodded.

"I'm going to tell you. His name is—"

Red turned in his chair, startled. Close behind him, the door that led to the front of the sheriff's office had squeaked ever so faintly. Red was a sensitive, wary fellow, and his nerves were on edge from the sheriff's story of a beautiful girl murdered, an innocent man hanged. The sheriff had talked in a low voice that could not have been overheard very clearly at either door.

"Yeah," said Red, jerking up a warning finger at the sheriff, who was noiselessly rising, "I sure

49

want to hear the name o' that fellow, because—"

As he spoke, Red was getting out of the chair quietly. He turned, facing the door, drew a gun, and was just reaching to push against the door when—*snap! click!*—the door that the eavesdropper had held faintly ajar was shut, and the bolt on the other side was shot home by an unknown hand.

Instantly Red's shoulder hit the door with all of his weight, but it was a strong door, now bolted. He stepped back and drew his knee breast-high, then drove his foot against the lock with jarring blow.

He was just raising his foot to kick again when, behind him, he heard the sheriff's voice, high-pitched in astonishment:

"My God, *you!*"

The sheriff stood face to face with a man at the rear door. Two guns went off almost together.

As Red had moved toward the one door, the sheriff had made for the other at the back, hoping, in spite of his stiff knee, to run out and around the house in time to catch sight of whoever it was that had been listening inside of his office.

Gun in hand, he had jerked the door open, to find himself almost breast to breast with the second eavesdropper, who had not only been listening, but, by the look on his face and the gun in his hand, was determined to kill somebody.

This fellow, surprised by the suddenness with

which the sheriff appeared, and startled, too, by the tone of complete understanding in his voice, jerked himself back as he shot. Otherwise both men, at such point-blank range, would have dropped dead.

"It is my deputy!" the sheriff gasped, turning to Red, who had spun about and come up to his side. "That's why—everything known—he sold out to—quick, boy! Onto that horse and go!"

"What? Go? You're hit! An' he was—"

"I'm not hurt. Go! Take word to Rand and Wilkins—go!"

"Hell," said Red, over his shoulder, "they was another at the other door—"

"Go, I tell you!"

The sheriff gave Red a shove that sent him almost headlong out of the door. As Red brought himself up with a running stagger there in the alley, he turned, amazed and a little angry, with: "You got funny notions! And me, I—"

The next moment Red was looking straight into the sheriff's gun, and the sheriff was saying in a cold hard voice:

"Onto that horse! Think it over as you ride! You'll soon see I done right!"

"Well," said Red coolly, "I'll go. But damn your soul, if this game ain't square, you'd better shoot me now—'cause I'll be back!"

All at once in the distant darkness there were inquiring shouts and loud calls; then, on the hotel veranda across the way, were heard a clatter of boot heels and the rattling scrape of spurs.

With quick sweeping glance, Red could see the hazy, shadow-like shapes of men who were coming out of the hotel barroom. Having heard the shots, they came eagerly curious. High-pitched voices shouted vague questions.

Red, on the impulse and even without the sheriff's leveled gun, knew this was no place for him. Things might look bad with a deputy dead and the sheriff wounded.

He caught the reins, swung them deftly one to either side of the horse's neck, and with hand to horn leaped, straddling the saddle. He reined about, drove his spurs into the horse's flanks, and for a moment or two wasn't quite sure as to whether or not he was going to stay in the saddle.

This broad-chested, long-limbed black had the gift of speed and a heart of iron, had seldom felt a spur and was indignant. He bolted as if thrown, and Red rocked back with much the same snap as if the horse had bucked.

Old Joe Richards, king cowman of the Tahzo, loved horses as some men—the better sort—love their wives. He had spent thousands of dollars and half his lifetime in building up the breed from which Blackie came; and, thinking that an honest sheriff should have as fast a horse as any horse thief was likely to ride, had sold him at the price of a mustang. In that way the stern sheriff didn't feel he was taking a gift, but Richards knew that he was making one.

Red had never been on such a horse, not even as a kid when he rode bareback in the Tulluco races, carrying every dollar that old José and all his Mexican relatives could bet.

Also at the first jump or two, Red found his feet groping about in air, unable to reach the stirrups. Red was a fair-sized fellow, tall enough to stand anywhere among men; but the sheriff was long-legged and rode straight-legged in the saddle. The flap of the stirrups was like the thumping of clubs against the sides of the frightened horse; and these, together with sting of spurs, put fear into the horse's speed.

Red said hazily, "Gosh A'mighty!" grabbed the horn with one hand, his hat with the other, and bent low, getting his balance. Then he groped down and gathered up the flopping stirrups, bringing them up to the horn; and, getting settled, hooked his spurs into the cinch and lay forward.

He could hear the *pop! pop! pop!* of a gun, as if lead were following him, but there was no whiz near his ears. Maybe the sheriff was just shooting to make folks think Red had bolted on the sheriff's own horse, and taking care to aim wide.

"I'd be danged hard to hit on this here whirl-wind anyhow!" said Red to himself, pleased. He jammed down his hat and stared back.

As nearly as he could tell, it was just about as if he had ridden peaceably out of the town. Seemed mighty queer, so about a mile out he pulled up, letting the horse breathe, and looked back along the dusty road.

It was a clear, warm, starlit night. The road, with lazy squirming, seemed to flow back toward Tahzo; and the town, far in the distance, lay like a toy town of black blocks, flecked with points of light.

Red swore softly, mystified, watched and strained his ears with listening. There wasn't the faintest glimpse or sound of pursuit. That just didn't seem possible.

"Maybe as how they know it ain't no use to waste time followin' Blackie's heel. But shucks, now! My dad, if he couldn't-a rode, he'd-a walked out, just for to make sure the other feller kep' goin'!" He reached over, stroking the horse's neck. "Gosh, Blackie, you're sure a nice feller. An' you're goin' to like me, too—see 'f you don't. I'm sure goin' to fix them stirrups while I got a chanct."

He turned the horse's head back on the road, the better to keep watch. Without leaving the saddle, but with many upward and watchful glances toward the town, he began to adjust the stirrups. It was not easy, sitting in the saddle and dividing his attention between what he was doing and what the townsmen might be doing. But from the height of the saddle he could see farther along the road and have a quicker start if there were any shadow flashes of horsemen coming after him.

Then, from some direction hard to place, Red dimly heard the vague throb of hoofs, scarcely louder than the heartbeat of a dying man. He knew what it meant, but he couldn't understand why the pursuit was not over the road along which he had just come. He had keen ears and knew he was hearing just one horse, and that was strange. But the sound grew louder, and as it grew louder he began to hear, faintly, other vague and hurried hoof throbs.

"That just can't be so," he said to himself. "Who the gosh-danged hell they chasin' if not me!"

He looked all about, a little uneasy and wondering. It surely sounded as if the posse were giving chase to some man who was in the lead by a mile, and they weren't coming at all along the Tahzo road.

Red whistled, mystified. "Maybe they're hittin' out cross-country to try to cut me off?" He asked the question without feeling that it could be so. This road, he had been told, went straight through the Tahzo hills into Lelargo. Bad country, that Lelargo. He had heard a lot about it. Being a hard-working, law-abiding boy, he had never had much hankering to venture in; but now, being on his way, he felt a kind of tingling hopefulness

55

that maybe things would happen; and he had all the cockiness of a young rooster about coming out on top after things did happen. So far, he always had come out on top.

He was straining his eyes in the starlight over toward the right, from where, as nearly as he could judge, the sounds came. Sounds were deceptive on the rough desert-like plains at night; and, all in a flash, in the distance, he saw the black shadow form of a lone horse and rider go over rising ground and vanish into the darkness as if a pebble were tossed into black water. But the horse had been headed as if making for this very road.

"Yessir, our comp'ny's comin'!" he said aloud, and to the horse, "Let's go!"

He pulled Blackie about, rubbed at his sides gently with the spurs.

Red had an affectionate weakness for horses. It wasn't a common range weakness, and more than once in his turbulent life he had poked a man's nose for sneering at the way he petted and nuzzled a horse. He would not prod a willing horse, and he had never seen such willingness to go fast as Blackie had. The horse flashed off up along the road and set the wind whistling in Red's ears, but now that he had his feet in the shortened stirrups he didn't care.

"The sheriff, he give this here horse to me, didn't he? He did. Yessir. An' he's goin' to have one big fat hell of a time coaxin' me to give him back. I ain't that kind of a cowboy! I've plum' fell in love!" He glanced backwards. "Cut *me* off? Bah! This here horse has got winged feet!"

He leaned forward and rubbed Blackie's neck.

CHAPTER VI

"A SUCKLIN' BABE OF A FOOL?"

It was not easy to meditate on a galloping horse, but Red made the best job of it he could. He had a habit of talking to himself, not so much out loud, but with mental questions, answers, and comments, quite as if to a companion.

First off, he had big regrets that Sheriff Martin had been so agitated by the discovery that his deputy was an enemy that he had forgotten to name the fellow over in Lelargo who had really killed the Rand girl, caused one man to be hanged, and for a time made everybody suspect the old outlaw, Leon Lenard, of having had a hand in it. To kill a girl, just any girl, was something almost unthinkable in Red's simple-minded head—just as, for instance, striking your mother in the face.

Red had no religion to speak of, but he did have a primitive range-born faith in the downright justice of God. He had never said a prayer in his life; but he had the feeling, like faith, that sooner or later justice would catch a mean, dirty dog of a man, whoever he was. Usually it did.

Red's was a simple range code of honest men:

Don't steal nothing; don't tell no lies, needless; don't hurt nobody that don't deserve it. Doing those things, then do whatever else you feel like doing and it will be all right.

Fifteen minutes later Red reined up the horse, turned in the saddle, rose tiptoe on the stirrups, listening. When he was sure there was no sound of pursuit, he swung from the saddle, quickly loosened the cinch, and said, "Go to it, Blackie. Get your breath. Now me, if I had to run with my belly all cinched up and a feller on my back—even a good-lookin' feller like myself!—I think I'd make a ruckus."

The horse shook itself, snorted, thrust forward its head, breathed deeply, heaving. Red kept one hand on the saddle horn so the saddle wouldn't shift, with the other stroked Blackie's neck, murmuring in admiration, "Not even hardly a sweat up yet!" In a few minutes the horse lifted its head with ears perked and swung its neck about as much as to ask, "You ready?"

Red listened again. The night was still, sound carried far, but he could not hear even the faintest drumbeat of hoofs.

He flipped the stirrup up over the seat of the saddle, felt to make sure the blankets were in place, and drew the cinch, hit the saddle, sat listening for a moment or two, and shook his head, puzzled. Still no sound.

He set off at a trot, went into a lope, now

and then drew rein to listen, and every twenty minutes or so stopped to let Blackie rest. In that way he kept the horse more or less fresh in case something happened that called for speed.

When they began to get into the hilly country, Red slowed down to a walk, stopped often in the shadows of hilltops to watch and listen. He had ridden out too many times with his father not to know that the hardest man to catch on a long chase is the fellow who rides slowly; and while this couldn't now be such a very long chase, because he was getting nearer and nearer to Lelargo County, he took his time.

He was poking along when, about midnight or a little after, he heard sounds on the road ahead. His heart gave a jump at the thought that maybe, somehow, the posse had sneaked by a short cut away ahead of him through the hills and were coming back along the road. Somebody for sure was coming and not far off. He stopped, tense and listening, then grinned. There was a wagon coming. Chasers of horse thieves didn't go after 'em in a wagon. That shrill rasp in the distance would be the squeak of wagon or stage brakes on the downgrade. After a time he heard the jingle of harness and the crack of a whip.

"Stage," said Red and pushed the horse off the road and up into the dense shadows of scrubby timber.

A few minutes later the Lelargo–Tahzo stage

went by with a guard beside the driver and a gun in the crook of his arm.

"Now the stage fellows'll say they didn't see me on the road, and maybe that'll help make folks think I ain't got here yet. If it was allus this easy to run away from sheriffs, I wonder, now, would I be like I am, or act more natural when they's horses like this to be took for the ridin'?"

He decided to take the saddle off Blackie and give him a real rest.

The horse shook himself gratefully, snorted, then began to nose about, nibbling. Red, holding the reins, found it pleasant to sit down and try to tease himself into a glimpse of how a real outlaw felt to be on the dodge. It was much more easy to meditate out of the saddle. The night was warm, fine for idling in the starlight that dimly winked through the trees; but he had scarcely got comfortable when his stomach began to ask questions about something to eat. He poked about inquiringly, but without much hope, in the saddle bags to see whether or not the sheriff had put in some ham and eggs; but found nothing. So he sprawled out, restfully meditating on the happenings of the last few hours; then he exclaimed, "Ho—lee smoke!" and, stung by a sudden thought, jumped up quite as if he had been sitting on a wasp.

"Maybe I'm being just a sucklin' babe of a fool! Me—sure as I'm a foot high, that sheriff'll say I shot his deputy!" he said indignantly, then asked: "Good gosh, will he?"

He summoned up his most vivid pictures of the tall, grim, calm sheriff, gathering reassurance from the vivid memory. "Oh, he wouldn't do a thing like that! No, sir. I bet he'll just say I took the chance durin' their gunplay to slope! If that's what I thought he'd— That's what he'd *better* say, though, Gosh A'mighty, how I'll ever live down the story o' me killin' a dep'ty sheriff, 'specially," Red added, with a lot of imaginative worry, "if the sheriff hisself gets killed so they'll be nobody's word for it but mine! Y'know, I'm quite liable to have myself in a pickle! I wonder. H'm-m-m."

And Red, greatly troubled by so many possibilities of bad luck, brooded. But soon he grinned in the starlight, said, "Shucks! I'm allus lucky. Bein' in a little hot water is good for a feller. Makes him get up a sweat!" And, jeering himself, "Look at the times you been scairt needless in your life before!"

Had anyone who knew Red overheard his self-reproach, there would have been a good deal of wonder as to just when these needless scares had happened. He was just about the most unscarable scalawag in ten counties.

He patted about in his pockets, wanting tobacco. But he already knew he didn't have any, because he had searched his pockets before.

He wanted something to eat, too. A lot to eat! He thought a little sleep would come in handy. "And," he suggested to the horse, "how about some nice long drinks o' cold water?"

Then he was set tingling and alert by the far-off *cloof-cloof, cloof-cloof, cloof-cloof,* of a jogging horse, coming from over Tahzo way. After listening critically, he knew it was only one horse.

"Trottin' his horse upgrade, too!" Red's opinion was unfavorable. The only time it was right to push a horse uphill was to stop a runaway cow or save your own neck. Surely this fellow wasn't after any cows, but could it be he was on the dodge, too? "Maybe he's hurryin' over to Lelargo to tell 'em about me?"

He continued to listen carefully, making sure there were no other horses coming. "I wonder"— he had the saddle on again, and a hand to Blackie's nose to check a whinny or a snort—"is he comin' lone-handed after me?"

Then Red remembered that just outside of Tahzo he had got a quick and shadowy glimpse of what looked like some other man being chased cross-country. On the other hand, this rider in the lead might have been merely some better-mounted and more reckless fellow in the posse. It seemed too much of a puzzle for him to figure, so he decided, "I'll just lay low and have a look as he rides by."

Red took a good hold on Blackie's nose to keep the horse quiet, and waited, peering from the shadows.

Horse and rider came into view and passed quickly. The horse was breathing as if wind-broken. Man and horse were just blobs of shadow jogging by, but Red saw one thing clearly: the man's head was turned backwards; and the flap of his quirt was heard lashing the weary horse up the grade; and when they had passed he could still hear the *slap, slap, slap* of the quirt.

His opinion of the man who would push a horse so hard and keep his head turned back when there were no sounds of pursuit was very low. "Sheepherder," Red called him. He didn't know any sheepherders, had never known any, didn't want to know any; but his prejudiced contempt for sheepherders had been sucked in with cow's milk, so, to his way of thinking, "sheepherder" had a fine abusive sound, fit for the unfit men of the range.

"Huh!" Red snorted, now convinced that this fellow was on the dodge. "I wonder what he done so quick about the time I left town? They ain't no doubt he is the slumgullion they was chasin' instead o' me? But I wonder, did they think they was chasin' me? I ain't goin' to set down an' feel sorrowful about that!"

He led the horse down onto the road, got into the saddle, and sat listening. After a time he shook his head. "I bet they've turned back. Nobody ain't comin'. But now if I push on I'm liable to get clost enough to that fellow to scare the peawaddin' out o' him. Be just like him to sneak off to the side of the road and try to plug me—just to get my horse. Maybe I oughtn't have let him get ahead of me thataway. Ho, well—

"F'r I'm a lady, you dang galoot!
An' oh my gosh but she was tall!
An' the way she'd cuss made you feel small;
With great big feet an' bright yaller hair—
An' all the manners of a sore-tailed bear!"

Red stopped his humming, told himself to shut up, said it wasn't the thing to sing before you were out of the woods, and rode on slowly with an ear cocked backwards and his eyes watching the road ahead, and especially watching the horse's ears. He figured that a horse was smarter than a man and could see better in the dark. Whenever those ears twitched forward alertly, Red straightened, dropped his hand toward a gun butt, and made ready. However, Blackie was a sensitive and inquisitive horse that nosily spied out all sorts of interesting things and pointed at them with his ears, so Red rode with his hand near his gun a good deal of the time. But nothing happened.

CHAPTER VII

THE WOMAN WITH THE RIFLE

Shortly after sun-up Red came along to a wide place in the road with a clearing off to one side, and at half a glance he knew it was a run-down sort of place and did not look particularly hospitable.

Two or three sheds and houses of rough-hewn logs and a corral spraddled out in wobbly lines as if they had been set up by drunken men. "Yeah, an' they frequent changed their brands o' whisky on the job!" he suggested.

Above the doorway of the large old house, also of rough-hewn logs, was a faded sign with letters burned deep into the wood. The letters had a zigzag wobbliness as if the same drunken men had written with a red-hot poker.

A weary horse, with head down dejectedly, stood picketed near the corral. The horse had been unsaddled. The sweat marks were not quite dry. That told Red just about how long the rider had been there. The saddle had evidently been set up on the hitching rack, but by somebody that was too careless and tired to do it right, for the saddle had fallen and now lay on the stony ground.

Red grunted to himself. "Most likely my unknown friend, he is here. I bet as how maybe he won't want to see nobody as comes over the road from Tahzo. All right, then—he can look the other way! But let's see what this here sign says."

He rode close and spelled out:

Crow's House

While he was deciphering the old and now but dimly seen letters, an old woman noiselessly appeared in the doorway and stared at him in silence.

She was mostly skin and bones, with a bend in her back and a face wrinkled and colored like crumpled butcher's paper. Age and worry and work had certainly written a hard story on her face. Her bedraggled mother-hubbard was not clean, and the tail of the skirt trailed. Her thin gray hair hung uncombed about her face. Her eyes were bright, with a lot of latent fierceness in them. She stared up at him sullenly.

"Mornin', Mother!" Red said cheerfully and pulled at his hat.

"What'd ye want?"

"Well now, Mother, you've had a lot o' travelers in your time at this here roadhouse, so mus' know that when a fellow's real polite an' smilin', like me now, he's tryin' for to get on your good side. Ain't that so, h'm?"

She grinned sourly and struck at her hair as if brushing away a fly.

"What'd ye want *here?*"

"Fact is," Red went on, "I set off from town, back there Tahzo way, in such a big lot of a hurry, Mother, that I had to borrow a hoss—"

"I knowed that!" She spoke, then snapped her lean jaws together as if unwilling that another word should be pried from between them.

Red felt a little startled that she should know so much. The traveler who had just arrived must have told her; but how could he know? And if he knew, would he want to do something about it? Red was too hungry to care much about the puzzle or his suspicions.

He went on, cheerily: "But when I took the hoss, I forgot to borrow me some money at the same time. An' me and my horse here is a wee mite hungry. So if I can light down and do some chores for some oats and hay, with a piece o' bacon and a cup o' coffee thrown in, just you say the word an' I'll pile off."

She stared, sullen and suspicious, but Red sensed that she was weakening a little. "Whar ye from?"

"Tahzo, Mother."

"I knowed that. Whar else?"

"Tulluco."

She nodded, eyeing him. Then a sour shrill

voice, "Menfolks ain't to home. Too many folks comin' round here this mornin'. But you light down, fill up my barr'l from the well, an' you can eat. Then git!"

"Thanks, Mother. You go put side boards on your barrel—I'll shore fill 'er!"

As Red reined to one side to ride around back, he saw the blur of a face vanish from the open window. It was a man's face. What the face looked like he could not have told, though he hoped soon to see. The fellow had evidently been carefully listening.

"Oh, I say, Mother!" Red called.

She appeared again in the doorway, silent and suspicious.

"Just where am I? Me bein' a stranger, you know."

She cackled, grinned, then said half savagely, "You crossed the county line five mile back. So yer in Lelargo now—'f that's what ye wanted to know. An' afore sun-down, I'll bet you wisht you hadn't come!" She bobbed her head by way of emphasis and disappeared.

"Huh!" Red mused. "Now that's what I call a cheerin' welcome."

He rode around back to the stable, watered Blackie, took off the saddle, laid the blankets in the sun, found brush and currycomb, oats and hay, then about twenty minutes later he appeared at the back door of the house.

"Whar the tarnation ye been?" the old woman snapped.

"Rubbin' down my horse, Mother. Case you didn't notice, he's a mighty fine hoss!"

"I seen," she said, not looking at him.

"Where's the barrel an' a bucket? I'm powerful hungry." He eyed the stove, sniffing.

She sat peeling potatoes, thriftily just taking off the skin. She jerked her head toward the kitchen barrel and kicked with her foot toward a big wooden bucket.

Red took the bucket and went out singing. He staggered back, sloshing water, heaved up the bucket, poured and went out—singing. The woman eyed his back with a curious stare.

He filled the barrel clear to the brim, then brought in another bucketful of water, just for good measure. After that he took a pail and brought himself water to wash with on the bench out back of the kitchen.

He splashed away with his shirt off, scrubbing neck and hair, all the while spluttering something about the "yaller-haired girl."

He glanced up and saw the old woman standing in the kitchen door, with arms akimbo, eyeing him.

"What's the matter, Mother? Don't you like my singin'?" he asked, rubbing his cheeks and wishing for a razor.

"I ain't used to seein' menfolks happy 'less

they're drunk. Then not fur long. Come in an' set!" She raised her voice shrilly, as if she wanted to be overheard. "But you gotta eat in the kitchen 'cause you ain't payin'!"

"Shucks, I'd jus' as soon set down out here," said Red, but she gestured, beckoning, and stepped back.

Red sat at a kitchen table with his back to a wall and to one side of the open door that looked out toward the stable.

The old hag heaped his plate with potatoes and bacon. "You wasn't stingy with the water," she said crossly, as if somehow she had to explain why she was generous.

It wasn't good bacon, and the potatoes weren't quite cooked through, but it tasted preciously good to him.

She came from the stove with a big cup of coffee, bent low over his shoulder as she set it on the table, and pointing toward the door said quickly:

"Watch out there!"

Red didn't reply, but the next instant her voice went up in shrill anger: "If you don't like coffee plain, don't drink it! That's what I say. Here me feedin' a lazy no-count worthless feller—"

She disappeared into the next room, slamming the door behind her while Red gaped over his shoulder, wondering if she was crazy or something. He hadn't said a word about the coffee, liked it plain and strong as lye. He eyed the big, thick coffee cup, couldn't understand it, so shook his head and went on eating.

He was a little uneasy, but he was also hungry. Things might not be just right around here. The way she acted, and the warning about watching the door, together with a sensitive feeling that this old Crow's House was a good place for murder, made him think something might happen—but that was no good reason for missing breakfast. He switched his fork to his left hand so his right would be free, and he kept his eyes on the door.

The woman came back. She appeared to be still in a temper. He looked at her inquiringly. She eyed him with furtive sullenness and walked to the window, looking out. Something was wrong. She had very plainly given him a warning about keeping watch on the door, and he began to think that she half regretted doing so.

Suddenly she faced about and almost screamed: "All right, you come along into the bar an' I'll give ye a drink if then you'll go chop me some wood!"

"Make it tobacco an' papers, Mother," he said quietly, "an' it's a bargain. Me, I don't drink no more like I uster!"

He arose and turned to go into the next room, but she caught his arm with a pinch that hurt. "Wait!" she said, low and tense.

She held to his arm and turned back and peered through the door. A moment later she moved quickly to one side as if not wanting to be seen. She flung a scrawny arm toward the door:

"He made me promise to git you outa the kitchen. Away from this here door. He's gone out thar to steal your hoss. If he gits away, you'll be dead afore sun-down! Me too, 'cause he'll guess I tol' ye!"

"He'll do his guessin' in hell!" said Red. "Good place for bad guessers. Lots of 'em go there, Mother. Anybody steal my horse—that horse *is* mine! No matter what folks think, that there horse is—" Red checked himself. Forgetfully, he had been on the verge of giving away the arrangement between himself and the sheriff.

"I knowed that!" she snapped, glaring at him strangely. "Know all about you an' that sheriff."

"You what?"

"They ain't no time to talk now." She gave Red a shove. "Go out an' stop 'im!"

Red muttered, "Gosh A'mighty!" and went, though with misgivings. It seemed that this queer, savage old woman knew a lot of things. Was she plumb crazy? Or—how the devil could she know what had passed between him and the sheriff in but little more than whispers?

But he believed her when she said a fellow was about to steal his horse, and that had to be attended to first. He felt of his guns, settling them

73

well down on his thighs, and rose to his tiptoes, walking warily, as softly as he could.

The stable was nothing but a shed with some stalls on one side. The back of it opened into a corral. He crept up near the door, put his eye to a crack, and peered through. At first he could see nothing, for the sunlight was still in his eye, but his eye cleared and he saw that the horse was bridled and the saddle was on, being cinched.

Red's first impulse was to walk in and say things; but thought, "If he sees me he'll get behind the horse most likely, an' it bein' sort o' dim in there, I may make a miscue. I don't wanta make no miscues when I'm argyin' with a horse thief! 'Sides, this here door is too low for him to come a-ridin' out. He'll come leadin' Blackie. Yeah. Now it's all clear. He means to hop and go while the ol' lady's givin' me a drink. It's lucky I've quit drinkin'—for a spell!"

Red edged right up against the side of the door with his back to the wall, pressing stiffly, standing motionless. He knew that the shift of a shadow reveals the presence of a man when otherwise he wouldn't be noticed.

It wasn't long until he knew the fellow was coming. There was the scrape and tinkle of long-shanked spurs and the slow, almost dragging *plop, plop, plop* of the horse's feet. The fellow paused within the doorway, trying to keep well out of sight while he peered through to see if the road was clear. Red was standing too close to the building to be seen.

The man then with snapping jerk and tug at the reins came through, passed right by Red, looking in the other direction. Red simply leaned out and caught the reins, yanking them out of the man's hands.

Red had intended to say, "Thanks for saddlin' up my horse!" and so hold some conversation. He, being curious, wanted to learn something about this fellow and ask questions as to how he learned about Red's understanding with the sheriff back in Tahzo.

But the terrified man with a look of astonishment snatched at his gun, fired as Red lunged to one side.

"So that's it, h'm!" said Red, even as his hand was snapping at a gun butt, and with low side bend of his body he shot from the hip.

The horse thief reeled forward with arms upflung, the gun dropping from lax fingers. A staggering lurch and he pitched face down into the dust.

Red, still holding the reins in one hand, stepped forward, peering. He kneeled to turn the body and have a look at the face, but a voice squawked at him from the stoop of the kitchen doorway:

"Leave 'im lay! I want 'em to find 'im jes' as he is."

There she stood, a wild hag of a creature with a rifle in her hands and her thin face aglow with fierceness. Her thin hair was in straggling wisps about her face, the back of her skirt trailed the stoop, the barrel of the rifle rested in her left hand, and the butt was almost shoulder high. She seemed a strange, wild, mad woman.

"Good Lord!" said Red, wondering. He slipped his gun into its holster, hooked the reins over his arm, and walked toward her.

"You never saw 'im before," she said. "An' I'm almighty glad f'r to see the last of 'im! You come right along in here an' finish yore breakfas', an' I'll tell ye all about it! I can talk free now with him not listenin'!"

"Thanks, Mother. But I sorta ain't hungry now. I ate a lot before you—you shore done me a mighty big favor!"

"I know that!" she said with snap of lean jaws. She turned to the doorway, reached inside with the rifle in her hand, put it away. "I was goin' to kill 'im if you didn't!"

"I maybe wouldn't if he hadn't got rambunctious all of a sudden an'—"

"Well, you ort've. He knowed I don't like 'im. He'd have suspicioned I told ye about 'im, an' he'd've told my man Crow. An' Crow, he'd've knocked me over the head like he's threatened for to do more'n onct!"

"They'd better not, never, nobody!" said Red,

76

with feeling. She was a queer, fierce old hag, but she had been his friend.

"Now with him dead, boy, they ain't nobody but me knows why you've come over to Lelargo, an' hell'll freeze a foot thick afore I tell a livin' soul! I'm good sick an' tired o' the goin's on here! Been sick an' tired a long, long time. An' if the sheriff of Tahzo sent ye, I reckon you're hones'—the which is more'n can be said f'r one man in ten 'r twenty in this tarnation country!"

She had flung it out with rapid flash of tongue, all in one breath; and now, being out of breath, she gasped once or twice as if with so much more to say that she didn't know which words to let come first; then, flinging out a scrawny arm, pointed.

"He's Cliff Hammon, an' a no-good ornery varmint that poison 'ud have been too nice fer! Folks as won't dirty their own hands have used him, an' he's been makin' a fool outa Crow, though Crow ain't got sense enough to know it! This here uster be a tiptop roadhouse an' stage station, but after he got Crow into all the low-down mean goin's on an'. . ."

On and on she went, scarcely drawing a breath, pouring out her ten-year grievance against Cliff Hammon who had, she said bitterly, pulled her husband down into dirty work of a kind that she did not name.

Red had a sort of cold chill run up and down

his back. What she said was like a fierce chant of justice, long delayed, but come at last. Seeing how bitter she was, yet how unwilling to name just what Crow, at Hammon's instigation, had been doing, Red guessed that there must have been some murders.

Finally she got to the part that interested him most:

"Cliff Hammon rode in here about two hours afore you come, plumb scairt white!"

"Yeah," said Red, not loud enough to interrupt, "he passed me on the road—me off in the bushes!"

"The menfolks was away las' night, so nobody was here but me. I got up an' let 'im in. First off, he wanted to know 'f I'd heard anybody ride by."

Red nodded, attentively.

"Me, I don't sleep much. Nary a hoss goes by nighttime that I don't lay an' listen, a-wonderin' what devilment is up now! When I tol' him I hadn't, he poured hisself a big drink to stop his shiverin'—he was that scairt! He said the sheriff of Tahzo had sent a feller over here on his own hoss to pertend to be on the dodge an' make some trouble. Said he'd heard purt-nigh ever' word by listenin' at the door, right in the sheriff's office!"

Red whistled softly with great understanding.

"He said the sheriff had shot some to make folks think you was escapin'—an' that brought fellers runnin' just as he run out the front of

78

the sheriff's office and made for his hoss. Said somehow instead o' chasin' you, ever'body hit leather an' took out after him. Said he headed outa town the wrong way, an' so he had to take a long-about cut across country to get back to the Lelargo road. An' 'f he hadn't had one o' the best hosses in ten counties, he'd never a-made it. His hoss was dead on its feet, an' the menfolks had took all our stock, so they wasn't nothin' f'r him to ride. When you rode in he knowed you by the hoss. He wanted that hoss so he could get to town an' tell folks you was comin'. He wanted me to set with you here in the kitchen with yore back to the door while you et so he could sneak up an'— But I wouldn't! I tol' him I jus' wouldn't!"

She paused to get her breath again.

"I jus' wouldn't an' he couldn't make me! A nice-lookin' hones' boy like you. Somehow you didn't seem like no stranger to me—an' I ain't been called 'Mother' before in twenty years! There ain't been no man to carry water f'r me, either. Not since the stage quit stoppin' here. Before that I had a nigger f'r to do it! I had to sort o' pertend to help him steal yore hoss, but I made up my mind that he wasn't goin' to ride off alive an' tell them killers thar in Lelargo about you so they'd be layin' f'r you!

"So now, boy, nobody knows who sent you over here to Lelargo but you an' me. An' you may tell—but me, I won't, never! So light out an' git done with whatever 'twas the sheriff sent ye over here to do. Good-bye!"

Red pulled off his hat, reached out, took her withered, hard, dry hand and squeezed it. "Good-bye, Mother. You sure have played white with me, an' I'm alive, I bet, 'cause you've been a friend to me. Gosh, I wish there was somethin' I could do."

"Thar ain't. You've done it a'ready. You've treated me like I was a human bein'! Now git—an' God bless ye!"

She stood gaunt and savage, pointing; but there was a glimmer of moisture that dimmed the glow of her fierce old sunken eyes.

CHAPTER VIII

"INNOCENT BYSTANDER"

Red meditated fully and from all angles as he rode along. He felt pretty much at ease now about the sheriff. The sheriff had sent men after this Cliff Hammon who had been seen running from the office about the time Red hit the saddle. That seemed to show that the sheriff was playing square all right. Red grinned widely as he figured that the sheriff not only had wanted him to get away all right, but would have felt some better and a heap more peaceful if Hammon had been knocked right out of the saddle.

"Well, he has been—only not a saddle!"

And this Cliff Hammon had gone to hell with never a chance to learn that his friend the deputy was already there, or pretty close—having had so much head start.

"Yeah," he confided to Blackie, who twitched his ears as if with understanding, "the two of 'em was hangin' around, waitin' to see if anybody got hit by them snakes. Nobody did, which made 'em sorrorful. Then before me and the sheriff got settled down to talk, Hammon, he got in there in the front office to listen, and the deputy he went to the back door.

81

"H'm-m-m. Um-h-m! You know what I bet? I bet that deputy got all het up with suspicions that the sheriff was almost ready for to guess just who'd put them bobtailed rattlers in there. So Mr. Deputy up an' says to hisself, 'I'll kill me two birds with one stone. I'll put a crimp in 'em. Yessir, I'll nail the sheriff, then drop that Redhead, an' I'll say Red, he killed the sheriff, an' me, I killed him! Who's to know? Just fire Red's gun onct an' leave it layin' by his hand. Simple. Yeah. Then I'll be sheriff myself and get all them nice wages that's been promised if the sheriff has a funeral!' "

Red chuckled. "Nobody ain't ever goin' for to know just what that deputy did think. But that's my bet. It was a darn-fool notion an' a bigger mouthful than Mr. Deputy could chew. Some fellers have to be shot before you can learn 'em. I bet when the devil, he pokes his pitchfork into that deputy, he says, 'Son, now if you was smart like me, you'd stay away from hones' men!' Yeah, an' to that Hammon, too. I sure wanted for to have a little talk with him, but he got plum' overhet from bein' so bad scairt. Yep. A feller ortn't ever to get so scairt he don't know what he's doin'. That's bad.

"An' she said, 'Sir, you're talkin' through
    yore hat,
So hit your horse an' go like a bat,

82

'Cause I'm a lady an 'f you stick here,
I'll bite a piece right outa yore ear—
You danged galoot—oo—oo—oot!' "

Red stopped his humming, fell sober. "An' that pore old woman back yonder. See? You can't never tell. I thought she was just achin' f'r to take my head plum' off an' all the time she was meanin' that I wasn't to get hurt. Yessir."

Jogging along, Red rode into the town of Mekatone shortly after noon and, looking it over, shook his head, not charmed.

Mekatone was a sort of headquarters and amusement place for Bill Powell's big outfit and such other cow outfits as were friendly to him. It seemed a right good-sized place. Not far off up in the hills were some mines, and they sent a lot of men with wages down to the saloons and gambling places.

The sheriff had said that Leon Lenard had gone to work for Powell; and that the dead Rand girl's brother and his friend Wilkins would be pretty sure to be sticking close to Lenard, watching him, waiting for a chance to get him off somewhere in a lonely corner and ask questions.

Therefore, the thing for Red to do was find Lenard and sort o' look over the men about him. But Red knew that he was going to have to be mighty careful about asking questions. Lenard, an old-time outlaw, dangerous as a wolf and twice as suspicious, who for some reason best known to himself had bolted from Tahzo suddenly, might take it as unfriendly curiosity to have a stranger inquiring as to his whereabouts.

Red rode along into town until he came to the unpainted front of the stage office, which had a barn and corral out back.

He rode into the barn and sang out, loud and saucy. The barn boss, who had been dozing in the hay, came yawning, stretching, and blinking. The minute his eyes fell on Red's horse he woke up, stood stock-still and stared. The barn boss didn't say anything, but looked a lot; and he looked carefully at Red, too.

"Howdy," said the barn boss in a cautious tone with much respect, which was significant because barn bosses are mostly as bad-natured and fretful as camp cooks.

Red, still in the saddle, said, "You've guessed wrong! This here *is* my horse!"

"Have I said he wasn't?"

"You've looked it."

"Awright, awright, but I can't he'p how I look, can I?"

"You orta try. Then maybe yore kinfolks 'ud be prouder! Now listen clost. This here is my horse. An' if I put him up here, I'd better find him when I come back. Have I spoke plain, or do you need some more information?"

"Why, I didn't say nothin'—"

"Don't, neither. An' if anybody wants for to *borror* him, don't let 'em, an' send word right over to me at the—Where's a good place for to put up overnight?"

"The T T House is a right nice place."

"T T? That's Powell's brand, ain't it?"

"Yeah. Folks say the Old Man built the hotel so he'd have a good place to stay when he come to town."

"Then," said Red, "I reckon it'll do f'r me. So a'right. An' if anybody starts meddlin' with my horse, or askin' questions—same as you look like you'd like to!—you send word over to me at the T T House. My name it is Red Clark."

There was a sort of good-natured half-bantering earnestness about the way he spoke that made the barn boss scratch the back of his neck and meditate. Red didn't have the earmarks of an outlaw, he didn't have the look of a fellow trying to act bad, but he had a lot of something about him that made the barn boss feel respectful. And he had ridden in on the horse of the sheriff of Tahzo, which was more than any of these other bad Lelargo *hombres* had ever done.

Red walked down the street a piece until he came to the T T House.

It was a pretty solid two-story frame building. Most of the downstairs was given over to a saloon and gambling place, with a dining room at the side.

Red went into the narrow front office, looked about, whoo-whooed, didn't arouse anybody, so he picked up the triangle gong used to call the guests when meals were ready. He meant to hammer the gong, then decided he'd better not lest a lot of people think it was time to eat, and fellows get peevish when they think they're going to eat and don't. So he struck the gong just once but struck it hard.

A fat, sleepy-eyed man, with rumpled hair, came in sort of hastily and shouted, "Hey, what you mean—"

"I'm lookin' for somebody to talk to about a place to sleep," said Red.

The fat man grunted, looked reproachful, and crawled up on the stool behind the counter. He leaned forward as if getting fixed to go to sleep again, but asked drowsily, "You want a room?"

In Mekatone folks stayed up most of the night, or at least a lot of them did, so they dozed during the quiet of the day.

"Me," said Red, "I jus' rode in. I'm flat broke. But I been thataway lots o' times, so it don't mean nothin'. I'd like some board an' room till I sorta get straightened around. An' I give you fair warnin' that I eat a heap!"

The fat, sleepy man eyed him from boot-toes to ear tips, then yawned as if trying to swallow a full-grown apple:

"Number Ten upstairs there, back to the end of the hall, right hand."

He waved his arm vaguely and yawned again, making a sound that sounded to Red like a dying calf.

"Thanks," said Red and started toward the stairs.

"Hey, you!" the sleepy man called, beckoning. "I ain't done yet. Are you lookin' for a job?"

"Why?" Red asked, a little evasive, not sure whether or not he wanted to stay in this country longer than to attend to the sheriff's business.

"If you want work you can get it. Mr. Powell, he is havin' a rumpus with some fellers over west as is hornin' in on the T T range. An' he's hirin' right an' left. Good man to work for—'f you're a good man yoreself. If you ain't, he ain't. Do I tell him about you?"

"Well, maybe so, though I ain't yet quite sure what I want to do. My name it is Red Clark. I'd sorta like to stick around a couple o' days an' see what's what before I jump to a job that takes me outa town."

"Yeah, I know," said the sleepy man, with understanding. " 'S o.k." He was quite used to having strangers drift in and stick around for a few days, then slope. "Only," the sleepy man added, not concerned but as if he thought he ought to say something about it, "but supposin' now yore expectations don't shape up—who's goin' to pay this here hotel bill?"

Red slapped his holsters. "Claim my guns. How's that? If you look close, I think you'll think I'll get me some money somehow before I give 'em up. Now me, I'll just go an' have some pleasant dreams. I shore need 'em."

"Luck," the sleepy man grunted, looking after him, rather taken with the young fellow's lanky litheness and good-natured face.

Red went to the room. It was a little affair about seven by ten, more like a good-sized packing case than a place to live in, and furnished like a cell, with an iron bunk, a very small pine table, a lamp, and some rusty nails in the wall to hang clothes on. The room was hot and stifling with stale air.

As he started to undress he heard a man moaning in the room across the narrow hall. Red grinned, thinking: "He's had a good time an' he's now wishin' he hadn't! He's promisin' hisself that he won't never do it again. Me, don't I know them symptoms?"

Red struggled to get the sash window open, then propped the lone chair against the door which had neither bolt nor keyhole and sat down on the bunk to pull off his boots.

" 'Pears to be some purtty nice folks over here at that," he thought, reflectively. "The barn boss he was plum' quick to understand. An' this hotel man, he was nice. I reckon maybe I can get along 'f I take pains to behave myself." He paused, listening. "That fellow cross the way seems to be sufferin'—louder. Yeah, much louder."

Red drew the chair from the door, opened it and listened. "Maybe he et something an' has got the cramps. Sure bad, cramps is. I've stole enough green apples for to know. Anyhow, if I'm goin' to sleep he has got to be woke up!"

Red crossed the hall and tapped gently. No answer. He knocked. The moaning stopped. Red knocked again, lightly. A voice like a sick man's said, "Come in."

Red opened the door. A dark, good-looking young man, somewhat peaked and thin, with clear bright feverish eyes, looked up at him with mild surprise. He had raised himself on an elbow. There were the sort of smells that a doctor leaves in a room and some cloths on the table that looked as though they might be bandages. One glance at the man's face and anybody would have known he wasn't getting over a jag. He was sick.

"Pardner," said Red, almost coaxingly, "you sounded a little like maybe you'd like somebody to do something for you, so I thought I'd ask. Ain't there a little—you know—anything—"

The man looked at him carefully. He didn't have the sort of face that suggests a suspicious nature, but he seemed aware that Red had had some other reason for knocking. He said wearily, "Yes, I know. I jus' dozed off. I carry on that way when I'm half asleep. Keep ever'body else awake. They ain't many as is as polite about it as you."

"Aw now, shucks," said Red. "I just thought—"

The sick man smiled a little. It was a sad, tired smile. The look in his eyes was as if he had more than sickness the matter with him. "You might just hand me some water. They's a glass there this side the pitcher an'—"

"Surest thing. But wouldn't you like it fresh? An' ain't they no ice in this man's town? An' where in hell's the doctor that he'll let you lay an' suffer?"

"Ho," said the man with weary patience. "I been like this for near three weeks. Only worse. Purtnear the first night I got here I played innercent bystander—an' got it right in the belly. Sure tough. And," he said, with lift of eyes toward the ceiling and deepening haggard look, "bein' shot ain't the toughest part of it. I got things as ort to be done." He paused, looked down at a hand, then up at Red. "But the doctor, he does give me special care 'cause my pardner keeps steppin' on his tail. But if I try to get up I fall down, like I was dizzy drunk. An' I just gotta get well!"

"Oh, you'll get well a'right," Red offered with friendly assurance. "My name is Red Clark. An' I jus' rode in about an hour ago."

"My name is Ra-Ramsey, an'—an'—" Then fiercely: "An' I got special reasons of my own for knowin' I just can't die yet awhile!"

He took the water Red poured, drank a little, handed it back, nodding. "Thanks."

"Well, I'll be over 'cross the hall if you want anything—jus' you sing out."

"I'll try for to stay awake so I won't bother you. I don't do it only when I'm dozin' an' sorta half dream about somethin' that—that—" He choked up.

"Bother me?" said Red, pretending not to notice the man's emotion. "Oh, I can sleep in a thunderstorm with a buzz saw goin'. I got that there sorta conscience! So long."

CHAPTER IX

"DAMN IT, YOU'RE HIRED!"

Red tossed about for a time with all the recent happenings trying to crowd up into his thoughts and be looked over again and thought about, but he didn't want to think of them; so he turned this way and that—then slept.

He was awakened by a thumping as if somebody were trying to drive his fist through the wood of the door. Red thought he had been awakened just a minute or two after getting to bed, but it was dark, with only a glimmer of starlight coming through the open window, and from down the street was the tinkle of a piano in some dance joint. The night life of Mekatone was in full swing. He had slept for hours.

When he realized that the heavy knocking was against his own door, he shouted, "Hey, what's the matter?"

"Say, you in there!"

"How do you know I'm in here!"

"You Red Clark?"

"Yeah, I think that is my name. Purt-near sure, in fact. What you want?" Then quickly, "You from the stage barn?"

"Naw. Mr. Powell he wants to see you *pronto*—or a little sooner!"

"Yeah?" Red grinned. "What I ever steal of his?"

"Nothin'. Or he wouldn't have sent me. He'd've come hisself. He's in his room, waitin'. You comin'?"

"Hey, you gotta match? I can't see my nose before my face nor find my britches."

"Maybe you got 'em on!" the shrill and good-natured youthful voice suggested.

"I ain't," said Red. "I've spanked myself for to see." He pulled the chair from the door, pulled back the door.

A splinter of a kid stood there, a lean boy, with much the same sort of body and face as Red's. Except for the hair's color, they might have been taken for brothers, one some years the older.

The boy struck a match, crowded in, lit the lamp and turned, eyeing Red with staring curiosity. "Gosh," he said, "not many fellers could sleep like that—not if—" The boy stopped, somewhat embarrassed.

"Huh? Not if what?" Red asked a little sharply, noting the peculiar hint in the boy's tone.

He was a nice-looking kid, and Red right off liked him.

"Nothin'," said the boy; then he smiled. "On'y the Tahzo stage has jus' come in. That's all!"

93

"Comes ever' day, don't it?"

"No. Three times a week. An' 'tain't often it brings so much news, neither!"

"Um-m-m," said Red, enlightened.

"An' Mr. Powell is waitin'. He wants to see you mighty special. His room's in front. At the other end this hall. I'll go tell 'im you're comin'."

The boy backed out, still curious and admiring.

Red closed the door and rubbed his head with his knuckles. If you wanted to wash at a hotel like this you went downstairs and out back to the washroom. "All same as a dry camp," Red commented. No looking-glass. He rubbed at his cheeks. Felt he must look pretty scrubby and in need of a shave.

"H'm-m-m. So the Tahzo stage has come in? With news, h'm? Say, maybe Sheriff Martin underguessed the admiration these fellers over here have got for a hoss thief! In the which case it would be just too bad, wouldn't it? If I tried to tell these people the sheriff, he drawed a gun, told me to climb his horse and go—say, maybe they don't hang folks they think is crazy! Oh, well.

"Her chin wasn't much, but her mouth was
   big,
An' she had a nose like the snout of a pig,
But her hair was yaller an' her tongue was
   sharp—

She'd-a looked like an angel if she only
    played a harp,
You danged galoot—oo—oo—toot—toot!

"Yessir, you danged galoot, this here is a time
when you don't dare tell the truth. An' bein' as
you ain't no great shakes of a liar, you'd better
mostly keep yore mouth shut."

Red strapped on his guns, shook himself, tied
down the holsters, slipped the guns in and out to
see that they moved smoothly. He didn't expect
any trouble. It was just habit.

Stepping out in the hall, he looked about. No
one was in sight. He walked down the length of
the hall and tapped on the door at the end.

The door opened under the hand of a tall slim
man, well along toward the upper sixties. His
hat was pushed far back, and close-cropped gray
hair showed about the temples. His lean, closely
shaven face was deeply lined and had the color
of sun-tanned cowhide. He stood with a straight
back, and there was a hard look in his narrow
eyes.

"You Mr. Powell?" Red asked, feeling respectful, for this was a man and no mistake.

The man looked into Red's face. Those bright
narrow eyes were not easy to meet. There was a
searching drive in their glance. Red knew right
then and there this man was one bad *hombre* to
monkey with—one of the old-time breed, silent,

hard, and quick. "Are you that Clark boy?" The voice was mild, low, not unpleasant, but by no means soft. These soft-spoken men were the fellows you wanted to look out for. Red's own dad had had that same kind of a voice.

"I am," said Red.

The tall lean man stepped back and pointed: "There's Mr. Powell."

Red felt a little disappointed. For no particular reason at all he had sort of wanted this to be Mr. Powell.

He came through the door, walked into the room, a good-sized room, well lighted, well furnished, but with no knicknacks or bright colors. There were a half-dozen or more solid chairs, a table, and against the wall a desk with pigeonholes.

Powell was in a chair by a window. He stood up, and Red saw a thickset man, not tall, not short, with thick shoulders, thick muscular neck, and jaws like a pair of clenched fists. His nose was a little hooked, and his eyes had the perpetually half-angered look of a hawk. He was known to be, though he didn't look it, somewhere around sixty years old, and most of his life had been spent in the Lelargo country.

Like many of the old-time cattlemen, Powell had fought his way up with rope, gun, and saddle iron, had stood by his friends, had refused to forgive his enemies, had dealt out a rough-handed justice, but could not be checked or crossed without making a row. He frowned on the law-and-order party as a tricky device of weaklings to get affairs into their own hands. His was a violent temper, he rode roughshod over people that got in his way, drove a hard bargain, and was erratically generous.

It was said that if you happened to get on the blind side of Powell he would never see your faults or believe anybody that tried to tell him about them. And the men that rode with him were, as near as he could pick them, of his own breed.

"Clark?" Powell snapped.

"Yessir."

Powell came close, fastened his hawk eyes on Red's face, looked hard, then said, "All right, young fellow. What you got to say for yourself?"

"Plenty."

"Let's hear it."

"Well, sir, I got drunk in Tahzo an' they locked me up, which was right an' proper. Next night the sheriff, he took me up to his place for to have a little talk. He's plum' inquisitive, that feller. So, him bein' the next thing to a cripple with that leg o' his, I made a jump an' hit the nearest saddle. I lit out. An' here I am. My name—right name, I mean —it is Red Clark, an' I'm from up Tulluco way."

Powell laughed, not pleasantly. He simply

dropped his thick jaws and "Huh huh huh!" rolled out, loud with sarcasm. He looked Red up and down, then:

"What's the matter? Scairt to tell it all?"

Red glanced aside and saw the keen lean old slit-eyed man who had opened the door watching him. "I don't feel talkative, an' that's a fact!"

Powell grinned with noncommittal look. "You killed that deputy, shot the sheriff, an' stole his horse. That right?" There was nothing in the tone to indicate whether Powell was making an accusation or unreproachfully reciting facts.

Red settled back on his heels with head up. He was a little startled and had the impulse surging up to blurt out a protest; but he set his jaws and said nothing.

Powell gave a fellow the feeling that there was a lot of power behind those quick hawk eyes. Just by standing before him, anybody would have known that he was dangerous. They might be bad men in this country, but they were hard men, too.

Powell looked across at the other man, the tall lean fellow with thin mouth and narrowed eyes.

Red followed the glance but could not detect any flicker of expression between them, and he didn't know in the least how they felt about him.

But Powell nodded. "All right," he said with gruff friendliness that sounded mighty pleasant to Red's ears. "I'll tell you something. What a man does in some other part of the country—that's his lookout. Most men, they have the good judgment to go somewhere else than Tahzo to do it, though! You can be sure of it, that Tahzo sheriff is not going to sleep well o' nights till he gets his hands on you. He's a mighty honest man, that Sheriff Martin. He was man enough to say you got off fair and square, without shootin' when nobody wasn't lookin'. Jus' quick an' lucky, he says—so the people tell that come over with the stage."

Red took a deep breath and felt better. "Yeah," he murmured earnestly, "I shore am lucky. Allus was."

The lean old slit-eyed man looked at Red with much the same steady expressionless stare as a stone image with human eyes.

"But," said Powell, and his voice deepened, yet there was no sound of blame, just a recital of fact, "after you got over here—what about Cliff Hammon, there at Crow's Place?"

"Ask the old lady. She was watchin'!"

"Cliff Hammon, he was on my payroll," said Powell, calm about it, making no threat.

"Man pulls a gun on me, I don't ask what payroll he's on!"

"Though what the hell Cliff's been going over to Tahzo so much for lately, I don't know. But I know damn well he's been doin' some other things. He deserved killin'!"

Red's look brightened at that.

"Right now," Powell went on, "I need men.

Need 'em bad. Since you knocked Cliff off the payroll, I'm puttin' you on!"

"But listen—say—I—"

"Damn it, you're hired!" said Powell, jerking back his head, glaring with a kind of angered wonder that Red didn't seem to understand that when Powell said something it was just that.

"But wait a minute, Mr. Powell. I'm a heap appreciative an' all that, a heap, but—"

"Otherwise, back you go to Tahzo!"

"You mean you'd—"

"Just that!"

"Holy gosh!" said Red.

"I don't often do a sheriff a favor like that. This time I will. I'll give you just a half a minute to make up your mind." Powell pulled out his watch, a big thick watch on a heavy link chain. It was merely a gesture of emphasis. He did not look at the watch. He looked at Red, asking: "How about it?"

"You shore got me out on a limb! I was thinkin' some of kinda likin' to be my own boss for a spell an'—"

"I'm your boss, either way you want to jump!"

"An' besides, Mr. Powell, I'm just a wee mite nervous-like that I won't stack up quite so high as you 'pear to think because, honest, I don't set myself up as a bad man 'r anything similar, so if you think I'm—"

"Listen here, Red. I've been hirin' an' firin'

men for close on to forty years. Don't you think I know something about 'em by this time?" Powell demanded in a tone that sounded, but certainly wasn't, angry.

Powell had troubles, lots of them, and these days he was likely to seem irritable even when he didn't mean to be.

Red frowned thoughtfully. "Me, bein' a little cur'ous, I'd like to ask how long am I hired for?"

"Long as we get on well together!"

"But I was thinkin' of a little what you call *personal* matter that I need to be footloose to attend to," said Red, quietly.

"That's fair enough," Powell told him with frank understanding. "Your business is your own—just as soon as I get some of mine attended to. So you're hired till I learn some fellows that think they've got the Old Man down to stay off my range. May take a week, may take a month. You see I'm—"

There was a clattering rattle of knuckles on the door, and a kid's voice sang out, "It's me, Johnny, Mr. Powell!" and the same boy that had aroused Red from sleep opened the door and looked through with excited and urgent air, saying breathlessly: "He's just raisin' hell, Mr. Powell! Nobody can do nothin' with 'im an' Mack said for to tell you—"

Powell glared at the boy. With an oath, "Tell

Mack to hogtie 'im and—oh, well, I'll go!" More oaths.

Powell started for the door with the air of being on his way to break somebody's neck. At the door he paused abruptly, said to Red, "You stay here with Leon till I come back." Then Powell shifted his look to the tall, lean, slit-eyed man and said savagely in Spanish, "Why the hell couldn't I have had a boy like"—he jerked an arm toward Red—"instead of—well, you know!"

Powell turned about and went on, pushing Johnny roughly aside, and slamming the door with a bang.

CHAPTER X

"—OR LIE SO CONVINCIN'
I BELIEVE YOU!"

Red, left alone with Leon Lenard, took another look at him and reaffirmed his opinion that he was one bad *hombre* for to have trouble with. Red, if at all roused, was about as timid as a sore-tailed bear, but he was glad he wasn't set for trouble with this old outlaw. For one thing, he liked the look of him.

Red's thoughts and feelings were in rather a jumble because of that story that had come over from Tahzo about his escape and the way Powell had taken it; in more of a jumble over the way Powell had offhandedly accepted the shooting of Cliff Hammon, which seemed downright queer. But Red was clear-headed enough to be downright glad that this Leon Lenard with the sinister eyes, who seemed mostly bone and rawhide, was no longer suspected of having killed the girl. No doubt about it, Lenard would kill 'most anybody quick enough if riled, but in a man's way, shooting through smoke. "No, sir," said Red to himself, "them eyes never looked over no knife at a girl—'less to fight *for* her. You jus' bet yoreself that!"

Leon Lenard had his eyes still on Red and kept them there as he rolled a cigarette, a slim one, not much thicker than a match. He did it quickly. He held the cigarette about an inch from his mouth and said to Red, "Set down. Mr. Powell may be some little time gettin' back."

"Thanks." Red had an uneasy sense that something was coming. He sat on the edge of the table with one foot on the floor and the other dangling, didn't feel happy and wondered, what the hell? This old fellow wasn't the kind to look at a man that way just for the pleasure of trying to scare him. No, sir; something was coming.

Leon Lenard stood near the door with his back to it. He scratched a match, lit the cigarette, not taking his eyes off Red. He smoked, not saying anything, just watching and studying, and Red felt his hard-hitting eyes could pretty near look inside of a man and see what kind of bones were holding up his body.

Lenard tossed the cigarette away, narrowed his narrowed eyes until there was nothing but little points of glinting light, then asked gentle and low:

"Jus' what you doin' over here?"

Red caught the danger signal in that voice. He didn't stir except to waggle the dangling foot and say offhand:

"What's most anybody doin' that's crossed the line on a borrowed hoss?"

Then Lenard, not excited at all, but just as if stating a plain fact in a clear, cold, low voice, said, "You are a liar!"

Red didn't move. He stopped the waggle of the dangling foot, let it hang motionless. To be called a liar when, in a way, he was a liar did not make him angry; but it did make him a little anxious. He sat tight and grinned, wondered how the devil Lenard knew that, and asked: "Well, how you figure it?"

"I figure well," said Lenard.

Red looked inquiring and hopeful. "Let's hear."

"You're wearin' your own guns, ain't you?"

"Sure am!"

"How'd you come to have 'em when the shootin' started? Most sheriffs, they don't tie guns on pris'ners—they want to keep!"

Red couldn't think of a thing in the world to say, so he said nothing, looked calm, but wasn't quite.

"How'd you get 'em if the sheriff, he didn't give 'em to you?"

Red tried to look wise but thought he'd better keep his mouth shut.

"An' why'd he give 'em to you," Lenard went on, "if he wasn't turnin' you loose?"

"You've heard the story that come over from Tahzo," said Red. "I'll stand pat."

"All right," said Lenard and, coming over to

the table, sat on another edge of it, face to face with Red. "Then let's have a showdown. 'F you are smart as you look, you'll tell me some truth."

"I ain't no much of what you call a hand to lie," said Red, modestly.

"I got a little edge on you. I'm from over Tahzo way myself. I know that sheriff well—from a distance. I never get intimate with sheriffs. But he's no fool. Fact is, he's a pretty smart fellow— for a sheriff."

Red looked blank and listened attentively.

"I'm one of the few men," said Lenard, "as know that deputy o' his was a damn skunk, though I didn't learn it complete till I come over here. Him and Cliff Hammon was throwin' in together. Both of 'em are dead. You done it."

Lenard stopped, expecting Red to say something. Red didn't say anything because he felt that somehow this lean gray old range wolf held all the aces.

"I'm not wipin' away any tears. 'Cause o' something learned just late, I'd have killed Cliff Hammon myself just as soon as he come riding back here into town. That's why Mr. Powell took it so calm. Usual, a stranger shoots one of his men an' the stranger has regrets."

"Then I been lucky," said Red with sincerity.

Lenard nodded a little. "So far. But I want to know what happened there in Tahzo. You seen my cards. Now show your hand!"

Red took a deep breath and met Lenard's gimlet-eyed look:

"Well, sir, the deputy was right there at the back door of the sheriff's office, gun in hand, about the time I was leavin'. He shot first. There was some more smoke, an' me, I hit the nearest saddle. Over to Crow's Place, Hammon was a-leadin' my horse outa the stable an' I stopped him. 'Fore God an' cross my heart, I never see that deputy or Hammon before!"

"You," said Lenard coldly, "stick to what I ask. I didn't ask how many times you'd seen anybody before."

"I was just tryin' to tell how it all happened."

Lenard eyed him with unwavering look; then, softly, "Son, you don't lie worth a damn!"

" 'Course not. I'm speakin' truth!"

"No, you ain't," Lenard told him calmly. "You're wigglin' round the truth like a cripple snake round a stump. There's something wrong some place. I use to be quite some hand at puttin' things together an' sizin' 'em up. You goin' tell me you don't know who I am?"

Red shook his head, admitting, "No, 'cause I do know."

The old outlaw, with just a little calm pride, said, "All right, then. I'm Leon Lenard, an' in my time I been far-hunted an' never caught. That was mostly because I knew how to figure things. I'm figurin' now. So you just listen to the story that's

107

come along over here. You check me up as I go along an' speak out when I tell it wrong.

"First, you rode into town an' give over your guns to a barkeep. The which means you are just a kid puncher with some more sense than most. It means you wasn't wanted for anything anywhere, an' wasn't lookin' for or expectin' trouble. Right?"

Red nodded. "Purt-near, I reckon."

"You got drunk an' raised the devil. More kid puncher carryings-on. All you done was to play some pranks that was plum' annoyin' to a few folks, but all in fun of a sort. No harm done. The marshal an' the sheriff, they rounded you up an' dropped you in the old calaboose to sleep it off. That right?"

Red admitted, "I couldn't tell it near so well myself."

"There was nothin' agin you anywhere. You wasn't on the dodge an' you hadn't done nothin' to make you scairt. So the sheriff must've been lettin' you go, since you was wearin' your guns. You're not a trouble hunter. You're not a killer. You ain't got the earmarks. You're a good-natured, mostly honest, an' halfway likable young puncher. That right?"

"I shore hope so!"

"Then why, all of a sudden, for no reason a-tall, did you start shootin'?"

Old Lenard had put him right up into a tight

corner with no room left to wiggle. Red's lips felt dry. Think as fast as he could, he couldn't seem to hit on anything that seemed worth suggesting to this hard-eyed, perfectly calm, wise old outlaw whose lean, wrinkled face was as inscrutable as a pine knot. Lenard did seem just a little favorable; but he was the sort of fellow that might seem that way just to get what he wanted out of a man.

Red didn't know which way to let his tongue jump; and he thought he was likely to be luckiest if he just grinned and said, "Me, I guess I'll stand pat!"

"All right," said Lenard, standing up and walking around in front of Red. "I've done more talkin' to you in the last ten minutes than I've done before to any stranger in the last ten years. So now listen to some final words. Beginnin' right now you either tell me the truth—or lie so convincin' I believe you! Else I tell Mr. Powell how I got things sized up. Goin' a-talk?"

Red shook his head, feeling pretty helpless.

Then Leon Lenard started to draw, but in the queerest way Red had ever heard of. Lenard reached for the gun on his right hip; and he reached for it with a kind of wide slow swing of arm as though he had rheumatism. He set his hand on the butt and pulled slow. When the gun was about halfway out, Lenard stopped, then pushed it back, dropped his hand, and eyed Red queerly.

"You'd set there still an' let a man pull his gun on you, h'm?" Lenard asked, not sneering.

Red had stiffened and set both feet to the floor, but otherwise hadn't moved. He didn't feel happy and wasn't angry. He couldn't shoot it out with a man he didn't dislike and even half admired for so logically calling him a liar when he was one. Lenard had treated him downright decent and square.

Besides, though he wasn't going to say so out loud, he hadn't been really scared, because he couldn't believe that Lenard meant business when he reached for a gun just about as a man would if he had a stiff shoulder. He knew there wasn't anything stiff about Lenard except his backbone. He carried himself straight up and down as though he had been a soldier all his life; and Red would have bet everything down to his boot heels when Lenard reached for a gun, and meant it, all you'd see would be a flash of movement and a spurt of fire-colored smoke.

Red shook his head, still refusing to talk; but he debated with himself just how much, if anything, of the truth he could tell, when Lenard backed off a step or two, frowned, and spoke:

"I don't know jus' how you an' that sheriff have stacked the cards to give you the name of a killer on the dodge. I reckon the sheriff must've killed that deputy for good reasons of his own, then maybe said you done it to make you welcomed by some folks over here. But your name is Rand. An' you've come over here for to get *me!*"

"My name's Red Clark. An', hell, nobody thinks *you* done it!"

"That sheriff, he does!"

"No, sir! He don't. He told me so!"

"Then that *is* why you come over here! Lookin' for the man that killed your sister?"

"My name ain't Rand. But you're guessin' mighty close, Mr. Lenard!"

"They got reasons for to think I done it," Lenard told him.

"I don't know nothin' about the reasons. All I know is the sheriff, he said he knowed damn well now you didn't."

Lenard eyed him cautiously, suspecting a lie, thought maybe Red was afraid to speak up to his face. Then, "You don't know why I been suspected?"

"No, sir, I don't. But I know you never hurt no woman—not in your life, you never did!"

"How you know that?"

"I jus' know it, that's all—to look at you. Your eyes, they say so."

The reply pleased old Lenard, but he wouldn't show that it did. He said, "They hung that poor cowboy 'cause it was his knife they found by her body. When they hung him they didn't know that I had borrowed the knife off him some time

111

before an' never give it back. But the sheriff, he found out. That's how he come to suspect me." Lenard waited, but Red said nothing. Then: "Not long back, Bessie Rand's brother showed up from Texas an' swore to get the man that done it—meanin' me!"

"Who's been tellin' you?"

"Cliff Hammon."

"I wonder," Red suggested hopefully, "could Hammon have done it hisself?"

"Might've, but I don't think so. Some low things even a no-good man like Hammon wouldn't do!"

"You borrowed that cowboy's knife an' never give it back?"

"I did." Lenard frankly acknowledged the incriminating statement.

"Then who borrowed it off you? Or stole it?" Red asked eagerly.

"I don't know. But I got suspicions. I'm goin' slow. But even if it was my own father that killed that girl, I'd kill him! She was to me almost like if I had a daughter, but Bill Powell, he has been my best friend purt-near all my life!"

Red gasped, pointed at the door, vaguely trying to show whom he meant:

"It can't be—*him!*"

"Who?"

"Mr. Powell!"

Lenard's thin mouth moved into a hard, cruel

curve. "Don't even ever halfway say a thing like that again long as you live!"

"A'mighty gosh, didn't you hear me sayin' it couldn't be him when 'twas his name you spoke?"

Lenard reflected, said, "Oh" vaguely, as if he had somehow been pinched a little by his own kind of close reasoning. He nodded with aloof approval: "You got right smart of a head on you for a youngster."

"Listen," said Red, eagerly. "The sheriff knows now just who did do it. I'm goin' tell you, tell it all, an' she's truth—ever' word! It was thisaway . . ."

Red told it all, from beginning to end. He liked, he trusted, this lean old wolf that had put him into a tight corner, and so talked freely.

Lenard listened with motionless expression and not a flicker in his slit eyes to tell what he thought. When Red had finished, he nodded:

"That there is a hard story to swallow. But at that, it goes down easier than the other one. The last thing any sheriff's goin' to say is that his prisoner got off fair an' square because he was smart an' quick. That ain't the way sheriffs talk. I know. I've been the cause of some talk among 'em. When I heard Sheriff Martin had said that, I started in to look for the joker. Pretty soon I figured out he had *sent* you. Then I guessed you must be the Rand boy, though you ain't quite old

113

enough, an' I never heard that he had red hair. So I knowed most likely it was me you'd be after."

"That there is jus' why I come, Mr. Lenard. To tell Rand an' Wilkins it wasn't you by no manner of chance."

"Then I guess maybe Rand is that fellow that's sick back there at the end of the hall. His pardner is called Wilkie, which is nearly like Wilkins. They let on as how they'd come up on the dodge from Texas. You can stop in and have a talk with the fellow."

"I shore will. An' do you think you know who done it—the killin' of the Rand girl?" Red asked, almost begging.

"Son, I know no more'n I did before. And I 'most near hate myself for the suspicions I got."

"Meanin'?" Red asked.

"Meanin'," said Lenard coldly, "I keep 'em to myself till I am plum' sure. Then I won't need no help for to do what I think ought to be done. I loved that girl like she was my own daughter.

"Now then, son, when you get word to that sheriff, you tell him to keep a good grip with both hands on that Mexican witness he's got. Valdez ain't so damn honest. Why he stopped over to Tahzo an' give hisself up, I can't figure. It's more than suspicioned—it's said that 'twas him that shot Powell's old paymaster in the back an' lit out of here with near ten thousand dollars, 'bout ten days ago. Keep that under your hat.

114

Personal, I ain't so sure Valdez done anything of the kind. But if Bill Powell knows Valdez is over there at Tahzo some place, he'll go over an' get him, sheriff or no sheriff. Bill Powell has fought his way up through hell—where-as that Sheriff Martin has only smelt a little brimstone an' smoke now an' then. I sure feel sorry for him. He was my friend when I never had but the one in the world. An' the only other I ever thought half so much of was Bessie Rand—"

Powell with unexpected suddenness flung open the door. He strode in angrily and sent the door shut with backward sweep of powerful arm.

"That Rand girl, h'm?" he muttered. He walked across the room, turned, and began to pace back and forth. "Seems like I hear her name ever' place I go." He drove fist to palm and strode on as if determinedly walking somewhere, stopped abruptly near the wall, turned back, still as if purposefully on his way. "I just overheard that fellow Wilkie talkin' of her. Then you, here now." Again fist and palm cracked. "Hangin's too good for the dog that done it. The old Apaches had some right ideas about some things! Ought to be staked out on an anthill, fellow who'd do a thing like that!" Back and forth he went with heavy tramp and clatter of spurs. "First thing Buddy wanted to know when he come down from the hills yesterday was if anything had been learned—though they caught that fellow next thing to red-handed, didn't they, Leon? An' hung him quick!"

"It's the sort o' thing the range don't soon forget," said Lenard.

"They sure don't. I keep hearin' it, hearin' it, hearin' it! If they hadn't caught the fellow right off, I'd have chipped in on the reward." He turned to Lenard: "An' I know you too damn well to think if they hadn't got the right man that you'd not be out on the scout!"

Powell stopped short, whirled about, looking at Red, stared a long time, then in silence reached down into his pocket, took out a buckskin bag, opened it, and offered Red a twenty-dollar gold piece.

"Thanks, Mr. Powell."

"No thanks about it. Be took outa your wages. But I hear you're broke. Now don't go an' get drunk first thing. We're ridin' at sun-up."

"I'll be ready; any time."

Powell waved an arm, dismissing him.

When Red left the room, Powell dropped with all his weight into a chair, sighed and leaned forward, elbows to knees and face down. He spoke without looking up. "I don't know what I'm goin' to do with that boy."

"This redhead, you mean?" Lenard asked a little evasively.

"No, you know I don't mean that kid. I mean

Buddy. Leon, I'm beginnin' to think that son of mine is damn near worthless."

"What's he been doin' now?"

"Just took a bottle an' swollowed till he was fool drunk. When I got down there he was cussin' out men the devil hisself would speak respectful to—or get hurt. Cussin' 'em to their faces!"

"An' they took it," said Lenard calmly.

"Yeah, but why?" Powell lifted his head, stared with a hurt and angered look. "Mack, Pete, Slim, and Harry Bates, standin' there sour-eyed an' silent, takin' it! Why? Why would *you* take it, Leon, if Buddy made a fool of hisself an' stepped on your toes?"

Leon Lenard growled softly without speaking.

"You fellows that would fight a she-bear bare-handed for her cubs—you know he's all I've got. An' if anything happened to him, I'd be all broke up. You take it off him because he's my boy. Yet somehow, at times, it don't seem he can be my boy. Take that kid Johnny Howard—just a stray I picked up. He acts more like a son ought to than Buddy hisself! An' ever'body likes Johnny, though he's a sassy little devil!"

"Well, you see, Johnny's had to ride his string as she comes," said Leon Lenard, trying in an oblique way to show Powell that he had overnursed that boy of his by trying to make things too easy. "Like you an' me when we was kids, Johnny's never had gentled horses for to

117

ride. An' when he's been throwed, he's hit the ground. Didn't land on none o' them feather beds that, in a way of speakin', you've drug around for Buddy to fall on. Put Buddy on wages an' make him earn 'em an' he won't have near so much time to get into devilment."

Powell did not appear to listen. He never seemed to listen when anybody hinted that his son wasn't what he ought to be. Yet now the old cattleman was deeply hurt, not by what Lenard had said, but by something his son had done.

After glowering at the floor for a time, he looked up at Leon Lenard: "He was down there in the bar tellin' what-all he was goin' to do, an' how he was goin' to run things, when I cashed in! Talkin' to my men, that ride for me an' fight for me, about how things would be if I died! Crazy drunk, an' of course he didn't know what he was saying. Good God, but you don't suppose he can wish I was dead!"

"Some folks as he calls his friends," said Leon Lenard, calm and unflinching, "probably do!"

"What's that? What's that!" Powell leaped from his chair, glaring.

"You heard me, Bill." Lenard stood unexcitable and with slit-eyed gleam striking against the face of the big cattleman. "But I'll tell you some more. The which is this: The bunch Buddy runs with keeps him broke, don't they? They prod him into doin' all sorts of things for to get money.

Then *they* get it away from him. When you cash in they'll mighty soon get it all away from him. As 'tis, every time you clamp down the lid of the money box on Buddy a lot of other fellows' fingers get pinched. Take just one. Cliff Hammon was his best friend. An' you know now Cliff was a-selling you out over on the Nelis range."

"Right," said Powell, dropping his glance.

"An' the time Buddy was a-stoppin' over 'cross there with me till you fixed up some of his troubles here, his friends was ridin' over or sendin' word, wantin' money. That's all most of his friends want outa him."

"By God," said Powell as he straightened and struck the table a rattling blow with heavy fist, "he's man-grown an' he's got to do a man's work in a man's way from now on. I'm through lettin' him go about as he damn well pleases an' runnin' wild. He rides with us tomorrow. An' he rides with fellows I'm goin' to pick. I'll put him stirrup to stirrup with that Red Clark an'—"

"I wouldn't do that," said Lenard quietly. His narrow eyes seemed to grow more narrow.

"Why not?"

"Well, because—um-m-m." Lenard meditated as if, having spoken before he thought, he was now having to shape up his words a bit carefully before venturing to go on. "Well, I got me a suspicion they won't hit it off well together. That Buddy'll—well, just sort o' take a dislike to 'im."

"Well, I've taken a likin' to him!"

"Um-m-m. That Red's a deceivin' sort o' fellow, Bill. He's a gentle sort of boy, good-natured an' near honest, but—"

"Go on. But what?"

"I knowed his dad," said Leon Lenard, and almost grinned. "His dad was sheriff of Tulluco an' give me more trouble than any half-dozen other sheriffs. His dad had a way of ridin' alone. An' them are the hardest sheriffs to dodge. This boy rides alone an' 'll go into trouble without battin' an eye—an' come out grinnin'!"

"Just the sort of boy Buddy needs to be with! They're about of an age. Red's come through smoke on the sheriff's own horse. An' not braggin' about it!"

"No. He ain't bragged," said Lenard enigmatically.

"Buddy's got an admirin' weakness for the wrong sort of bad men, so—"

"He ain't no bad man, Bill, that kid."

"Why, he shot the sheriff, killed the deputy, dropped Cliff Hammon, an' you say—"

Lenard made a slow gesture. "Never mind what he done. He's a reckless fool kid. Get him riled an' he's dangerous. An' he's redheaded. Bein' a teetotal stranger, he may not understand Buddy's ways at first! 'Mong the fellows he's rode with he ain't met many like Buddy."

"Well, I like him," said Powell. " 'Tain't often

I misjudge men, Leon. But it 'pears I sure did on that Mexican, Valdez. I liked that fellow, too."

"Maybe," said Lenard. "I didn't see him, but he was over my way the day Bessie Rand was—"

Powell swung his arm as if to slap the words from his ear. "I don't want to hear her named. I just can't stand it, Leon. Ever' time I hear her name seems like I see her layin' right there dead. A woman—murdered like that! A man—or half a dozen men—if they are killed—well, they're men, an' carried guns or ought've! But a girl, out alone, an' killed with a knife just so she couldn't never name the man that—God, it makes my tough old hide creep to think about it!"

"Yes," said Lenard. "I know. You ain't near as hard some ways as folks try to think. I mind when your wife was sick, dyin'. You was gentle an' almost tearful, too."

Powell breathed deeply. "An' I guess I've been pretty soft about that boy of mine. But you'll see from now on. By God, he's got to hit the collar or I'll skin him alive!"

"Yeah," said Lenard. "I know. A collar with a lot o' paddin' in it."

"You'll see. You'll see, Leon."

"For near thirty years, Bill, I been lookin' straight at you. An' I ain't never seen you hurt a friend yet—no matter what he done. An' Buddy's your son. You'd cut off your hand before you'd paddle his rump!"

121

CHAPTER XI

RED DODGES
LETTER-WRITING

After he left Mr. Powell and Lenard, Red learned
that he had slept clear through the supper hour,
and that made him talk to himself, reproachful.
But he scouted around and found a restaurant,
had some steak, eggs, potatoes, prunes, two
pieces of pie, and three cups of coffee, so he felt
like a man again instead of like a half-empty
sack.

He strolled over to the stage company's office
to have a look at his horse.

"Yeah," said the barn boss who, being through
with the day's work, was sitting out front
smoking, "you ain't got no business 'bility
a-tall. 'F you'd charged a dime a throw we'd
both be well fixed tonight. 'F you'd rode in on
an elephant, folks wouldn't-a been more cur'ous!
Too late to start chargin' now. Ever'body's seen
'im!"

Red went back to the hotel. The fat manager,
still looking a little sleepy, was at the desk. He
was busy with some figures—having such a time
with them that he had got ink on his fingers and
wiped his face.

The manager eyed him with a sort of admiring interest. The Tahzo stage had rolled in since Red had rung the gong and asked for a room—on credit.

"I'll jus' pay up what I owe—an' for tomorrow's breakfast. I'm ridin', come sun-up. An' I'd like me some paper an' a pencil, envelope an' a stamp. 'Mong the duties I don't like is letter-writin'. I'm a heap more to home writin' with a hot iron on cowhide than on letter paper."

The manager beamed. "I told you Mr. Powell was needin' men. Ridin' out with him, h'm? I reckon you an' him'll get on. Come along into the bar an' I'll interduce you to some of the boys. T T boys."

Red went in and met old Mack, Pete, Slim, and Harry Bates, with some of the other T T men and their friends crowding around.

Everyone eyed him carefully, though in a quiet way they were not unfriendly. He knew he was being sized up with steady watchful glances that glimmered with just a trace of distrust. No doubt of it, they had expected him to strut some and maybe talk loud. Young killers were likely to. The talk was of cows, weather, feed. There was no hint of what they had heard of him. They weren't at all the sort of men to throw their arm welcomingly about any stranger's neck.

Red smiled a bit and listened, said, "Yeah, I reckon," also, "Maybe. 'Pears so," and such-like things, carefully not talking of himself. He went away, leaving behind him rather favorable comments; such as:

"He don't fourflush none, nohow."

" 'Pears to take it as all in the day's work."

"Seems mighty young."

"Yeah, but them guns is low-hung and tied down, an' he looks sort o' limber, too."

"Well, in a couple days or so maybe we'll know better what to think. The Old Man's sure got a fight on his hands. That right, Mack?"

Old Mack spoke slowly: "Hope so. An' me, I've followed the Old Man through fights aplenty. He don't send no man where he won't go hisself. Usual, he goes first!"

"Yeah," said young Johnny Howard, who had just come in and piped up with the shrillness of a youngster who meant to be heard, "Mr. Powell'll go horseback where most o' you tough *hombres* can't walk an' carry a bridle!"

They grinned tolerantly at Johnny. He was one of the toughest little devils in Lelargo County; sassy, full of grit, hard-riding, hard-working, too. Men who knew him well liked him too much to do more than cuff him about as a she-bear teaches a cub good manners.

When Red left the group he went up and knocked on the door across from his room.

It was opened by a black-eyed young man who gave Red a careful looking over, then said, "Oh, you're Red Clark. Well, I didn't know that sheriff you winged well enough to feel bad after Charley here told me how nice you was to him. Come in. Ain't much more'n room for one skinny man an' his shadder in these cubbyholes. Here's your visitor come again, Charley—an' he's that Red Clark I was tellin' you about."

Wilkie pushed the chair toward Red and leaned against the wall.

Red looked at the sick man, asked a few questions, then he said:

"Fellows, I got a delicate matter to talk over with you boys. Matter o' fact, I got some news for a man over here named Rand an' a friend o' his'n called Wilkins."

Red pretended not to notice the surprised and slightly alarmed exchange of glances. He stooped to adjust a spur strap, straightened, went on:

"An' bein' as I'm ridin' at sun-up, I thought maybe I'd better leave my message with some-body as would pass it on to the right parties."

"We'll see it gets to the right parties or keep it to ourselves," said Wilkie.

"Well, sir, if you get a chanct, just let 'em know that Sheriff Martin over at Tahzo says he *knows* now who killed that girl an' that all his previous suspicions is wrong!"

Silence followed. Red leaned back and thought-fully looked at the ceiling.

"How come," asked the sick man, "*you* 'pear

to know so much about what the sheriff knows?"

Red grinned. "Things is queer. That there is a little detail I can't explain 'cept to Rand an' Wilkins themselves."

Long silence. Then the man who had called himself Ramsey said, "See here, we're them!"

"An' you knowed it!" Wilkins added, not quite sure there wasn't a trick somewhere.

"No, no, sir, I didn't know. I just suspicioned. An' suspicions, they're like poker hands. You may be willin' to bank on 'em a heap, but you can't be sure till after the showdown. 'Less you hold a royal flush—an' me, I don't never. 'F I did, 'twould be penny ante with a nickel limit!"

"Who are you an' why you here?" Wilkins demanded, doubtfully.

"Well, sir, I got to spoil my nice repytation for bein' a hell-bender an' tell you boys some truths. You maybe won't believe me, but facts is facts, and these are them! . . ."

When Red had finished, Wilkins nodded, looked at his partner, and said, "You know I've told you that from watchin' an' listenin' careful, I just couldn't figure Leon Lenard as the man that done that killin'. He'll kill. But not with a knife, an' no woman."

"I know. I've been some doubtful myself," said Rand. Then, explaining to Red: "Just the day before they found Bessie'd been killed, my kid brother, he asked Tom Terry—he's the boy they

126

hung—for to borrow his knife. Tom give him one, but the kid said, 'No, the stag-handled one with the spring blade. I want it.'

"Then Tom he said, 'Gosh. I almost forgot. Glad you 'minded me. I loaned it to Leon Lenard the last time I was to town. I'll sure remember to ask Leon next time we meet.' "

Rand cleared his throat, propped himself more firmly on an elbow while Wilkins bent over and fixed a pillow behind him.

"The kid and a couple of neighbor boys went off that day up in the hills to hunt and fish for a week 'r ten days, so the kid didn't know nothin' about what had happened till he come home.

"An' as Tom an' Bessie—he was in love with her—had a quarrel that very mornin' she was killed, why, when the knife was recognized, well—folks thought the world and all of Bessie! They jus' didn't waste no time listenin' to poor ol' Tom who'd been drinkin' some. On account o' that quarrel, I reckon. They jus' up an' hung 'im.

"By the time the kid had come down from the hills an' told Dad, and Dad had told the sheriff— why, Leon Lenard was gone. So soon as me an' Wilkins rode in, we jus' followed him over here, hopin' for a chance to get him where he'd be willin' to talk.

"But me, I got plugged by a stray bullet, an' I been laid up ever since. But the doctor, he says he's goin' to make a stab at gettin' the bullet out.

He's been scairt to try till somethin' or other happened to my insides. I'm feelin' a lot better. An' I just got to get well!

"But say, don't you reckon Leon hisself has got a pretty good suspicion as to who got that knife away from him?"

"I know dang well he has," said Red. "An' me, personal, I wanta have a plum' clear conscience if I ever see them slit eyes of his peerin' at me over a gun barrel."

Rand lay back weakly, but seemed mildly content. "I'm powerful glad it ain't Lenard. Bess, she was awfully fond of him. Said when you got to know him he was plum' different from what he looked. She called him Uncle L'on."

Red began to fish about in his pockets. "Now, boys," he said, coaxing a little, "I got here all that's needful for to write a letter. I done all the sheriff sent me to do—mostly by luck. Listen. Here's pencil, paper, stamp, ever'thing. You just write him. An' if you think maybe you hadn't better address it to no sheriff—'specially over to Tahzo—for fear the postmaster or somebody gets careless an' loses the letter, why, send it over to your dad an' let him take it to the sheriff. How's that? Moreover, I know plum' damn well what the sheriff is goin' to make you promise. He's goin' to make you promise to help him get the feller that done it over to Tahzo an' stand trial."

"I know," said Rand, with disapproval, and Wilkins growled.

"After all," Red insisted, "he's sheriff, an' if he's responsible f'r catchin' the feller—don't you see? Well, then, you boys write the letter an'—you can do it a lot better'n me."

Red crossed over to his room with a weight off his chest. Letter-writing always gave him indigestion, due to nibbling so long and thoughtfully on the end of the pencil.

As he undressed he hummed to himself:

" 'Now you listen here, you danged galoot!
Maybe you c'n ride an' maybe you can
    shoot;
But straddle yore horse an' a-git outa town,
Cause I'm a lady an' I'll knock you
    down—
You dang galoot!'

"Yessir, I'm lucky. Allus was. An' bein' as now I ain't goin' to play cards no more, or ever get married, maybe I'll stay lucky!"

CHAPTER XII

SMOKE WITH LEAD IN IT

The next morning Red was up early, and by sun-up he had given Blackie a good cussing just to offset the half-affectionate scrape of the currycomb and rub of the brush. And so Blackie, having ears, knew that he was a slab-sided, sway-backed, underdone piece of knock-kneed crowbait; but having plenty of horse sense he didn't seem to pay much attention to what Red said. He munched oats and switched his tail, quite at times as if he thought Red too had some flies on him that needed switching off.

Blackie was saddled and ready to go, but he stood in his stall, shaking the bridle and stamping the flies off his feet while Red tossed the sheriff's rope along the runway, shaking out the kinks and seeing that it was suitably limber. He was an artist with a rope and knew a rope had to be well looked after or an artist might look like a chump.

A voice behind him said, "So you're the man that shot Cliff Hammon—when he wasn't lookin'!"

Red dropped the rope end and spun about on a dime-pointed heel with hand to hip and gun out, ready to drop knee down or lunge aside, expecting to face a gun. To his ears the tone meant trouble and the words fight! But the man who had spoken staggered with much the same expression as though unsuspectingly he had kicked a piece of dynamite and it exploded under his nose.

He yelled anxiously all in a breath:

"Hey, there—look out what you're doin'! My God, man, don't!—I was jokin'—and hones'! I'm Buddy Powell, so don't—"

"Yeah? Well, whoever the hell taught you to make a joke musta had some coffin nails for to sell! Now listen to me!"

Red put away the gun and stepped closer, stepped up very close so there would be no chance of not having everything he said clearly heard.

He began to talk fast and fluently. He used words and phrases that have never been in print and never will be. It was such a cussing as probably no man on the range had ever taken before without trying to do something about it. When he finished, or rather tapered off into repetitions, Buddy Powell had been called everything that a redheaded cowpuncher, who had been in almost every kind of a place where bad language was used, could lay his tongue to; and Red put feeling, inflection, and emphasis into the words, holding a fist doubled at his side ready to work on the dissipated pudgy soft face and shape it up like the splatter of a dropped egg if young Powell so much as grunted in protest. All young Powell did was to open his mouth and eyes in a long gasp of stupefied amazement.

"You," said Red in disgust and out of breath, "ain't fit to be used for wipin' out a sheepherder's skillet, an' except that I don't want my boots to stink, I'd kick you all over this here town! Why, you ain't got the spunk of a broken-backed jack rabbit ner the sense of a drunk lunatic, you—" Red paused for breath.

Young Powell, with a kind of whining snarl, said, "You'll wish you hadn't talked to—" He started to go away.

"Wait a minute! I ain't done. I jus' got a little outa breath, that's all!" Red grabbed his shoulder, jerked him about, peered hard at his face, said softly: "You're sorry Cliff Hammon went out, h'm?"

Red with high contempt examined young Powell's fancy range finery, from silver-studded hatband to silver spurs, silk shirt, embroidered vest, fancy-worked chaps, broad belt and ivory-handled guns; then spoke:

"Yore dad's a man. I'm admirin' of him. But I been underestimatin' of his power an' influence in this here community. But some day somebody will none the less jus' naturally wring your neck!"

"Oh, you're afraid of him, too, ain't you! You wait till I tell him!"

"Tell 'im what?"

"What-all you've said to me!"

"You can't remember it! It's all been wasted on you. But me, I'll go right along with you an' repeat it to him. Lead the way!"

That seemed almost to jolt young Powell's back teeth loose. He held his mouth open as if afraid to close it. He had never in his life been talked to like that. Men either sort of coaxed him to be good-natured or else took his talk sullenly for the Old Man's sake.

"Aw, I was only jokin'," said young Powell evasively.

"Well, I ain't jokin'!" Red added a few choice cuss words by way of reaffirming his opinion of any man who would use fighting words, then try to wiggle out by calling it a joke.

"Oh, see here," said Powell with bad grace, but trying to make the best of it, "you didn't know about me. Other fellows understand. I'll forget it. I've got a big head this mornin' an'—but I was jokin'! Of course you got Hammon fair and square. An' I'm glad the dirty dog got it! He had it comin'. He was up to somethin' bad. Good job you done. Let's forget it. Come. Shake on it!"

Red promptly put his hand behind him and gazed at Powell with increase of suspicion and some uneasiness. He was startled by quick stabbing thoughts. Leon Lenard had felt sorry for old Powell when they were talking about the girl's murder. Could this be it?

"My gosh!" Red murmured, staring at him.

Powell drew away as if edging back from a man who was a little crazy, then he turned and went off, hurrying.

"Whew!" Red wiped at his face and felt trembly. He muttered, "It can't be!" A moment later, "Can be, too!"

He coiled up his rope reflectively. "That fellow's dangerous. Coward kind of dangerous. Them are the worst. Shake hands—when he'd like to have bit me! I reckon I ain't lived long enough to know much about some kind o' folks. H'm-m-m-m. There's just one thing I'm goin' to ask Leon Lenard. One little teenie weenie question. If he answers me, 'Yes,' then I'm goin' to have a little private talk with this feller an'— My God, now I'm beginnin' to feel sorry for old Mr. Powell—well, he ort to be felt sorry for, havin' a thing like that for to call him Dad! Ho, well.

> "And she had a front tooth like a picket
>   peg,
> But her hair was the color of a new-fried
>   egg;
> Her foot wouldn't fit in a No. 10 boot—
> But she was a lady, you danged galoot!"

134

Red rode along up to the hotel, where horses stood thick at the hitching rack. Men were riding up and dropping off to saunter about with scraping thump of high heels and long-shanked spurs. They fell into groups that leaned against the walls or squatted, as if aimlessly waiting for something.

Johnny Howard came jogging up, leading two horses, nice, big, strong horses that trotted along with their noses out and their ears back as if their feelings were hurt at this undignified way of being pulled along.

Johnny called out, "Hey, you picture-book punchers! Make some room for Mr. Powell's horse here at this rack!"

Jibes flew back at him. He was told to set and hold 'em—maybe hatch an egg at the same time! He was told to get the same fellow he was usin' this time last year for to do his biddin'; also, to ask polite, 'cause the practice of so askin' would be good for him; and other things similar.

"Bunch o' pore ol' one-legged cripples! Grub sacks and bunk wallopers!" Johnny's tongue was quick on the trigger. He grinned at Red, who had come along, and raised his voice the better to be heard: "Not half these hosses'll stand hitched to the ground—that's how shamed they are of the men that ride 'em! Now 'mong real cowboys, hosses foller you like a dog! Hold these two, will you, Red, for a minute?"

He tossed the lead rope to Red and got off, making a place for Powell's horses. One of the mounts carried a fancy stamped saddle. The saddle wasn't new, but there were no marks of rope burn on the horn. Men looked at the saddle and knew the Old Man was dragging that worthless kid of his along on the ride today.

Johnny and Red crossed the street together and tied their horses on the other side. Red did not yet know how well Blackie would stand without hitching; and Johnny, as nearly always, was on a half-wild bronco. That was the way he liked his horses. Sometimes they spilled him. Johnny said so; and got right down deep into Red's affection by explaining, "An' 'f I was a hoss, I'd buck my head off to make dang good an' sure a feller was worthy for to set on *my* back—wouldn't you?"

A voice bellowed from the hotel doorway, "Come an' get it, wolves!"

"That's our breakfas', an' let's hurry, Red. Their idea of enough to eat is ever'thing in sight!"

Johnny was among the first into the door, scrambling with prod of elbows; and he bolted through the narrow door of the hall toward the dining room, where an early breakfast had been set for the T T men who were riding soon.

Ordinarily Red, too, was always among the first when the grub call sounded; but now he was among strangers, and so sort of brought out his best manners and didn't push and jostle, just fell in behind and took his turn as if eating didn't mean much in his young life.

As he started in the door, a man who had been waiting stepped up:

"You Red Clark?"

Red looked him over carefully, saying, "Me? Sure!"

The man was in store clothes, with nice white hands and the sort of face men have when they live mostly in lamplight and sleep daytime. He dropped his voice, confidentially: "A fellow down to Bundy's wants to see you. Jus' rode in hell-for-leather from Tahzo an' is waitin' there. Asked me to come an' tell you. He don't want hisself seen by any o' these fellows."

"Better be something mighty 'portant for to make me miss my breakfast. I ain't good-natured till I've et. Give any notion of what he wants?"

"Said it was mighty important. Rode like hell to get here."

"H'm-m-m-m." Red gave the man a slant-eyed stare and thought carefully. Maybe the sheriff had sent somebody over. Somebody that was bringing the name of the man that had killed that girl, seeing that had been right on the end of the sheriff's tongue, then had slipped back down his throat when the commotion started.

"Did he say who sent 'im?"

"No. He said you'd understand. An' he wants to

light out back for Tahzo before folks get onto his bein' here. You comin'?"

"I reckon, but—" Red turned, sniffing. He could hear the clatter of dishes and chatter of voices. "If I miss my breakfast—how far is it to this here Bundy's?"

"Just round the corner."

"Come on, then. I gotta get back *pronto.*"

Bundy's was a barnlike saloon with numerous poker tables and, toward the back stood roulette, faro, and crap tables.

The front door was closed. If there was any reason for it, such as a big pay day on the range or celebration of any kind, Bundy's ran night and day.

Red's companion opened the door. It was dim inside. No lights were burning. The place hadn't yet been swept out, and there was the strong odor of stale tobacco and spilled liquor; and dirty sawdust lay in the tiny drifts scuffed up by men's feet.

Three men were talking together down near the lower end of the bar. One was the bartender. He had his apron tossed back across his shoulder and at once started up behind the bar, and pulling the apron off his shoulder began to use an end of it to wipe a clean place for Red and his companion to put their elbows.

"Gosh!" Red thought. "It's dark in here. And the stink—whoof!"

"The feller that wants to see you is back here," said the man who led the way. "Come on back. Why you stoppin'?"

"Wait a minute. I ain't no danged owl. I can't see."

Red stepped back and put out his hand to pull open the door and let in a little light; but the movement was misunderstood. Voices rang out:

"None o' that!"

"Stop 'im, Jack!"

"Don't let the dirty skunk get away!"

"Give it to 'im!"

"Ho, so that's it!" said Red. "An' me innercent as a lamb!"

Red, with the hand that had reached for the door latch, jerked out a gun; but the gambler Jack was right by him and whipped his arm around Red's, bearing it down and straightening it out, at the same time calling for help.

The gambler, with his free hand, tugged at Red's gun. The two other men started forward on the run with guns out and curses rippling.

Red locked his teeth and with all the strength he could put into his right arm he jerked, swinging the gambler half off his feet and around in front. Then Red's left hand came up from the holster. With a long-barreled, overhand sideswipe he rapped the gambler's head hard through his high-crowned hat.

"I tol' you"—another crack—"on empty stomach"—*crack! crack!*—"I'm peevish!"

The fellow's fingers had loosened at the first whack, but Red continued to pound his head. The man stood as if dead on his feet, held by Red's arm and leaning against him. Then with lunge of his breast and shove of his arm, Red sent the gambler's body against one of the two men who had run up close with guns out. They were afraid to shoot while their partner was tangled up in Red's arms. But as the gambler's body struck one man with a hard-driven toppling lurch that sent him staggering back, a gun went off. The powder burned Red's throat, and the bullet skinned the side of his neck as neatly as if it had been taken off by scissors. The flashing jar of the bullet's force knocked Red's head up and back and brought a curious, hoarse, half-strangled grunt out of his throat.

Red's left gun blazed into the fellow's face as the fellow was leaning far back in a futile dodge. His knees sank like melting wax, and with backward fling of arms he went over.

The third man that had joined in the fight did not have the stuff in him that stands up when smoke is laced with lead. With long jumps and backward glances of terror he made for the back of the saloon, pumping hasty shots behind him.

Red felt a little dazed, couldn't swallow, was choked and seemed to have lost his voice; but he swung up both of his guns and let them go. The fleeing man bumped into a poker table, sprawled half across it, flung his arms loosely to one side. The gun fell. He lay there as if drunkenly asleep.

Red peered about, trying to see who else was in the fight and wanted something. Then he made for the bartender, who had ducked down with only his eyes and pasted-down hair showing above the edge of the bar. Red tried to shout, but his voice wouldn't come. His throat was numbed by the blow of the bullet that had nipped his neck. He gasped, squeaked, gestured.

The bartender understood sign language and obediently rose, with hands high. His face was that of a man who has not only seen a ghost but expects right soon to be one.

"Cliff Hammon's friends!" said the bartender with husky breath. He knew what Red wanted to know; and added indignantly, as if he had never liked them anyhow, "Damn fools! They might have knowed you—a feller like you—hell afire!"

Red made more signs, impatiently squeaking. The bartender shut up and with sudden understanding asked, "Whisky?" at the same time reaching for a bottle.

Red nodded. The bartender grabbed at a glass with the haste of one eager to please.

Red put his guns away, poured a little whisky into his mouth and tried to swallow. He spluttered and choked and coughed as if strangling. Then he tried it again, just as several men who had heard the shooting threw open the door. But they, having good manners in matters of the kind, did not venture in until sure that all was quiet again.

Heads appeared cautiously, then shoulders and legs followed, with eyes stretched wide. The room was very dark for anyone just coming in out of the sunlight. At the door, almost under their feet, they found two bodies.

"Wha-wha-what h-happened?" said a voice, stuttering timidly.

Red squeaked, "Aw, go to hell!"

His voice was coming back. It sounded curiously strange to his own ears, as though it were not he who was doing the talking. But he made the best of it and, with finger leveled at the bartender, he said:

"You're yaller as the feet of a dead Chinaman! 'F I done right, I'd plug you, an' me, I allus try to do right!"

Red reached toward his hip, and the bartender simply closed his eyes and dropped out of sight on the floor behind the bar. Red pulled the handkerchief from his pocket, dabbed at his neck.

Men scrouged belly up on the bar, looking over. The bartender lay as if he had been shot.

"My holy gosh," said one, "he's fainted!"

Red turned about, pushed by men that gaped at him, and went out.

For a moment he blinked blindly in the sunlight

as he got his bearings. His hat was gone. His shirt was torn. Powder burns scorched his throat. Blood trickled. He felt hazy. His thoughts were in a jumble of wonderment: Cliff Hammon's friends? Yeah, and maybe, too, Buddy Powell's?

CHAPTER XIII

DANGEROUS MISSION

Old Bill Powell, with some of his men about him, was out in front of the hotel, giving some of the boys a little more time to get through with their breakfast, when Red came up. He was followed by some of the men who had started down the street to see what all the shooting was about.

Old Powell looked him over with hawk-like glance. "Well, what's happened to you?"

Red gurgled, twisted his neck, patting it with the handkerchief. "Had an' argyment an' lost my voice!"

"You hit?"

"No. Scratched." Red pulled away the kerchief and put his head to one side, pointed. "Spoiled my singin' voice!"

Powell leaned forward, looking closely, pulled a little at the skin, making sure it was a scratch. "Narrow call."

Kid-like, Johnny Howard had been among the first to dash out the back way and go to see what had happened. Now he came up the street on the run. His face blazed with excitement, and crowding up close, he shouted:

"Three of 'em down, Mr. Powell! An' the

barkeep fainted! Red here, he done it. Cliff Hammon's friends!"

Men murmured and whistled softly as they looked from one to another:

"Three!"

"Holy gosh!"

"They shore drop when he shoots!"

"Thunders of hell!" said Powell, astonished. "An' you told me you wasn't a killer!"

Old Leon Lenard stood close by, keen of eye, grimly blank of face, making no move, giving no sign. "An' you, too, Leon!" Powell said. Lenard parted his thin lips, spoke softly. "He ain't. A killer picks his men. *He* takes 'em as they come."

"Yore damn right I ain't!" said Red, hotly. "They sent word up a man had come from Tahzo for to see me special. An' me, bein' a cur'ous fool, I traipsed along down there. Missed my breakfast an'—gosh, I can't talk. Sound like a young rooster learnin' for to crow!"

The men eyed Red with curious respect. He was neither dour like most killers nor preening his feathers, like some. He acted pretty much as if it were just part of his morning's work to walk into a trap and shoot his way out; and he seemed merely a good-natured boy who didn't feel quite at ease when being admired. They credited him, of course, with having done all that shooting over at Tahzo—that is all except Leon Lenard, who watched closely and said little—and so they thought he had just about topped the record for lone-handed work in two days' time.

"Go in," said Bill Powell, "an' wash up, an' get your breakfast. I'm goin' to step around to Bundy's an' have a look. A long look. Come along, Leon."

Red paused, searching the crowd with quick glance. The man whose face he wanted to inspect was not there; and not seeing Buddy Powell, Red pushed along through the crowd that parted respectfully, making no comment but staring after him.

Johnny Howard tagged Red into the washroom, saying:

"Oh, a lot of fellers can shoot an' do! But gee, in this man's town, to make a barkeep faint! That's got 'em all beat!"

For days Johnny was to sass men and jeer at them with: "Give a barkeep heart failure—shoot at that one, you wall-eyed *hombres*. Then maybe I'll take off my hat to you!"

Red drank much hot coffee, and that eased his throat a little. It hurt to swallow; but he said it would hurt more not to; and that it was better his throat should suffer than his stomach.

When Mr. Powell came back, Leon Lenard brought along Red's hat and handed it to him without a word, but there was a steady and not disapproving look in the old outlaw's eyes.

Johnny had tied a rag about Red's neck to help

146

stop the blood, and much to Red's embarrassment was proudly solicitous at trying to play doctor.

" 'F you don't stay 'way from me, I'll bite you!" said Red.

"The last man as did went into a spell of fits!" Johnny told him. "Stand still while I tie that rag tighter 'cause—"

Red's shirt was torn and covered with blood. Mr. Powell sent a man to rouse up a storekeeper and get a couple of new shirts, together with some other things, such as underwear and the toothbrush Red said he had forgotten to buy when he was over to Tahzo.

"Only one thing wrong with your job, Red," said Mr. Powell, drawing back his head and cocking it a little to one side, critically. "That fellow you whacked over the head may get well. 'F he does, he'll get outa town faster'n he rode in. 'Cept for that one mistake, you done noble. Bundy's crowd'll keep their tails between their legs for quite some time. I didn't know Cliff's friends thought so well o' him as 'pears they do." Then he called out, "All right, boys. Let's be ridin'! Where's Buddy?"

Somebody said he was in the barroom, and a man went to fetch him. Buddy came, looking unhappy, and did not glance at Red.

"Hop to the saddle, son," old Powell told him. "What you lookin' so down-at-the-nose about? If somebody'd plugged them tin horns long ago, you'd have more money in your pocket!"

As they rode out of town, Red discussed things with himself:

"Maybe, now, Buddy didn't have nothin' to do with my invitation down to Bundy's place. 'Twasn't much more'n twenty minutes from the time he left me there in the barn till that gambler feller showed up at the hotel—in the which case, Bundy's men shore work fast. But I got me a suspicion it was all hatched last night. Which don't keep me from thinkin' maybe Mr. Buddy knowed all about it—an' was hopeful. 'Cuse me of shootin' a man in the back—then call it a joke! Yet somehow I sorta feel maybe it was hatched in them twenty minutes, seein' as how I tried hard to give him reasons for wantin' me to feel bad. H'm-m-m! Funny, my throat feels more sore inside than out. Oh, well, that'll help me to keep my mouth shut an' 'pear smarter'n I am."

Red knew nothing about the lay of the range or about Mr. Powell's plans. He simply rode along with the others and kept his ears open. There appeared to be no particular hurry. It was jog-and-walk, jog-and-walk, with an easy lope now and then for a spell.

In the course of the morning, from what he overheard and more clearly from what Johnny Howard explained, Red understood that the trouble lay over in the west in what was known as the Nelis Range. Some highbinders over there had decided that Mr. Powell was trying to hold altogether too much range, and they had thrown in together against him.

It was war, real range war. They had raided the Nelis Valley bunkhouse, sneaking up on the men Indian fashion, getting the drop, and telling them to go and never again dare to show up.

Then the highbinders—that was Johnny's word for them—had set to work stealin' some cows and running others of the T T out of the rich, well-watered valley and into the open, dry, desert-like country.

Johnny said, "Most o' that country over there is where hell uster be, but it was too hot an' rough for Old Nick, so he moved. But she shore is a pretty valley—'f you don't get lost on the way. Like heaven, I reckon!

"Me, I was almost born over there. My dad was a-prospectin'—an' a burro was my nurse. Cradle too. Soon as I was big enough to steal one of Mr. Powell's hosses, I done it. Later on I stole a better'n. Say, they chased me back'ards and forward for days. Lot o' fun. An' when they caught me, they jus' stood an' looked. They was expectin' a full-growed hoss thief, an' I was only a little nubbin of a kid. Mr. Powell, he put a hand on his hip an' eyed me a long time. He said I was too young to hang an' too good a judge o' what hosses to steal to turn loose, so he put me to ridin' for 'im. I don't know how old I was, but that was 'bout five year ago. Dad—oh, hell, he was glad for to be rid of me!"

More of Johnny's chatter followed. He was heart and soul devoted to Mr. Powell, the finest man that ever lived.

"His boy take after 'im?" Red inquired, casual.

What Johnny said was just about like an echo from the remarks that Red had passed that morning in the barn. It was odd and not nice to hear a kid cuss venomously, but it didn't ruffle Red much.

"I'm glad for to see the Old Man is draggin' him by the scruff of the neck into this fight." Johnny was gleeful about it. "Why, Red, this here is war! An' we're going into it same as into a round-up! Two chuck wagons pulled out yesterday, an' the horse herd, too. I been into fights before with Mr. Powell!"

Johnny put on the airs of a veteran, and probably had a right to them. He continued to explain:

"Some of us is goin' to put up at the home ranch tonight. An' some'll push on. Us as stays closest to Mr. Powell will have the most fun. He allus saves the warmest spot for hisself—an' maybe he thinks I ain't goin' to foller him, but I am! I know that country better'n he does. I'm drawin' man-sized wages, an' he ain't got no right to try to keep me out of fights for his range.

"He's waitin' for some word to come. Then

he'll make a start. Be right plumb sure, Red, ol' son, that the devil is a-greasin' of his fryin' pans!"

Shortly before noon some six or seven of the riders, with old Mack at their head, waved their arms in vague parting flourishes and without further ado left the road and headed cross-country. The remaining six or seven now set forward a little faster, and in a couple of hours came to the home ranch where men were waiting for Mr. Powell.

At the Powell house much talk went on, with men coming and going.

Red patiently loafed in the shade of the bunkhouse, listening to whatever was said, but offering no talk. He knew he was much talked about because men who had ridden in would stroll by, eyeing him. It made him a little embarrassed, because the last thing he wanted in the world was the name of being a "killer." He had grown up in the shadow of his dad's contempt for killers, most of whom were nothing but cold-blooded murderers that simply jumped the draw.

After supper he returned to the shadows of the bunkhouse. Some time went by, then he heard Johnny's high-pitched voice asking for him. Red got up and walked into the lighted doorway.

"Oh, there you are," Johnny called and came up. "Listen. Tag right along with me. You're wanted!"

About halfway to the house, Johnny pulled at

151

his arm. "This way, Red. Over to the blacksmith shop. Somethin' nice is bein' cooked up for you an' me!"

A dim figure detached itself from the darkness of the blacksmith shop and spoke:

"All right, Johnny. Go in an' tell Mr. Powell we're waitin'."

It was Leon Lenard, and Johnny turned about and went with stumbling haste.

"Nice kid," said Red.

Lenard didn't say anything, but Red had the feeling that he nodded in the darkness. Silence. "How's your throat?" asked Lenard.

"Feel like I had a crick in my neck. Sore some, but better. Turned husky, as you can hear. Ain't easy for to talk, but say—listen. I want to ask if—"

"Be easier on your throat if I do the talkin'," Lenard suggested calmly. "You told me you was lucky. An', son, I'm beginnin' for to think you don't lie much. Got any notions why you got into a dust storm over to Bundy's this mornin'?"

"Cliff Hammon must-a been well thought of."

"Yes. Some folks was right sorry for to see Cliff quit his orneriness. But it wasn't only that Bundy crowd. This mornin' even I had me some doubts. Just recent now I've heard a man say as how he'll never get over thinkin' you shot when Cliff wasn't lookin'."

Red grunted, saying nothing but being expressive.

"Son, have you by any manner o' means had a run-in with young Powell?"

"Sure have."

"Let's hear."

Red told him. ". . . Why, when I turned around after hearin' that, a hair-weight more on my trigger an' he'd-a been shot. So I just naturally said some things, fluent-like."

Lenard spoke quietly: "Buddy's no nice boy for to have dislike you. An' he's gettin' more an' more that way."

"See here. Will you answer me just one thing, Mr. Lenard?"

"Maybe."

"That stag-handled knife with the spring blade—could *he* have took it unbeknown to you?"

"What's give you that notion?"

"You yourself."

"Uh. Me? An old thin-lipped gook like me has been talkin' too much, I reckon."

"You was plum' het up over that matter we talked about yesterday. An' 'mongst other things, when you was thinkin' of the girl an' how she died, you said you was sorry for Mr. Powell. After I seen this here Bud Powell, I thought maybe I understood why." Red had spoken as softly as he could and stood up close to Lenard, waiting for his answer.

Lenard took a lot of time before he said, "You

got some reasons for to like Mr. Powell, too. Remember this careful. You might just as well take a gun an' shoot Bill Powell as for to make him ever believe a thing like that of his son."

"I know. But if Bud done it, then he must-a been usin' Cliff Hammon most confidential an' personal for to learn if the sheriff—"

"They're comin'. Mr. Powell, he wants for you to do a little something."

Mr. Powell came out of the shadows with Johnny at his side. It was dark where they stood, but no light was needed.

"Red, how's your throat?"

"Awright, awmost."

"I got a little scoutin' work for you. You're a stranger, an' you'll be ridin' a horse that'll help folks think they understand why you've come their way. Now I don't want you to go 'less you want, 'cause a man that's sent 'gainst his will ain't likely to be worth a damn. What about it?"

Red said promptly, "When I draw wages I wanta do what the man as pays 'em wants done."

"All right, boy. I'm trustin' you more'n I'd trust some mighty good men that have been with me a long time. They'd try all right an' be honest. But they'd likely be reckernized as my men. An' shot. You understand?"

"I reckon."

"All right. Over in the Nelis country they may

154

not know just where your horse come from, but they'll know it ain't off my range. An' bein' as it is a fine horse, they'll have their own notions about how you come to be ridin' him.

"Now listen close, Red. I want you to go to Nelis City. It's got three houses in it. Maybe four, not countin' the saloon. Over there they'll shoot a T T puncher on sight. I just got word that old George Robbins an' the fellows that's throwed in with him to clean me out is to meet there in two or three days for to make themselves some plans. I want to be among them as is present an' them that speaks up, seein' as how it is sure my business that is to be discussed. An' they sure don't expect me."

Red said, "Yessir."

"Now then," Powell went on, "I'm sendin' you in alone. Me an' some of the boys are goin' to be layin' back in the hills, waitin'. When George Robbins shows up, I want you to start a little fire, somehow. Burn down a house, saloon, hotel, anything—just so it makes a nice big blaze for a few minutes. We'll be watchin'. An' a few hours later I'll show up.

"If things go well, I'll pay damages for what you burn. If not—well, I just won't. But you be careful. Just us fellows here know I'm sendin' you in. Me, Leon, an' Johnny.

"Johnny here he'll be your guide tonight an' point the way tomorrow. You ought to get

155

in about sundown tomorrow. Even if George Robbins is there, don't start no fire the first night, 'cause I won't be ready. But for the next half-dozen nights I will.

"If I can catch Robbins an' the locoed ringtails that's throwed in with him, I reckon that'll be quicker an' better than skirmishin' about, pottin' riders that are doin' only what they're paid to do, same as my men. With this job, your wages is doubled, an' here's somethin' for you to make a splash with while you're loafin'."

In the darkness Red could hear the clink of coins, and his fingers groped toward the outstretched hand Powell offered. Red dropped the coins into his pocket, thinking it was a handful of dollars.

"May interest you for to know, Red, that in discussin' who to send, Leon here says, all things considered, he'd risk you. 'Pears like some years ago—I can tell 'im, can't I, Leon?"

Lenard spoke softly. "Go 'head."

"Well, 'pears like some years ago there was a certain sheriff over in Tulluco that give Leon a heap of trouble, an' Leon here allus sort of admired the way that lone-handed sheriff worried him. Leon says you got enough earmarks like that sheriff for to be well trusted to ride alone an' get done what you're sent to do.

"An' you see how much I am trustin' you, don't you, Red? Some fellers might tell Robbins what was up—then start the fire, an' coax me to come ridin' in!"

"In the which case," Johnny Howard snarled, "such a feller'd better jump in it. Be easier on 'im!" Then, hastily, "But Red's square—ain't you, Red?"

"When I don't think so, me, I'll quit usin' my dad's name!"

CHAPTER XIV

THE MEN OF NELIS CITY

Red and Johnny rode quietly off into the darkness, with Blackie on a rope, being led.

There was a rifle under Red's leg, the saddle bags had been stuffed with grub, and two big canteens, now empty, clinked. Johnny chattered like a squirrel that has found a woodpecker's cache. Red listened drowsily.

At last they got into the hilly country, and though it was pleasant enough by starlight, the rocky barren hills looked as though they would be a bad place under the noon sun.

Johnny explained with great detail what they were doing, waving his arm about and naming distances, but all Red understood was that this was a short cut. " 'F you know where we goin', what's the use of me bein' burdened with knowledge?" said Red.

Now and then they paused to let their horses breathe. Shortly after midnight they ate some sandwiches, and about three o'clock Johnny stopped his horse, slid off, said, "Light down. This here is your last water till you get to Nelis City. I ain't never seen a real city, but I hear tell some of 'em have two or three main streets with stores on both sides!"

"You hear a lot o' things that ain't so," Red suggested.

They scraped about in a sandy mudhole until the canteens were filled with dirty warm water. They smoked two or three cigarettes, let the horses drink, then pushed on. An hour or two later they looked down from a high barren hillside upon a wide sandy basin that ran on and on toward far-distant hills.

In the dawn, Johnny pointed toward the basin:

"You'll think a baker's oven is a nice cool place in the shade afore you're across this basin, so you'd better make as many tracks as you can while it's cool. See that sharp-nosed peak across yonder?"

" 'Bout fifty mile off, ain't it?"

" 'Bout. Ride straight for it till you strike the road, then turn right an' keep goin'. It'll bring you to Nelis City. But don't go dozin' in the saddle, Red, 'cause you may walk right across the road, which ain't a thing in the world but a trail. I don't know just how you are for stayin' awake, but if you just have to take a nap, roll off, face down, and take 'er under yore hat. There ain't no other shade till after you go a long ways up the road."

"Long as I'm sober I can stay 'wake."

"Me, I get sleepy ridin' slow in the heat. Now you comin' in thisaway, they won't suspect that maybe you've been near Powell's ranch. Nobody but prospectors and fellows as get lost ever get into this country."

Red changed his saddle to Blackie's back. Blackie had been led so as to be rested and fresh. Then Red began to feel through his pockets to make sure that he had matches, tobacco, and papers. In doing so he fished up the coins that Powell had given him. They were not dollars but gold pieces.

"Holy jumped-up Judas!" said Red huskily. "Mr. Powell shore ain't no piker in dishin' up spendin' money! My gosh, I'd have to chase cows purt-near six months for to earn this. Here, Johnny, have some!"

Johnny waved the money aside. "I get my wages reg'lar—even if I don't earn 'em! Mr. Powell told me to hustle back to the ranch—but I ain't goin'. Usual, I do what he says, prompt. But this time he's tryin' to keep me out of the fun. I know where he's makin' for, and I'll be around up there, layin' on the trail. He'll cuss hell outa me—an' take me along with 'im! So you and me'll meet in Nelis City, an' maybe fit a pair o' wings to old George Robbins. Devils has wings, too, ain't they? Sure! S'long."

Red went on slowly, walking down the steep rocky hillside that led into the basin. He walked, not because he distrusted Blackie's legs, but to save the horse. He knew it was going to be tough on both of them before the day was over.

When he reached fairly level ground he mounted and rode on, slowly, lifting his eye now and then at the peak that had been pointed out as his landmark.

The sun rose higher and was hot. At about eight o'clock he washed Blackie's nose and mouth because he wanted a drink himself—and he wouldn't cheat on a partner. His throat was sore and dry and felt feverish, so he filled his mouth and let the water trickle down.

An hour later he poured some water into his hat and gave Blackie a drink, took a small one himself, just a mouthful. And so it went, a little water at a time but often. If you let yourself get too thirsty, then a whole bellyful of water wouldn't satisfy you, which was the mistake a lot of people made in trying to save their water. Red knew there was no danger of really suffering from thirst in this day's ride: it was just a matter of keeping as comfortable as possible.

About noon he was pleased to notice that his throat wasn't nearly as sore, though it seemed scorched. The only real hard thing was staying awake. Blackie went forward at a steady walk which, to the saddle-raised Red, was like being in a hammock. He grumbled, "Here I am out where I could sing my loudest an' not trouble nobody— an' I've lost my singin' voice. Life's sure tough, ain't it, kid?"

Blackie flecked his ears forward by way of

reply. Red slid off, took a swig, emptied what was left of the canteen into his hat, and gave Blackie his drink. He threw the canteen aside.

Along in the middle of the afternoon, Red struck a trail running across his path. He eyed it for some time, doubtfully. "Johnny, he called it a 'road.' Good thing he told me to keep my eyes open. This here looks like a jack-rabbit run."

An hour or so later he drank heartily from the second canteen, filled up the old hat, and told Blackie to get busy. "Yore last chance, son!"

T T had been painted on the canteen, probably to prevent disputes when two outfits came together and water was scarce. He didn't want to run any risk of having himself associated with the T T, so he rode well off to one side of the trail and flung the canteen into a patch of cactus. He thought it better to be a little thirsty during the rest of the afternoon than possibly have to try to explain about the T T.

Now that he had found the trail, Red settled in the saddle, put his hands on the horn, gave Blackie his head, and went to sleep. Every few minutes he came to life, took a look about, and promptly dozed off again.

Late in the afternoon they climbed out of the basin, passed through some scrubby timber, and presently saw Nelis in the distance—its few buildings looking not unlike some badly baked biscuits that had been tossed away by a disgusted cook.

Red scanned the surrounding country, trying to figure out just where Mr. Powell was most likely to stop, waiting for his signal. There seemed to be a lot of half-grown mountains scattered about the narrow valley in which the town stood.

He wondered how the devil he was going to start a fire without getting suspected of being up to something, or of being crazy. "Yeah, Red, just go ahead an' set fire to something! Sure. Burn down a house—an' have the owner catch you! Well, Red, you're gettin' better'n wages"—he jingled the gold pieces—"for doin' what you're told. So start figurin'." He took a long look about the lonely, nearly barren landscape. "If Johnny used to play in this country for his front yard, I don't envy him none his childhood. Be danged if I seen enough feed yet to fatten a cow, so why all this rumpus over it for a range?"

He slapped Blackie's neck: "Come on, old son. We got to look all frayed out an' travel-sore— pertend we're exhausted-like. So just you hang your head down between your front legs like you was ashamed of yoreself. An' me, I'll let my tongue hang out and pertend I'm dyin' o' thirst!"

Mr. Powell had guessed that Red would get into Nelis City in the cool of the evening, but there was nothing cool about it. Not a breath was stirring. All the heat that the sun had poured down during the day now seemed to be oozing up from the ground and from the buildings. A hot haze simmered over the valley.

A few men on backless chairs—their backs and heads propped against the wall—sat in front of the saloon. They had watched him from afar; and now, as he came near, they straightened in their seats and looked closely, with the silent staring scrutiny of every detail, and no friendliness.

Red climbed off with weary slowness, staggered, gurgled, and pointed toward his mouth. It was a pantomime well understood in Nelis City. Strangers who came out of that basin were usually half dead. Whether or not Blackie had understood his instructions, he put his nose almost to the ground and looked woebegone.

A big, powerful, broad-shouldered man went into the saloon and came out with a tin cup full of water. Red drank from the cup, licked his lips, and pointed toward his horse, and with great effort, or so it seemed, barely whispered: "Water for him, too."

"Why, feller," said the big man in an unfavorable tone, "yore tongue ain't swole an' that hoss ain't desert dry!"

Red nodded, gurgled, and pointed to the bandage on his throat, then made a gesture as if writing. The men stared distrustfully but with interest. One went next door and came back with paper and pencil.

Red wrote, *"Shot—throat—can't talk."*

They eyed him and eyed one another. These were troublous times, and they were distrustful men. More than likely most of them were wanted at some place or other. The law's men were up to all sorts of ruses and shenanigans. But there was the color of blood on the bandage about his neck.

" 'F they get too inquis'tive," Red reflected, "I may have to sprain my wrist!"

The men looked him over with solemn doubt, dropped a few words in Spanish among themselves. Red pretended not to understand. They studied the horse, and some thought they knew why he had come; but they were curious as to how he had got here without being thirst-fagged and nearly dead like most other strangers who came. Bill Powell's name was mentioned, but the suggestion did not meet with much response from other men.

They were inclined to take him for a horse thief on the dodge. That was perhaps not quite all right with them, but did not give his presence an unfavorable aspect. Nelis City, like hell itself, was the sort of place where only bad men stayed. And, as a wolf smells a trap in every piece of iron, so they had doubts about every stranger who wasn't brought in and vouched for by responsible people.

Except for his youth, Red looked like he might

be one of their breed. He wore two guns and carried a rifle. His face was unshaven, and that gave him a rough, haggard appearance. There was dried blood on his neck.

Red wrote on the paper:

"Eat, sleep—where? Horse too."

Then he jingled his pocket, letting them know that he had money; could pay.

The big broad-shouldered man was the saloon keeper. His name was Mike. He had sunburned red hair and carried much of the lazy fat that often pads the bones of saloon keepers. He asked pointedly:

"You rode far today?"

Red shook his head and tried whispering. It seemed mighty hard to whisper even, so Red wrote:

"Prospeckter over there been keepin' me."

Mike spelled out the writing aloud and the men nodded. That seemed to explain. Somehow or other, this young redhead had fallen in with a desert rat and been taken care of, put on the right trail.

Red rolled a cigarette and lighted it, throwing down the match before he shook out the flame. Then casually he stepped on it.

Mike told one of the men to go along with Red and talk for him at the rooming house, and to show him where to put his horse.

"Gosh," thought Red as they walked along,

"start a fire in this man's town an' ever'thing 'dobe!"

The corral was at the other end of the town; but being at the other end of the town did not mean it was far off. There was a *ramada* where horses could have a little of something that looked like shade. A pile of hay was close by and not far from the blacksmith shop. The blacksmith had the corral as a part of his business.

Red lighted another cigarette and flung down the match. It touched a spot of meager bunch grass and awakened it into flame. He unhurriedly scraped out the fire with his foot.

"F'r a feller that looks range-wise, you're some careless thataway," said his companion, with reproof.

Red was taken over to a dirty restaurant, back of which were bunks and rooms. It was the nearest thing that Nelis had to a hotel, but was often so called by way of municipal pride. There weren't more than a half-dozen houses in the city.

Red wasn't hungry, having eaten well from his saddle bags. He found his throat so much better that he put a big pebble into his mouth just to help him remember that he couldn't talk when he went up to the saloon that night and sat about in a retiring sort of way trying to get acquainted.

A poker game was started, and since poker is well suited to pantomime, he sat in. During the game he sipped warm beer, having explained that whisky hurt his throat. He kept his ears open without seeming to listen and almost swallowed his pebble when he heard a man say, "Me, I sorta smell the stink of a polecat—or T T man. Can't tell the diff'rence."

Some of the men answered the fellow with growling sneers, unimpressed. Apparently he did not have a very high standing.

Red frowned over his hand and very carefully did not look up just then. He needed four cards to make his hand a good one; so he threw away four cards and, getting up with a kind of solemn grin, walked around his chair in the way that some fellows do when hopeful of tugging at Lady Luck's petticoats to get a little favorable attention.

The fellow who had the extremely sensitive nose was a little dark man with eyes like a pair of black beads; and, being slightly drunk, he sat on one chair, his feet on another, and was propped up by an elbow on a near-by table.

Red guessed that he had thrown out the remark just to see what would happen, as some suspicious men will shoot in the dark.

The four cards that the dealer handed Red were no better than those he had tossed away; but he played as if they were, got called, and so lost a nice tall stack of chips.

The saloon keeper, who won them, chuckled. "Bluffs is allus called in this here Nelis country!"

168

But winning the pot seemed to help him think that Red wasn't a bad sort of fellow.

The little dark man took another drink of whisky and announced in a loud voice, just as if somebody had asked him, "Powell an' his *hombres* ain't a-goin' git outa this here valley alive—none of 'em! No, sir!"

Red was dealing. The man's remark almost gave him a chill. It seemed to hint of knowledge that Powell was coming.

Red coughed real hard and went on dealing. When he looked down he spied four aces, and that made him feel cheerful. But even as he eyed them he grew sorrowful. Four aces, right off the bat, on his own deal? He was likely to be told that didn't go in this man's town, and an argument would follow. He wasn't over here to win poker pots. Couldn't risk having any arguments. Four aces and couldn't play them: that sure was tough luck. He picked out two of the aces and tossed them into the discard, lighted a cigarette and flung the match down—still flaming. The floor was plain adobe, so there was no danger.

Red quit the game rather early, being dead tired and having much to think about. But he did not go at once to his bunk. He walked down to the corral.

He rather suspected, and certainly hoped, that somebody would follow him just to see what

169

he might be up to. He sensed that the men had no dislike, but also that they were cautiously suspicious. He was a stranger.

He climbed on the corral and whistled, coaxing. Blackie wasn't sure, but smelt sugar, and came up with far outreach of neck. Red petted the horse for a time, stepped down from the corral. Lighting a cigarette, he threw away the live match, but quickly stepped on it.

He saw two tall shadows stir over by the haystack and knew that men had crept up just to see what deviltry he might be into. Well, they had seen him telling his best friend good-night. That was all; and they probably thought he was a pretty queer cuss to be taking the trouble to pet a horse before he rolled in.

In his bunk, Red lay wide-eyed even if dead tired and meditated. He was troubled. He had overheard much talk; but knew it was just the clipped, jerky, broken sentences of men who had talked the same thing over and over so much, and with such intimate knowledge of the country, that they understood one another perfectly. He did not see how it could be possible that they did know, yet they seemed to know, that Powell meant to raid the valley—and conceded that he might get in easy enough, but would never get out alive. That worried Red. There was no way for him to get word to Powell. On the other hand, could these men of Nelis City be so unconcerned and casual if they expected Powell? They just couldn't. So the thing was puzzling. He tossed about.

"My voice, it is sure got to get some better so I can sorta carry on some conversation an' maybe learn things. 'Sides, it makes me sorta lonesome, bein' dumb. An' I got to nose around on Blackie and get me the lay of the land some. I may have to get outa here in one gosh-awful hurry. An' if I ever do get outa this Nelis City I'm goin' to behave myself careful, so I won't have to come back after I die."

The next morning Red began to croak a little, but he pretended that it was hard work. He leaned his elbow on Mike's bar, said "Better!" pointed at his throat and nodded, joyfully.

"Must be awful, Dummy," Mike told him, "if you lose your temper an' can't cuss!"

" 'Tis!" Red squeaked, sucking in his breath and drawing in his stomach.

Then by much squeaking he made Mike understand that he wanted somebody to ride about with him, point out the trails and roads, give him the lay of the land. He held out a gold piece to show that he was willing to pay.

Mike eyed him thoughtfully and grinned.

"Was you wantin' to get anywhere special?"

Red shook his head, grinned too. "No, but if I do have to go, I'd sorta like to know where I'm goin'."

"Just have spells of the saddle itch now an' then, huh?" Mike suggested, looking wise.

Red nodded. "Only way to cure it is for to ride—fast. But the country is right troubled some at the present time, I hear tell."

"You heard tell right," said Mike.

Red looked attentive without appearing overly curious.

Mike said, "You'd sure knowed it if you'd rode in the other way. I don't understand yet how you made it. Not more'n two waterholes anywhere in the Basin. You must-a found 'em both. Plumb lucky fellow. An' a friendly prospector too! Sure lucky."

Mike explained to some of the men that Red had a hankering to ride around and look at some of the scenery. He said the Nelis scenery was the kind that sure was worth looking at, only a lot of people rode by too quick to get its full beauty. Men grinned understandingly and a little amused.

The little dark man with eyes like black beads, whose name was Pincher, eyed the gold piece and said he would go; said there was nobody anywhere that knew the country so well as himself and appealed to Mike for confirmation.

Mike growled tolerantly, "F'r me to call you a liar 'ud mean I'd have to hurt your feelin's. I don't hurt the feelin's of folks that look like you. No. I just step on 'em—same as on a cockroach."

Pincher took it as a joke. At a hint from him,

Red bought a bottle of whisky, and Pincher obligingly offered to carry it.

They rode out of town. Red soon saw that this Pincher was a waspish, savage fellow, chock-full of grievances against the world—but of the type that always had his grudge against men who weren't anywhere near. Before the bottle was half empty, he declared that he had taken a liking to Red on sight, and that Red was sure one white man. Yeah, you bet! Pincher was right there to tell the world.

Pincher told as much of the world as was within earshot what he was always willing to do for his friends—and with some zigzag sidling of tongue and hazy talk about what was coming to him and soon to be paid, he asked Red if he would lend him some money.

Red did. Did it just to encourage Pincher to feel good and keep on talking. Pincher took some more whisky; then, saying he knew Red was a good fellow and on the dodge, proposed that they hook up together and steal some cows. George Robbins was a good old cowman who never asked where range mavericks come from. He had a special liking for such as came off Powell's range.

Pincher cursed Powell up and down, and said he knew him well, having worked for him. Young Buddy Powell, he was all right, a fine fellow. The old man himself was nothin' but a sneakin', ornery cow stealer with no backbone a-tall. Not a-tall. Didn't even know good men when he saw 'em.

Anyhow, Powell's day on the range was done. He was heavily in debt. Didn't have a friend in the world. His men wouldn't back 'im up!

"No?" Red inquired innocently, thinking of old Leon Lenard, slit-eyed and calm as flint, just as full of fire; of young Johnny Howard, wild, fierce kid; of all the men, hard-eyed and slow-smiling, that clustered about Powell with more of a liking than could ever be bought with wages.

"Yeah, tha's right!" said Pincher. And what was more, Powell had been kicked off the Nelis Valley range, his cows run out; and if he so much as dared poke his head inside the valley, he'd be shot; an' all the men with him, too, because George Robbins, Pete Strodd, and Walt Wiggins had men campin' right at the mouth of the canyon, just waitin' for Powell to come bustin' in!

"But ain't this Nelis Valley?" Red asked, forgetting to be squeaky as he swept his arm, waving at the cactus-strewn stretch between nearly barren piles of rock.

Pincher didn't notice Red's change in voice. He was a little drunk and much excited. "Naw. You come through Nelis Basin into this here Nelis City valley where a burro would damn near starve. But down about twenty mile, Nelis Valley proper begins, and she shore is rich. The road into the valley is 'cross over yonder. We'll ride that way tomorrow if you want, an' I'll show you some trails. I know this country like I know my own hat. It's God's country an' no questions asked. The six-guns tells it all an' the law ain't got no ears!"

Red asked cautiously, "Does Robbins pay good wages?"

"To men like me an' you he would. Mike's told some of the boys up there to set an' wait; that maybe Robbins would be along pretty soon. He don't hire nobody but killers—an' me, I'm well knowed. Yessir!" Pincher waggled into dignified straightness in the saddle and scowled, letting Red see how a real bad man ought to look. It was too much effort to keep the pose, so he relaxed, put a hand on the horn, and lay forward. "Now then, do you an' me hook up together an' throw in with Robbins? Me, I'll vouch for you. What do you say?"

Red said, "Maybe."

Pincher presently told Red it was too hot to go any farther. Besides, he was beginning to get drowsy and almost fell out of the saddle two or three times on the way back.

An hour later, Pincher was dead drunk across a table. Mike, without any haste and without anger, dragged him by the scruff of the neck into a corner, dropped him all the same as a sack of oats, and let him lie.

"Pincher," said Red, with a kind of solemn irony, "he has been tellin' me how a lot of folks is scairt of him. An' seems to be pinin' for to meet an' old cowman name Powell——"

Mike chuckled, and, opening a bottle of beer for himself, said:

"If Powell showed up right now, Pincher there would either get down on his belly an' beg or light out cross-country on foot. Ol' Powell once held him out like that"—Mike extended his arm full length—"an' give him a quirtin' that plumb near skinned him, then set him on the toe of his boot an' invited him to git. Powell's got his faults, but bein' scairt to tell folks what he thinks ain't one of 'em!"

"What'd Pincher done to rile 'im?"

"I don't know. Stole a dollar off one of the girls there at Mekatone—mos' likely. His kind of a trick. He's stickin' around here thinkin' maybe he's goin' to work for old George Robbins. Old George wouldn't use him for to wipe out a skillet with!"

"Pincher said they was some range trouble 'tween Robbins and Powell."

"Plenty. Now me, I'm a Robbins man from toenails to hair tip, an' this here is war to the knife. Robbins an' Powell, they have been enemies from the time hell was first hot enough to cook eggs. An' this here is the final showdown. Now we've got the upper hand and are settin' pretty. But a lot o' damn fools, the which I ain't one, think the war is plumb over. That's 'cause they don't know Bill Powell. He'll win or die— an' die fightin'. An' me, son, when I stand up an' look down at him, I'm goin' to take off my hat. He's a man!"

Red looked steadily at the big old fat saloon keeper, spoke softly, very low: "And so are you to say that about a fellow that's an enemy."

Mike swore, a little embarrassed, cleared his throat, grunted, kicked at something he pretended was on the floor: "Personal, I think this here country is plenty big to hold both old George Robbins an' Powell. But they say 'tain't; an' me, I'm a Robbins man. That's all."

Red dozed through the heat of the day, as everyone else did; drank much warm beer, listened, said nothing, played poker, dropped lighted matches each time he rolled a cigarette, then slowly scraped them out with his foot. He ate supper, fed Blackie some sugar, came back to the saloon and played more poker, then rolled in and meditated.

Nobody excepting the unreliable Pincher had given him any hint that Robbins and his friends were expected to ride into Nelis City. He had stayed up late to make sure they didn't come. Orders were orders with him. Having satisfied himself that he had done his best, he slept pretty well. It was a little restful and soothing to know that Big Mike had grown almost friendly; but Red felt a warm flush, almost like shame, at what Mike might say when, and if, he learned that the redhead was a Powell spy. Red couldn't get any pride out of doing things underhanded, even when his reason and judgment told him they were all right, as now.

CHAPTER XV

THE MEXICAN STRANGER

The next morning Pincher had a bad head. "The fallin' sickness," Mike called it. "Falls over his own feet." None of the other men took Red's hint about liking some company.

His throat seemed much better. He could talk pretty well, and he sort of coaxed for company. He didn't want them to think he was snooping and really wanted to ride out alone. Also he really did want to get the lay of the land. That was only common sense. He might have to jump sudden and ride fast.

Mike drew some plans for him in the spilled beer on the bar and explained which way to head. Most of the travel came in up the other side of the valley.

Red rode over there and found a quite good road along which teamsters brought in goods to the city. He went along and found ravines, box canyons, and thick clusters of scrub oak beside the high wall of rock towering above the road. Here and there a thin trail left the road and went winding up overhead, past the sprawling cactus that had somehow got a toehold among the flat faces of the rocks.

"Good place to wait for somebody as ain't your friend," Red suggested, eyeing the broken rock ledges high overhead.

He went on slowly for an hour or two, then reined up quickly. There was the clatter of hoofs on ahead. Somebody was coming, riding hard. Pursued? Red listened. Nobody was very close to the rider anyhow.

Red started to get off the road and keep out of sight; then decided on second thought that he had better not seem to be hiding. If he were seen he might have a hard time explaining—" 'specially as my throat is still plum' bad!" He had ridden out openly, and as long as he stayed in the open, Mike and the men in town would bear out his story that he was just out looking the country over in case he wanted to hurry off.

He did not know what twists and turns the road took on ahead, so he went back some fifty yards, the better to be in plain sight when the rider came around the elbow of rock ahead. Red waited until he knew the man was close, then started up Blackie at a walk.

A horse and rider flashed on the turn. A Mexican was in the saddle. At sight of Red, he pulled up with a high swing of arm and jerk that sent the horse's head up with forelegs pushing stiffly on squatting haunches.

"Hi, *señor*, you are from the town?" the Mexican called eagerly, but in the tone of one who wants to be quite sure and somehow feels he ought also to be much welcomed.

"*Yo soy!*" Red sang out and drew his eyes down, squinting hard, not liking the look of the fellow.

The Mexican seemed pleased and, reassured, said rapidly in Spanish:

"You are the guard on this road, *señor!*" Red didn't deny the guess. "But an enemy is behind you, *señor*, there in the town! One with red hair who spies! You have seen him?"

"*Sí,*" said Red, thinking: "An' you got an enemy right here in front of you, too, Mr. Man." He pulled his hat down tightly, the better to keep the color of his hair from being noticed.

The Mexican talked fast, with excitement: "He is a stranger that has come across the desert, being guided by the son of the devil, so that you would not suspect him! And I have come to give you warning!"

"Well, now, ain't that nice of you," said Red, returning to English. "But he 'pears to be a right quiet pleasant sort of fellow. Yessir. An' how do you know about 'im? An' who the hell are you?"

"Ah, *señor*, I have brought you warning. And must now return. You will permit that an unknown friend departs in peace!"

"Pieces maybe!" Red muttered and, having lightly touched Blackie with spurs and checking him with reins at the same time, made the high-spirited horse seem restive. In this way he edged closer to the obliging Mexican; then whipped a gun from his holster with, "*Ven acá!*"

The Mexican protested, but came as told with hand half raised and palms out.

"Now listen, feller! She's a hair trigger an' I'm nervous. Powerful nervous! Get your horses off the road. Get over into that gully where you'll be walled in. They's goin' to be some talkin' done by a man 'bout yore size!"

As the Mexican moved by him, Red popped his mouth to see the T T brand.

The fellow rode in as told and faced about, palms still up and out. Red came near, said: "Now take a look an' tell me what you see!" Red pulled off his hat, held it for a moment above his head, clapped it back.

The Mexican swore helplessly.

"Yessir. You see, I'm him—an' you're it! Now talk. Who sent you?"

"*Señor* Powell, *señor!*"

"You're a liar! Another break like that an' you'll be a dead one. I don't like the shape o' yore nose anyhow!"

"Before God!" said the Mexican desperately.

"My gosh!" Red thought. "Would he play me a trick like that?" Then he answered himself aloud: "Not by a damn sight he wouldn't. I stand pat. You're a liar!"

"It is the truth, *señor*!"

"Old Bill Powell sent you over here for to tell—"

"No no no! The young *señor*!"

"Oh. Well, that's a what-you-call something else again. What's your name?"

"Manuel."

"Come on. Tell me a complete lie while you're at it. Manuel what?"

"Manuel Diaz, *señor*."

Red eyed him carefully, had never laid eyes on him before, but how was the Mexican to know that? So Red took a chance, said with conviction: "That ain't no more your name than mine's Susy Ann. You see, I'm smarter'n I look. Now try onct more, an' you better give me a name that fits your kind of face."

"Ho, *señor*, he is afraid of you! He ordered, he begged, he gave me much gold and many promises! He swore that I must come and—"

"Don't change the subject so much. We'll get around to that, maybe. I don't like yore looks an' I wanta know yore name. What is it?"

"Ramón Diego."

"Maybe so. Now you lis'n. You can't lie fast enough for me not to think the only reason Bud Powell sent you is 'cause he knows you like doin' the things he wants done. You an' him are snakes outa the same hole."

"But, *señor*—" Diego's voice rose in a pleading

183

whine. The sound of it did not soften Red, but irritated him.

"Shut up that sick-cat sound. I been round Mexicans all my life. Most of 'em are men an' more'n men, gentlemen. But when one turns bad, he carries a stink, same as you now. You an' Bud Powell are up to the orneriest low-downest trick that the devil with a bad bellyache could think of!

"I ain't talkin' about what you two are tryin' for to do to *me!* I'm talkin' about how you an' Bud Powell is tryin' to maybe ruin old Bill Powell's range war jus' for the pleasure of gettin' me shot. So you come a-ridin' in here to get me killed, didn't you? Awright. Go ahead an' do your own killin'! 'F you don't, I'll kill you, right here now. What you got to say?"

For a moment Diego looked like an angered fiend, studied Red's face, seemed about to snap; but he didn't have the stuff in him that it took to accept the challenge. He whined, he begged, he pleaded.

Red told him, "Shut up. God's lookin' at me, an' He knows I ain't goin' kill you to save my own hide. I'm drawin' wages to help Mr. Powell win his fight. I ought but I jus' can't shoot you down. So I'll back up out here on the road a piece. You can put your hand on the saddle horn an' I'll put mine. Then start drawin'—"

But the Mexican didn't want even that halfway

fair chance against the tense-faced, hard-eyed redhead who had a calm fierceness about the justice of the duel and confidence in his own marksmanship.

Ramón Diego began to talk hurriedly in Spanish, with something of a hurt dog's whimper in his voice. Red hated the sound. He had no use for men that whined. But Diego began saying things that made him listen. He was pouring out what he knew about Bud Powell as if he knew that more than anything else he could say would hold Red's attention.

He told how Bud robbed his own father, how he had men about him that killed and stole and hid behind young Powell whom his father couldn't suspect. Then Diego said with flattery:

"He has much fear of you, *señor*. And when he fears a man he hates him. You have killed his closest friend, thees Cliff Hammon. And at Mekatone others died who were to give you burial.

"Why he holds thees fear of you, I cannot say. Perhaps it is that you have met and talked with my cousin, Benito Valdez. Though Valdez and I were not good friends, he is my cousin. Valdez knows something that I do not about the young *señor*. He says it is what he saw one day when he looked down from a high ridge on a lonely trail. He, my cousin, talked to me about how God would curse him if he did not tell honest men

185

what he had seen. To me he would not tell. But one day he went away.

"Then the young *señor* came to me and said, 'Where is Benito?' I replied, 'I do not know, *señor*.' Said the young *señor*, 'He has been seen in Tahzo and talked with the sheriff.' Then I told him of the madness of Benito and how he feared God's curse; but why, I did not know.

"The young *señor* cursed until the froth flew from his lips and madness looked out of his eyes like a cat's shine in the dark. And he said, which I believed was a lie, that he had given Benito, my cousin, much money to carry and he had stolen it. The young *señor* said that Valdez, to keep us from following him, would tell the sheriff of certain horses that had been run off the Tahzo range.

"Ah, now plees listen. The young *señor* asked for one of Benito Valdez's gloves, and I found old ones. Then he went to Mekatone, and when it was night the young *señor* went to the bank where the old paymaster worked late. Being the old *señor*'s son, he was let in. I was with him. He wanted me to shoot the old man, but I would not. So he did it himself, in the back. He dropped the gloves on the floor. The young *señor* said, 'People will think Benito said he came with a message from my father and was let in here. Now we will have money, which I need! And Benito will be sorry he rode off to that sheriff in Tahzo.' "

Diego took a deep breath, let his glance rest keenly on Red's face as if to judge how much was believed and how far Red was off guard through being astonished. He went on, rapidly:

"All that is truth, with no word twisted."

Red said, "I ain't sure, but it sounds like it might be true."

"My cousin did not kill the paymaster at Mekatone! You have come from Tahzo—is it not that you met my cousin and so learned what he knew about the young *Señor* Powell?"

"I never seen him," said Red. He had turned his horse slightly and now rested his gun and hand on the horn.

Diego, in talking, had gesticulated and from much moving of his hands about had let them come to rest on his own saddle horn.

Red, being very perturbed, eyed him and thought:

"Now there seems to be purt-near as much reason for wantin' to keep him alive as there was a minute ago for not wantin' to! But what to do with him? I can't trust 'im. Maybe he's been lyin'. An' maybe he's been tellin' the truth in hopes that maybe I won't want to kill him. But a Mexican's word against Bud Powell wouldn't go far—not in the Old Man's ear. An' me, I'm sure all in a muddle."

Then Diego shrieked, *"Por Dios!"* and with

astonishment exploding on his face, pointed: "One listens and has heard every word!"

Red reined up with startled jerk and stared around, his gun muzzle poised across his breast ready to whip down.

No one was there. It was an old trick, but always a good one if well played. The jingling clink of bridle chains brought Red's head about as Diego skillfully made his horse rear then fired almost point-blank. The bullet, with the jar of a hammer blow, struck the hump of Red's saddle tree.

Red, with a snap shot that grazed the neck of the rearing horse, killed the Mexican. The mingling echoes rang from rock to rock. The horse flung its head wildly, then with a half-turn high in the air dropped forefeet to the ground and shook its head, trying to shake out the sharp pain of the bridle's bit in its mouth as Diego's body listlessly sprawled off, head down.

"So that's that," said Red, gazing down thoughtfully, and as a matter of habit began prodding out the empty shell.

"Funny now. I bet he felt he had to tell me some truth to make me listen close. He felt it would be all right for me to know the truth 'cause he was goin' to sneak the draw an' kill me. Sneakers of the draw don't have no luck—no more'n liars. Now what to do with him? I could poke *him* somewhere away out o' sight, but there's the horse. An' branded T T. An' how the hell did he ever get in here ridin' that horse?"

Red eyed the dead man and, unhurriedly, meditated some more:

"Now I wonder, did that nice little gentle boy Buddy know just why I am over here? Or did he happen for to learn that I'd been sent an' thought I was just scoutin'? Nope, for to be plum' honest an' reason'ble, I don't think he'd have busted up any of the Old Man's war plans like that. That'd be hittin' hisself right in the face, hard. An' he sorta likes the look o' his own face. Buddy? Such a nice, gentle-soundin' name! As for me, I'm gettin' plum' tired o' bein' shot at by folks I don't know an' never saw before. But at that, I can't blame Diego much for makin' a try. But," Red affirmed solemnly, "they is shore something about sneakin' the draw that makes fellows hasty an' not accurate." He nodded with serene faith.

Back in Nelis City men were waiting about Mike's doorway.

Somebody had seen Red crossing the valley, leading a horse with a body over the saddle. From the time they first made him out in the distance until he stopped in front of the saloon, Red did not change the gait of his horse, but came at a slow walk. He reined up, looked the men over, said nothing.

They eyed him with suspicious silence, waiting for him to tell what had happened while they heard critically. But they were face to face with a boy who, in spite of a tendency toward friendly chatter, knew how to keep his mouth shut when a shut mouth seemed wise.

The dead man lay stomach down, with face hidden. His hat dangled from a saddle thong.

Big Mike broke the silence. Very quietly, and with a hard look, he asked:

"Meet somebody you knowed?"

Red, still in the saddle, took his time about replying; then, coolly, "No. Thought maybe you fellows might know 'im. Right off, he 'peared to mistake me for one of you. So after our argyment, I brought him along for you all to have a look."

"Yeah?" Mike asked noncommittally.

"Yeah," said Red coolly, eyeing Big Mike with a long straight look.

The men came nearer, touched the body, having a look at the face. They grew excited in a calm sort of reserved way as they saw the brand, T T.

Then Pincher, not entirely sober, had a big moment: he only of all who looked at the face knew the dead man.

"Why, fellers, I know 'im, yeah! That's Ramón Diego! Yeah! An' a purt-near good fellow—for a Greaser!"

Red leaned slightly in the saddle, asked: "Are you hintin' at something?"

"No, no, oh no!" said Pincher, not liking the look and tone. "I jus' meant for a Mexican!"

Men sidled away quickly and with sparkles of hope in their eyes. As between this redhead and Pincher, they were all for Red; and though there wasn't one of them that wouldn't have put Pincher on a toe boot to shove him out of the way, they sort of hoped for a little gunplay that would let them see Red go into action. And there was nobody they would have buried with more cheerful feelings and peace of mind than Pincher. He, however, had other ideas on the matter, knuckled under, explained, wound up with, "Why, me an' you is friends!"

Red said nothing, but the way he looked at him called Pincher pretty much of a liar. Pincher didn't notice, or pretended he didn't notice. He hurried to say, "Diego was close in with Buddy Powell. One o' that bunch." He had the large manner of a fellow glad to give information. "Now me, I—"

Men pushed Pincher aside, asked questions, no longer suspicious, of Red.

He put his hand to his throat, letting them know it wasn't easy to talk, but said:

" 'Bout the first thing I knowed, there he was with his horse r'ared up, settin' on its hind legs, an' him shootin'—right there! See? Might have busted my saddle fork! Wasn't no time to ask questions, so I done what I could, the which was plenty. Then I brung him along over here for you fellows to do your own guessin'."

"A T T man ridin' in like that!"

"Damn funny!"

"Shore is!"

"I've told you *hombres*," said Big Mike with slow rumble, "them Powell fellows know more about this country than you think. They know trails you fellows never seen. This Diego knowed one an' was on the scout, understand? He bumped into Red an'—well, there he is."

Mike seemed to have explained everything, yet they stared up at Red encouragingly, hopeful he might add a word or two.

"Did sort appear to think I was from the town," said Red. "Which in a way o' speakin' I was. If he was on the scout he made a bad job of it."

Mike told the men to get out their shovels and put Diego up yonder on the hill with the rest of the bad shots, and had another man take the two horses to the corral. Then he got Red off to one side in the saloon and said:

"This here is like playin' poker blindfolded. But now me, I got a notion that Diego rode this way expectin' to meet somebody. Maybe hear something. An' he jus' naturally had the bad luck to meet up with the wrong feller."

"Yeah?" Red asked, interested and cautious. He was a long way from being sure just what Mike was driving at.

"All right," said Mike, and made a gesture as if laying out cards with one sweep of hand.

"Ever'thing's face up with you, son. I don't quite trust Pincher!"

"Oh."

"Yeah. Yesterday, did he by any happenchance say anythin' you could twist around to sort o' make fit the notion that he might be workin' for Powell?"

Red looked thoughtful, studied, shook his head. "Nope. He ain't the sort I'd trust with anything I wasn't hankerin' for to lose, but—"

Red tossed a live match away from the end of his cigarette.

"Don't you ever shake out your match?" Mike asked sharply.

"Must be from the time I burnt my fingers as a kid. Seems like I just got to drop 'em, quick."

"I noticed that. So you wouldn't suspicion Pincher if you was me?"

"Not from anything I know definite, no. He cussed Powell aplenty an'—"

Mike made a wry face. " 'F he was a Powell spy come in here, do you think he would be singin' his praise?"

"No. No, I don't. But you told me yourself, didn't you?—how old Bill Powell gave him a hidin' with a quirt that—"

"Old Bill Powell, yeah. But not young Buddy Powell, understand? They's a power of diff'rence. An' I reckon Buddy is as anxious not to lose any of the T T range as the Old Man. 'Sides, personal, I believe if even old Bill give Pincher twenty dollars to lick his boots, Pincher'd do it, notwithstandin' the hidin'."

" 'Pears like you don't quite approve of Mr. Pincher?" Red suggested, grinning.

"He's nosy an' he's mean. He'd steal candy off a crippled child an' hunt for somebody to grin when he bragged about it. You yoreself woke up an' took some notice when he said this Diego was a purty good fellow. That's what made my suspicions rise up an' take a look all around. I figger that remark just slipped out before Pincher thought how it would sound. I figger maybe Pincher would have knowed where to sneak out tonight an' meet this Diego an' tell him, for instance, they was—" Big Mike broke off to exclaim, "Now what the hell!" and hurry with heavy stride to the door.

Three or four horsemen were pounding into town, and they came with "Yippee-ki-ee-eye-ohs" ringing out like the cry of a wolf pack.

One bawled, "Hey, Mike! Pete Strodd an' two other hellcats is here!"

"Good! Fine!" Mike shouted, seeming really pleased.

The horses were jerked into a stiff-legged stop before Mike's place, the reins fell, men swung lithely from saddles. With loud and joyous greetings the newcomers stamped into the saloon as Mike hurried behind the bar, quickly set up bottles and scattered short thick glasses, then reached across the bar to shake hands.

Pete Strodd was a well-built hard-looking man; and a grin, ears wide, brightened his hatchet face as he came.

He thrust out his hand at Mike, saying: "She's all over! Powell's laid down. Plumb flat on his belly! He knowed he was licked!"

"So?" Mike asked, sounding a little more hopeful than certain.

"You bet, Mike. He's out there roundin' up them cows that we kicked through the canyon—run off thirty pounds 'r more from each cow, we did! Take a long time to fatten 'em back!"

"Good," said Mike, being agreeable, not wholly convinced.

"We been settin' up in the hills, watchin' an' waitin'. He ain't goin' to try to bust in. We hear he wanted to make it a fight, but his men, they quit 'im cold. Said they stood no show. The which shows they're wise *hombres*! They could've come in all right—but git out! Not without usin' the trapdoor to hell!"

"I'm rejoicin', Mr. Strodd," said Mike, and pushed the bottles about so each man wouldn't have to reach far for a second drink. "But y'know, if 'twas me, now, I'd keep right on watchin' and waitin'—hopeful. Bill Powell ain't one to disappoint somebody as is expectin' a fight."

"Sure hope not!" said Strodd loudly, though he

wasn't a loud sort of man. Echoes of the same opinion went up from the two men that had come in with him. "But he's done, Mike. He can't get the men as want to waltz in an' face the music. We got men settin' up on top o' all the trails an' hilltops. An' there ain't been a symptom of trouble—we'd have heard if he was up to anything. Cliff Hammon was keepin' us— Well, we learned things we wanted for to know!"

Strodd laughed, long and almost noiselessly. It was as if he knew a very good joke on Old Man Powell.

Big Mike in a very soft voice protested, "But 'f I was you, I wouldn't put no great lot o' trust in what news you don't hear. An' I'd put a lot in the kind o' man Powell's been known to be these thirty years or more. May interest you for to know a T T man was right in here close to town this mornin' and—"

"The hell he was! Who? Where? How'd he get in?"

"You mean close to town?" another asked.

"I usual mean what I say," Mike replied amiably. "This here young stranger"—he waved a hand at Red—"he was out for to see some scenery an' seen him over—"

Strodd and his men whirled about on Red, looking him up and down; and Strodd said with just a tinge of a sneer: "Oh, he *says* he seen him, eh? Well, now, I wonder was you—"

Mike spoke up, loud and a bit gleeful: "We all got a good chance for to see 'im, Mr. Strodd. One o' Powell's Mexicans. Name o' Diego. Red here, he brought him along in for us to look at."

The attitude of the skeptical listeners changed. They popped questions:

"Where is he now?"

"What's he have to say for hisself?"

"What'll you do with him?"

Strodd turned on Red, repeating: "What did he have to say?" but Mike answered: " 'Pears like Diego done his talkin' with a gun, hasty-like. Red here, he's got a sore throat from a bullet bite— got it some time ago. Can't talk much. But 'pears like he can shoot. Leastwise, Diego had all the symptoms of bein' dead when Red here brung him in, diamond-hitched over the saddle. The boys are up buryin' him now!"

Strodd and his two hellcats looked a little put out at having guessed so far wrong; but they eased themselves with a lot of wonder as to how the devil Diego could have got in.

Strodd, as if not quite liking having something of a joke turned on him, sized Red up and down and asked bluntly:

"Where'd you come from?"

Red smiled slowly, put his fingers to his throat, answered huskily:

"So far I ain't said!"

"Meanin'?" Strodd demanded.

"It hurts to talk," said Red, grinning.

Mike explained. "He come in across the Basin. Ridin' a horse no puncher's wages ever bought! He fell in with a prospector over back in them hills that put him through, so—"

"I asked," Strodd repeated, not taking his eyes off Red, "where did you come from?"

Red knew he was in a tight hole. He was afraid to say Mekatone or even Tahzo. These men would know that if he came from either of those towns he had pushed through Powell's country to reach the Basin—which would be a bad thing to admit, especially after the precautions taken to keep men from suspecting that he came in that way. But Red did not know the lay of the country well enough to lie. If he tried a cock-and-bull story they would trip him up quick.

So he smiled again and shook his head, saying:

"I come from far off an' most o' the way in a lope. For some reason or other, there was right smart smoke behind me. Once or twict, I traded horses—sorta coaxin' for to get the best of the bargain. Bein' a stranger an' not havin' no map, I don't know myself just how I got here. It ain't easy for to talk, an' I've said my say!"

"Aw, hell, Pete," said one of Strodd's men, "the boy here, he brung down a T T rider—the which is more'n I've done so far!"

"That's shore right!" said the other.

"Have a drink?" said Strodd.

"Thanks," said Red.

At that, Pincher, who had come hurrying back from the burial of Diego, and seeing Red now seemed taken into favor after some remarks that sounded doubtful, left his safe place by the door and said, importantly:

"I'll vouch for him, Pete. An' you know *me!*"

Strodd growled and snorted, but Pincher wasn't sensitive and so, lined at the bar, took his drink, then said, "See, kid, I told you how things would be—" He gave Red a hard companionable slap on the back.

Red whirled as if kicked. "Slap me in the face any time you like, feller! But keep yore hands off my back!"

Pincher whined an abused apology, lamenting, as if appealing to the sentiments of all present, that this was no way to treat a man who had just vouched for him.

Big Mike said, "Diego has done what vouchin' appears needful, leastwise for the time bein'!"

An hour or two later Walt Wiggins and another man rode in.

Wiggins was squat, dark, and an old-timer. He had the name of being about the deadliest gun fighter in that part of the country, where nearly every man was prompt; and Wiggins looked it.

It was known that Wiggins wore shortnosed guns with no sights and the triggers tied back. Wiggins would go for his rifle if the range was much over thirty yards, as it seldom was in any of the cowtown killings; and he was as quick almost with a rifle as with a revolver. Folks said that, face to face, he couldn't be beat on the draw—at least had never been!

He heard about Diego and brooded, giving Red a long scrutiny, admitted he couldn't make head or tail of it. Wiggins didn't have a loud mouth, and he had a jerky way of saying things; but even when he said them low-voiced they packed a lot of meaning and had much the same sort of effect as when some people shouted. He took his time about speaking up, then:

"If anybody was scoutin' 'twould be that old Leon Lenard. More sneaky'n a coyote. Mangy one. I run 'im outa this country onct. Give me some whisky." Pincher edged in close, hopeful of being asked. Wiggins moved his head, looked down. "You little wart off a pickle—git away!"

Pincher got, not even whining. Wiggins was morose and dangerous. Pincher drew off to the lower end of the bar and waited for the bottle to slide down within reach. He stood and drank by himself, nobody paying any attention to him.

"Now ol' George, he said we was all to be in here by sun-down," Strodd remarked. "He'd better hump hisself."

"Better," Wiggins growled. "I'm goin' to lay the law down. George Robbins is too easy satisfied. Kill Powell, an' who's to hold any of the T T range, huh? That kid o' his ain't got the fightin' guts of a mangy sheep. More whisky, Mike. We got Powell on the run. Run him clear outa the country. Some spoils o' war is what I want. An' when the smoke clears away, me, I'm goin' to be pushin' my cows clear over on the Mekatone range. You stickin', Pete?"

"You just bet!" said Pete Strodd.

"That there," Big Mike suggested mildly, "is a big mouthful for to chew."

" 'Tain't. More whisky."

"Before you begin parcelin' out the Mekatone range," Mike went on, carefully unangering of tone, "maybe you ought to wait and hear some of what George Robbins thinks. An' says."

"I know what he's goin' to say," Wiggins replied jerkily. "He's goin' to say whatever I tell 'im to."

Big Mike blandly let the remark pass. These men were Robbins's neighbors and friends. Good fighters. But they didn't have Robbins's common sense. Mike thought it bad that his friend should be hedged about by such reckless and unwise counselors: men who could make a war but didn't know anything about when or how to make peace.

They all drank steadily, with a lot of free talk, but nobody got drunk. They could carry a ton of whisky apiece. Most of their happiness was not from the whisky but from the fact that they had old Bill Powell on the run. Red looked on, tried not to appear too attentive, heard what was said, and, every time he could without attracting attention, passed up the whisky.

An hour later old George Robbins and six men at his side came through the dusk with stormy clatter of hoofs and gleeful "yip-yips." They swung with clattering stride into the saloon, shouted greetings, and there was a babel of congratulations among them: Powell wasn't even going to strike back. He must have heard, they said, what was waiting for him inside the canyon—and wasn't going to ride in. All sorts of reports were in the air. Some said Powell had left the range work to one of his men and gone back to Mekatone. He was trying to sell out. His men had quit cold—and so forth and so on.

Old George Robbins was much more puzzled and uneasy than Strodd or Wiggins had been over Diego. Old George was a gray wolf of the range who, like Powell, had fought every step of the way up, using fair means or foul, and was tricky and full of courage. He used bad men because they were the best men for his needs; and being a crafty, suspicious fellow, he knew that there was some reason more than mere guesswork had been able to discover why Diego had shown up on the road near Nelis City.

"Powell," he said wisely, "would never have sent in that Mexican on a T T horse for to scout.

An' right on the road, plain, where he was likely for to meet anybody? Never!"

But crafty and suspicious as he was, he couldn't figure just why Diego had come. He questioned Red, and Red gave him precisely the same story as told to Mike. It was a simple tale and plausible.

But Red, having a queer sort of conscience, reasoned secretly with himself: "An' it's so near the truth that I ain't much of a liar!"

As he stood there before the big gaunt form of old Robbins, answering questions, he dropped a live match from the tip of his cigarette. A moment later the cigarette went out, and another live match was flung to the floor.

"You look like a pretty good fellow," said Robbins, "but I wouldn't have you on my range till you learn better'n that!"

"I been cussed a lot for it, but I still got hopes. Maybe I'll stop smokin'."

Robbins said, "Be best 'f you did." He turned to Strodd and Wiggins. "I been expectin' word from over thataway. Cliff Hammon might-a sent Diego, but hell"—turning to Red—"you say he r'ared up an' let go at you on sight?"

"He r'ared up an' let go without no warnin' a-tall!" Red answered. "An' I'll say onct again, I never seen the fellow before in my life."

"H'm." Robbins sized Red up. "You lookin' for work?"

"I'm goin' to be if I keep on playin' poker with Mike."

Men laughed a little, and Mike grinned complacently.

"Funny," Robbins commented with vague accusation, "that you'd be ridin' off over there alone thataway!"

"He shore asked for company, Mr. Robbins," said Mike.

"Yeah? Well, Red, I hear you're ridin' a horse with a vented J R," said Robbins, not quite able to lay aside all of his suspicions. "A good one. The J R is a Tahzo outfit." He paused, waiting for Red to explain; Red did, evasively, with: "*Vented,* Mr. Robbins."

"That's so. Still—h'm. You got that horse over in Tahzo, didn't you?"

Red replied, " 'F you say I did, I won't argy. But I won't say I did!"

"Ho, so you keep a close mouth, don't you?" Robbins snapped.

Then Pincher squawked, "George, I've suspicioned him all along! He's been borin' into me with questions an'—"

Red half turned and with backhanded blow smashed Pincher in the face, knocking him backwards. Red jumped forward, jerked Pincher up, slapped first one side of his head, then the other; and, with kick and shove, flung Pincher at Robbins's feet.

"Once," said Red, not having any trouble with his throat now, "I picked me up a skunk by the tail." He dusted his hands one against the other. "I didn't get near so dirty as now. Question him good, Mr. Robbins. Hear it all. Ever'thing you think maybe he can tell you, so later on you won't think maybe I shut 'im up on purpose!"

Old George Robbins looked down at Pincher and poked him with a foot.

"Hit yore hoss an' git! Git clear outa town. Git off my range. Git outa the country. Up an' go!"

Pincher got up weakly, kept his eyes down, wiped snivelingly at his bleeding nose with a bare forearm, and staggered out of the door.

"Yeah," said Red, "them instructions is 'propriate as hell for a sheepherder, but just for to make sure he don't take the best horse by mistake in the dark, I'm goin' down along there to the corral till he's rode off! An' I'd like me some company. Witnesses is a good thing for to have when you're a stranger. He might stumble an' break his neck—then I maybe would be suspicioned some."

CHAPTER XVI

FIRE BREAKS OUT IN NELIS CITY

Three or four men walked with Red and followed Pincher down to the corral. On the way Red stopped, ran into the restaurant and got some sugar. He climbed on the corral, leaned over the top, and called to Blackie. It was a clear starless night, and they could see Blackie pitch forward his ears and switch his tail, quite as if asking: "Is that fellow to be trusted, or maybe does he want to throw a saddle on me?" But Blackie was tempted and came, got his ears scratched, nose rubbed, and ate sugar.

Pincher in sullen silence saddled and rode off, followed by some loud and casual-seeming remarks that must have made his ears burn.

One of the men said to Red, who was still on the fence rubbing Blackie's forehead, "I reckon if a feller was sleepin' on his belly in the dark, Pincher might shoot—from horseback!"

"He'll go over and work for Powell," said another. "Powell, he uses them kind."

Red said nothing. He stayed on the fence until the others said they all had better be getting back if they wanted to eat.

As they turned away, Red got down and paused to light a cigarette that he had rolled and stuck behind his ear. He hastily flung the match behind him, glanced to see where it had fallen, and went on.

A few steps farther there was a dancing light in the shadows behind him. He stopped, called out, "Holy smoke, I've went an' done it! *Fire!*"

He turned back on the run, grabbed the only pitchfork, and began frantically to pitch the burning hay about, making sure that the whole of the small stack would catch on fire before it could be put out. But as he worked he shouted: "Got to save this corral! An' shed! Keep the fire away from it!"

That was, after all, the sensible thing to do. Red did that all right, but in his frantic haste wasn't very careful where he flung forkfuls of burning hay. He had to work pretty hard to save the corral. It was dry as tinder and would have snapped into fire instantly if touched by the flames.

Men stood about watching him. Others came on the run. There was no doubt as to how it started. Chuck, the blacksmith, cussed a blue streak. It was his corral and his hay. He jumped in with a pole to help Red keep the fire away from the corral.

In the windless night the flames shot high, tossing sparks and lighting up the town with a brief glare that danced far out across the valley.

The horses whinnied and surged to the farthest side of the corral.

"That hay's all spoilt anyhow," said Strodd, "so you fellers better scatter it much as you can— burn it up. If a wind comes an' does the scatterin' the corral may go!"

Red leaned on the pitchfork, wiped his face, and announced:

"She sure is all my fault an' that's a fact. I done it. An' I'll pay."

"Twenty dollars I paid to have some Mexicans cut me that grass!" said the blacksmith, not now quite so angry and forgetting to add that many and many a horse had eaten from the stack since the hay had been stacked.

"I'll buy at that figger," said Red. "So now, boys, I'm burnin' my own hay! Step up an' enjoy the bonfire. Quite some expensive cigarette I smoked!"

"Quite some damn-fool habit you got, too," said Big Mike critically.

On the whole they thought Red was taking it like a man. He didn't boggle at the blame or try to make them think maybe it started some other way.

As for Red's own feelings, they were in a tangle. He was proud of having carried out orders, but had a sneaking sensation, like being a hypocrite, in thus tricking these men into unsuspiciously watching the signal fire that was to bring Powell and his men storming through the town. But he knew that if he had tried to start a fire otherwise than right out in the open these men most likely would have smelled more than smoke.

Some men soon hurried back to the saloon, others to the restaurant; and a few lingered, idly watching while Red scattered the hay as fast as he could, turning it over to make it burn faster. He wanted to be through with the job, yet couldn't leave as long as the corral was in danger.

He had really worked hard and was thirsty, hungry, blackened and singed. At last he pitched the fork aside.

"I call that enough. An' I think from now on I'll break a matchstick before I drop 'er!"

By the time he got to the restaurant supper was long over, but he was told some supper had been saved, so he and the idlers who had kept him company didn't lose out. Then they all went back up to Mike's, where the bunch was beginning to get a little tired of just talk and drink and were starting poker games.

Red drank a bottle of beer and looked around. "Where's Mr. Robbins?"

One of the riders said, "Him an' Strodd an' Wiggins are over to Chuck's house havin' a powwow. Why?"

"Oh, I just wanted to ask if he thought maybe I'd learnt my lesson. That's all. Now I think I'll go get me a big bucket of water an' wash up some more than I did for to eat."

He borrowed a lantern from the restaurant, got a bucket of water, stripped to the waist, and as he spluttered and splashed over the wash bench he hummed soft and low:

> "An' she said, 'Sir, yo're a man I hate.
> Yore eyes is crooked an' yore nose ain't
>   straight;
> You got bow legs an' yore feet, they smell,
> But I'll marry you—when it snows in hell,
> F'r I'm a lady—you dang galoot!' "

While he was using the towel, Red told himself a lot of things, all in discreet silence:

"I'm feelin' plum' some relieved. That's shore been botherin' me ever since I hit town. Let's see. Been over an hour since I started my fire. Powell can't have been more'n ten miles off, if so far. May have to come slow down outa them hills— in the dark. Maybe plans has been changed some an' he won't come a-tall. Well, that's his lookout. Me, I done as told!"

He scrubbed at his wet hair and swore under his breath as a new thought popped up:

"I got to take off my ol' hat to Mr. Bill Powell! He shore does know how to find out what other fellers is up to! He knowed o' this here meetin' days an' days ago! Well, then, ain't it funny he knows so danged little about what goes on under his nose? But who's ever goin' to have the spunk to tell 'im about Buddy? Would you? No, not by a damn sight! I ain't no hero. I reckon they call some folks 'martyrs' 'cause they get all marred up doin' what they think they ought.

"That Cliff Hammon seems for to have had his fingers into a lot o' pies. I'm sure lucky thataway.

"An' old Wiggins said he onct run Leon Lenard out o' this country? Yeah, he sure did! But did he? Maybe I ought-a called him a liar. Lot o' things I ought-a do I ain't goin' to do. Yessir. If Mr. Walt Wiggins wants to say he made Leon Lenard climb a grease' pole an' set up there all night, I'm goin' to listen respectful. That Wiggins *hombre* is a killer. He's got the look an' the cat-cautious way o' keepin' his muscles supple so he can jump the draw. But I'd sure like to be listenin' if old Leon ever hears him say it! He up'ards o' sixty, but all greased rawhide an' backbone. Be pretty, I bet, to have a nice tree stump in front o' you an' watch them two jockey for the split-second jump in the draw."

But try as he would, Red was not able to feel happy. A mean and sneaking feeling had settled down right in the pit of his stomach. He had done his job successfully, but he couldn't quite think it had been a real man's job. He had carefully pretended not to be a friend—though friendly, as became a sociable stranger—with any man. He

211

did not greatly like any of them except Big Mike. Mike was good leather.

Red admitted willingly, however, that all of them had treated him squarely. The more he studied about it, the less and less he felt like going back among them where he was sure to be asked to drink and play some poker—and his own friends, and employer, might come a-romping in any minute now for to hand out tickets to hell.

"I don't like bein' a hypercritter!" he told himself as he walked out into the starlit darkness, trying to think. Consciously, and unconsciously, too, he found himself listening carefully for the first faint pulse beat of far-off hoofs. Soon he realized that it was nervous work, just waiting.

He went around to the back of the restaurant and slipped to the bunk where he had been sleeping since he came to town. He took his rifle and scabbard from under the mattress and, taking care not to be seen, went down to the corral.

His saddle was there under the *ramada*. He thought about putting it on Blackie, and after some doubt decided it would be wise. Somebody might drift down and think it mighty strange, but that was a chance he would have to take. He called Blackie up, and the horse, with drooping head and a woebegone look, let it be known that his faith in mankind was shaken.

He let down the corral bars, led Blackie out, set up the bars again, and walked the horse around back of the corral where he was pretty well out of sight. Then Red went back near the road and settled himself in the shadows, watching and listening.

Up the street a blaze of light fell through the saloon doorway and was blotted every now and then by the shadows of men that moved about. Over at the house of Chuck, the blacksmith, he could see the lighted windows where old George Robbins, Pete Strodd, and Walt Wiggins discussed plans for running Bill Powell clear off the earth.

He rose to his feet, listening. From far off, very far off, he heard the faint muffled drum-like tattoo of horsemen. He couldn't place the sound well enough to tell from which direction they were coming. He climbed the corral fence and peered all about the shadow-dotted valley and saw nothing. Sounds carry a long way in the night silence. Even as he listened intently, the hoofbeats died away. He could not hear them longer.

"They've pulled down to a walk. My gosh, are they goin' to *walk* their horses into this man's town! 'R maybe they've left their horses an' 'll walk. Yeah, a bunch o' cowmen get off an' walk, don't they? Yeah, sometimes when a horse falls an' breaks a leg!"

He stayed on the corral fence, crouched down low and motionless, the better to watch. A coyote yelped as if in pain, and now and then an owl flew by like a sluggish shadow.

The strain of hard peering made shadows seem to move like creeping things. Time after time he seemed to hear the distant click of hoofs on pebbles and would face about, staring toward the arroyo below the town.

Then, at last, he saw the dim form of riders come slowly up the bank and into starlight. He made a move to get off the fence when the slow, dust-muffled *cloof-cloof cloof-cloof* of other horsemen drew his eyes along the road. Some were coming that way, too. Were these horsemen Powell's men or other fellows riding in? Maybe Robbins's men?

"I'm seein' things—or rather ain't seein' 'em very clear! Seem to be all about me, yet I can't make out more'n half a dozen all told. Three down yonder. Three more on the road. Oh, yes, they's a couple o' fellows laggin'. Why'd they be laggin'? This ain't no time for to want to be behind! Oh, but way 'cross there, too. They're comin' in from ever' side! An' walkin' their horses! But, all told, they ain't more'n ten to a dozen—but oh, is this goin' to be purty!"

Red ran for his horse, poked the rifle into the boot, and struck off at a slow trot toward the road where the nearest riders were coming forward at a bobbing canter—with the two laggers following.

A quarter of a mile out of town Red was stopped with a low, clear, sharp, "Halt!"

"You guessed right!" said Red as he pulled up. "I shore will!"

"That you, Red?" It was Powell's voice.

"Me!"

Powell rode up with Leon Lenard on one side of him and Johnny Howard on the other: one an old range man and the other a kid that would grow into a range man just like the other.

Leon Lenard was tall in the saddle and straight as if he had a brand-new ramrod stuck into his backbone. He crowded his horse up close to Red, but did not say a word or make a move. He just took care to be where he could hear every word, weigh the intonation, and perhaps, because he was a distrustful old fellow, might scan Red's face and see if he could tell whether or not Red had got into a jam and told of Powell's plans, then lighted the fire in order to bring Powell and his men into a trap. No lone killer wolf of the hills was more wary than Leon Lenard—the old outlaw that had never been caught.

Johnny Howard, in the low eager voice of one who didn't expect an answer just then, murmured, " 'Lo, Red!"

Powell pushed his horse up stirrup to stirrup, face to face, said sharply, "You've done well. Now who's in town? An' where?"

"Seven or eight fellows was here when I come,

loafin' round already. Then tonight Pete Strodd come in with two or three more. After him, Walt Wiggins an' another 'n. Then George Robbins an' a half-dozen. Most the men are over to the saloon, but Robbins, Strodd, an'—" Red broke off in a flame of curses.

The two laggers had come up: one was Buddy Powell, the other Pincher.

Over his leveled finger, Red demanded, "What's that skunk doin' back here!"

"Met him on the road," Powell answered. "He said he suspicioned you was my man. Said he helped you to play the game an'—"

"He's a liar! Mr. Powell, me, I'm doin' a foolish thing. I'm wearin' my guns cocked—same as I seen old George Robbins a-wearin' his. An' the very first shot that goes outa them is goin' into Pincher if he's anywhere near! The facts is—"

"Why'd you shoot Diego?" Powell snapped, and Red understood why he had been greeted with such coldness from Powell when expecting to have a little more of a pleasant and rewarding tone.

Red's lips trembled to blurt the truth. But this was no time. He knew in his heart that there would never be a time when he could tell Powell what he had learned about Buddy. So he said:

"I met Diego on the road 'cross there. He mistook me for a Robbins man an' said he'd brought a warnin' that the stranger who'd come in off the Basin was a red-headed Powell spy!"

"What!" Powell asked with a sort of gasping sound, as if he had been hit in a way that nearly knocked him out of the saddle.

"Yessir! So me, I took my hat off an' let him see what a mistake he'd made. Then he made another. Tried to shoot me. After the which I tied him 'cross his own saddle an' brought him in here to town!"

"Who the hell could have sent him?" Powell asked in the tone that doesn't expect an answer. "I know now that Cliff Hammon was one that might've, but Hammon is dead!" He brooded for a moment, then roused himself with: "Where's Robbins and them?"

Red shook his head, pointed again at Pincher:

"Me, I don't talk private with that feller around!"

"I know 'im," said Powell. "He ain't much of a man. But he's told me things an'—"

"You'd trust what a man you've quirted says!" Red snapped, leaning far over in the saddle to peer.

Pincher was not sensitive, but at that his face writhed in the starlight as if the shame and pain of the quirting had come back.

"Red is right!" said Buddy Powell, smoothly, with emphasis. "I'll stay an' guard him, Dad. No time to waste!"

"All right. Take him back there a piece,

Buddy," Powell ordered, then turned his head, watching, until Buddy and Pincher had moved out of hearing.

The groan Red smothered down almost broke his belt. He squirmed as if against a rope that tied his hands. "Ow, one side-winder watchin' another!" said Red to himself.

Powell told Johnny, "Kid, you ride up through town, slow. Tell Mack we're stoppin'. Tell 'im to go ahead as planned an' round 'em up in that saloon just as soon as he hears us makin' a noise. Ride slow!"

"Yessir, Mr. Powell!" said Johnny.

"An', Johnny," Red added, "tell the boys to go easy as they can on Big Mike, the saloon keeper. He's a Robbins man till hell freezes, but he's a man!"

That remark brought a staring silence; sounded like Red had some friendliness with the enemy. Powell's hawk eyes peered under a frown. Leon Lenard edged his horse a step or two nearer, asked softly, "Just what you mean by that remark?"

"I mean," Red told him, "that Big Mike, he says anybody that thinks Mr. Powell won't make it a fight is crazy. I mean Mike is man enough for to be respectful and admirin' of Mr. Powell, an' all these other dinguses from Robbins down have been buckin' 'emselves up by sayin' Mr. Powell is easy scairt, has got his tail 'tween his legs, an'

218

is layin' down. Mike has got some man-sized sense!"

"They are saying that of *me,* Red?"

"They are!"

Powell chuckled a little. "All right, then, let's mosey along an' maybe show 'em."

They rode on. Red's teeth were clamped. He was irritated by the way he had been a little suspected about Big Mike. He was more irritated by Pincher being in the group, even if somewhat removed. He glanced back. Buddy and Pincher sat saddle to saddle and were dropping farther and farther back. Buddy had got himself well in the rear where there wouldn't be much smoke; and Pincher too.

"Mr. Powell," said Red in a low and weary voice, "me, I was hired till you won your fight. I'll stick an' do whatever I'm told till then. But if this here showdown tonight does it, I'm through. You can keep my wages, 'cause I've got enough of your spendin' money left to more'n pay 'em. So I'm clear plum' through—if you win!"

"Why?"

"For one thing, Pincher. I wouldn't stay in heaven if he sneaked in!"

Powell took his time about replying. "I understand. But, Red, it was Pincher sent me word a few days ago about this meetin'. I didn't trust him. That's why I sent you in. I'm trustin' you, fully."

"You got no reason not to," said Red bluntly. " 'F I was drawin' you into a trap, would I be settin' here where you an' Mr. Lenard could poke some holes in me, first thing? But that Pincher—he could walk under a snake's belly without bendin' his head!"

"I know. An' it's 'cause I know he'd sell himself ten times an hour that I thought maybe he was sellin' out the other fellows. When you got an uphill fight you catch holt of anything that helps. If he'd known I was comin', he'd have sold *me* out. But I'm goin' to pay him spot cash for what he's done. He sneaked me a letter that Robbins had sent in to Mike. He'd sell the gold filling out of his dyin' mother's teeth—an' me, I reckon I'd buy if, f'r instance, I had to have something for to make a bullet!

"Now, Red, me and Leon is stoppin' here at Chuck's house. Do you want to come along in an' listen?"

Maybe it was a trap question to try Red's courage, to see if he would find some excuse for not joining in; and maybe it was just Powell's way of paying a compliment, of showing Red that he did trust him and thought him worthy to walk in and stand shoulder to shoulder with himself and Leon Lenard.

"Yessir," said Red, "I would. My ears, they'll be stretched out like a drift fence, too!"

CHAPTER XVII

THE SHOWDOWN!

Red had a strong liking for Powell; but nothing he had seen or heard of the man made him feel so admiring as the iron-nerved caution with which he walked his horse, and had instructed the men who were moving in from other directions to walk theirs, into this town. That was risky and took a rangeman's heart.

If they had sneaked in, creeping about on foot, Indian fashion, Red would have felt different, have done the same, stuck, tried to earn his wages; but to be with men that just rode in calmly and slowly gave him a nice warm feeling like doing something a fellow could be proud to do.

He had expected Powell and his men to come tearing up the earth, yelling their heads off to draw men into clusters about lighted doorways, and shoot it out just about the same as bank robbers on a raid. This was cold calm work— cautious, not sneaking.

Up the street, far up, he could see other men on horseback, riding slowly into the town; and still others were reined up like guards placed to check Robbins's men who might try to break through when the ruckus started.

Red's own heart was talking to him with high pulse beat under his ribs, and he had common sense enough to know that other men's hearts were bumping their ribs too, but nobody showed any haste at all. He said to himself, "And these fellows think Powell ain't got men that'll back him up! Ho-*lee* smoke, what a lot of wrong notions they have got!"

"Now quiet!" said Powell as he reined up before Chuck's house.

The three of them slid from their horses, letting the reins fall.

Red shook himself, settling the holsters, touching the gun butts, and glanced about. Quite a way off he saw two shadows that he guessed were Buddy and Pincher, playing safe. Powell didn't seem to notice, didn't look about. Perhaps deep down in his heart he knew his son would hold back, not keep in step, stand up, and take it side by side with his father.

Powell strode forward, walking light-footed. His spurs tinkled faintly. Leon Lenard was beside him, half a step behind. Red followed on tiptoes, holding his breath and so noiseless that the old outlaw looked around with quick keen glance, as if just to make sure. The thought, "It's sure going to be purty!" drummed through Red's head.

The hum and cackle of voices from within reached them through open windows. The door was closed. Without a pause, almost in stride,

Powell flung open the door and stepped through, hands at his side and head up. With hawk-faced scowl he confronted the four men half sprawled about the table.

Leon Lenard, straight as a soldier on parade, edged through and took two side steps that put him off to the left of Powell, with his back to the wall. Red crowded in and stood to the right, let his arms hang loosely.

The men at the table stiffened into attitudes of astonished awkwardness. Had the devil himself, horned and cloven-hoofed, walked in, they couldn't have been more astounded. Their eyes were blown wide by utter amazement; but Red's being there, backing Powell up, seemed an explanation.

A bottle of whisky was on the table, and glasses, some partly filled; a lamp and cigars, with chewed butts about the floor.

Robbins, gray and rugged, held a pencil and had been leaning forward over a roughly drawn sketch, parceling out the T T ranges throughout Lelargo County. He lifted his head with a startled jerk and sat motionless with elbow still on the table, pencil between his fingers. Strodd, with elbow half raised in frozen gesture as if to ward off a blow from his face, gazed with mouth open. The fourth man, a Robbins foreman, had leaned back in the stiff frightened posture of one who sees a snake's head near his face.

Of the four there, only Walt Wiggins had moved. He simply arose, kicking over the chair behind him the better to be ready to go for his guns, and stood half crouched with his arms hanging rigidly, palms backwards. He looked straight at Leon Lenard, not for a moment glancing aside at anyone else.

They waited, staring, with no word spoken. Powell, too, waited for a long moment, and when he saw nothing was going to happen with the promptness he had expected, he strode forward with long and heavy-footed stamp of heel and clatter of spur. He walked right up to the table, stared at the face of each man, then dropped his glance, saw the map sketch. He reached out, crumpled it between his fingers, and, flinging the crumpled paper across the table to the floor, said, "Up, Robbins! Fight it out!"

Leon Lenard, with a noiseless slithering of his long legs and but the faintest tinkle of spur rowels, went nearer, too, as Powell did, and kept his eyes on Wiggins.

Red, feeling his place was up closer, too, moved up with hasty clatter of heels and spurs. He wanted it known by everybody present that he was into this neck deep and was staying for the showdown—a showdown at almost point-blank range. Red, for a boy no older than he, had seen a lot of shooting. But most of it had been with sudden flash of guns before hot quick words had died away. This was the steel-nerved play of veteran killers, each silently jockeying for the split-second jump that meant sure death with the first bullet.

Robbins took a long time to speak. He was a hard man and a brave man, but he knew he was caught. He had a good deal of craft and much common sense.

"Bill Powell," he said, and without movement of his arm he tossed the pencil from his fingers, "this here is poker. Cows for chips, range for table. I reckon yore three of a kind beat our two pair. So you win!"

"Bah!" said Powell, jerking up his head.

"Yes, sir," Robbins went on, shifting his look, "that redhead of yourn hornswoggled us right— with his little fire. Sort o' sneakin' way to make a fight, don't you think?"

"I think so," said Powell, coldly calm and watchful, not in the least off guard because Robbins seemed to be yielding. "But they's been a lot of sneakin' and double-dealin' going on. An' to play *my* little trick, I sent in here the man that killed *your* Cliff Hammon!"

Old Robbins's head went up as if struck on the chin. Cliff Hammon being dead accounted for why Robbins had not lately been getting accurate information as to what was going on over on Powell's side. Powell seemed to have all the trumps.

Old Robbins eyed Red for a time as if seeing some things about him that he hadn't noticed before. For one thing, he didn't look now quite so much of a big, reckless kid. There was a man-grown hardness in his face; and the loose way he held his arms let Robbins know he had been through smoke before and had a lot of confidence in his ability to get his guns up and going about as quickly as anybody.

Robbins put his look back on Powell's face, then flipped his hands helplessly and let them lie, palms up, on the table. He was stalling for time and that split-second jump; and he knew that Powell knew it, but there was no other way to play the game and have any chance of winning. So he just gazed at Powell, saying nothing.

Then Leon Lenard spoke, calm and low, with his slit eyes widened just a little to show the gleam that flickered there like a bit of lightning. If ice had been melting in his mouth his tone could not have been more cold:

"Now that we've begun to talk, I'll speak. Walt Wiggins, I hear you've told more'n once that you once run me out of this country. The same bein' in a way truth. You pretended to be my friend. Then you sent a bunch of men up to catch me. An' I run. The world's too full o' dirty dogs for me to go huntin' up ever'one that needs killin', but when I meet up with one like yoreself I kill 'im!"

Lenard stopped talking and waited. Wiggins did not move. Then Lenard's right arm, palm back, began that slow away-from-the-body backward reach, as if he had rheumatism in his shoulder and was pretty awkward in making a draw.

Wiggins couldn't stand and let a man draw against him like that. Even slow as the movement was, once Lenard got that hand on a gun butt it was death. So Wiggins, with flash of hands and jerk of body that sent him into a forward hip-high crouch, whipped both his guns forward with thumbs on hammers.

There was an explosive roar. Wiggins pitched forward with both guns blazing into the floor. His body lay face down almost at Lenard's feet.

Lenard's slow-moving right hand had settled as if resting on the low-slung gun's butt. It was still in the holster after Wiggins was dead. But his *left* hand, with the winking flash of trained, wiry sinews, had pitched its gun hip high and smashed lead into the heart of the old killer who never before in his life had been beaten on the draw. Lenard's seeming right-handed awkwardness was just a little trick to test men's nerve.

Lenard's gun, held motionless, smoked over the holster. His long lean left thumb reached up and snapped back the hammer.

"Pete Strodd," he said, "you're next!"

The sudden suck of Strodd's breath could be heard, but he did not move.

"Since you won't draw, stand up an' take it!" Lenard told him. "You folks was aimin' for to kill Mr. Powell here, any old how you could. I ain't one to let mad dogs live just 'cause they won't bite at *me!*"

"My God—my God, Leon! You won't—shoot—me—like this!" Strodd gasped.

"If you fellows don't get on your feet an' fight it out, I sure as hell will! This is the showdown, permanent! I've let men live that tried to kill me. Not when they try to kill my friends! But if you want your chance, now take it!"

Lenard moved the gun in front of him, and, with his eyes on Strodd and using both his hands, he carefully let down the hammer. He slowly put the gun back into its holster and put his hands waist high in front of him, touching together the tips of his fingers. He stood straight and motionless, waiting, giving Strodd his chance.

At that moment shooting broke out up the street, with yells, the flying scurry of hoofs, and the *crackety-crack-crack* of .45's going like brazen-throated geese. The louder and less frequent explosive *whang* of rifles joined in. There were far-off curses and shrill yips.

The hub-bub was like a bunch of firecrackers going off in a tin wash boiler, with an Indian war dance thrown in. There were iron-shod hoofbeats of frantic horses, ridden by madmen; yells, the calling of orders, and the questioning cry of names to make sure of friends. Men rode by with thunderclap of hoofs, other men following, and stabs of flame winked back and forth between them.

Then old George Robbins, who had drawn his palms back to the edge of the table, with a hoarse cry of "Get 'em!" threw over the table, lamp and all, with a mighty fling as he dropped knees down to the floor.

Strodd, with a wild leap aside, put his back to the wall, and Robbins's foreman sprawled forward in a low duck, almost face to the floor.

The overturned lamp struck hard, but its body was metal. The chimney broke into the tinkling rattle of a hundred pieces. The smoke wick thrust up a yellow wisp of light and died.

The table, pushed over violently, struck Powell's legs, knocking him into a kind of stumbling jump backwards so that with a stagger he reeled aside.

Dagger-pointed flames from each side laced the darkness. The deafening burst of guns at close quarters between walls stunned the ears. Smoke, heavy with powder smell, stung throats and eyes.

Red, with one knee to the dirt floor and head drawn down into his hunched shoulders, fired both guns at once, then toppled as if hit—dodging bullets in the dark. Again he fired and lurched aside, coolly counting his shots.

Then by the winking blaze of guns he caught a glimpse of old Leon Lenard, still tall and straight, guns out at half-arm's length, coldly taking any man's fire for the chance to snap back. That made Red feel ashamed of his own wallowing antics, meant protectively; so he got to his feet, stood up, and tried to fight like the best gun fighter he had ever seen in his life.

After a deafening flurry and half-blinding lightning winks, the shooting stopped. For a moment the silence in the utter darkness seemed like a great loneliness to Red, and he wondered if he alone lived. The shots and cries outside continued. Red peered at the blackness. Some man groaned. It seemed far away. Red stirred, then called softly, "Mr. Powell?"

As he spoke, flame winked at him quickly as a knife thrust in the dark. The shot was answered, not by Red, who hadn't expected it, but from across the room where Leon Lenard stood waiting, wary, cool, watchful.

"Thanks!" Red called.

"Shut up!" said Lenard.

Minutes seemed to drag by, but they were seconds. Powell's heavy voice spoke from almost the center of the room:

"I think it's over, Leon!"

Instantly a nervous eager boyish voice shrieked from the doorway:

"An' a hell of a way to treat me! I've been

settin' here scairt to shoot for fear I'd hit one of you fellers!"

Johnny broke off into curses that would have shamed the tongue of a mule skinner, and came hastily into the room, scratching matches.

All the enemies were dead excepting Robbins's foreman, and he was dying.

Powell got up off the floor, asking: "Hurt, Leon?"

"I sort o' stumbled but picked myself up an' leaned against the wall."

"You, Red?"

"Not as I know of! But you, Mr. Powell?"

A howl went up from Johnny, who was almost singeing Powell with his matches: "Ow! Mr. Powell's all shot to pieces an' dyin'—covered—blood—ow—"

"Shut up!" Powell pushed at the anxious boy. "I'm hit, yes. But this here is ol' Robbins's blood, mostly. I jumped on him to make sure I couldn't miss in the dark!"

Red's knees felt pretty wobbly now that it was all over, and he fanned with a nervous hand at the smoke before his face. He said almost humbly:

"I thought I'd seen a little something in my time, here an' there. But I might as well have been blind! I never seen nothin'—nothin' like this. An' if I ever do again I won't be redheaded no more. I'll have gray hairs all over me!"

Old Leon Lenard, from against the wall where he stood on one leg, said calmly:

"All the gray hairs you ever get, son, won't disgrace nobody!"

And if somebody wearing a lot of gilt and plumes had come along and pinned a big medal on Red's breast he wouldn't have been half as pleased as at that laconic compliment from the grim, tight-lipped old outlaw.

Old Mack and some of the other T T boys came on the run, carrying a lantern. They crowded through the door, sniffing and coughing at the smoke, hunched forward in peering, and asked anxious questions as Mack stepped forward, holding the lantern aloft.

Old Bill Powell, with his right arm hanging loose, and a sort of sidling twist to his body, swept Mack aside with his left hand and stood before Red:

"Boy, while I got me a cow left, you—*you* can allus eat beefsteak!"

CHAPTER XVIII

"HE'S GOT TO
BE HUNG—LEGAL!"

Most of the night, and until well after sun-up, was spent in riding about after saddled horses, with reins trailing, that had scattered in the panic of wild shooting and the surging stampede-like clatter of the fight.

Somebody brought in Blackie with both reins snapped short. He had stepped on them, broken them off short, and bolted.

Red promptly took the reins off another horse, rode him over to the pump, gave him a drink, took off the saddle, skirmished some oats from Chuck's barrel, and put Blackie back into the corral. The cussing Blackie got was long and fluent for disgracing himself by running away.

Blackie laid back his ears and seemed to scowl, so Red apologized:

"I reckon you're right, plum' right, at that! If horses was a-shootin' an' a-cussin', an' me standin' with a bridle in my mouth—I'd run, too! Further'n you did. I never would have been caught again!"

Old Bill Powell of the T T had once again proved to all who took part in the fight, as well as to all the hopefully jealous cattlemen who, from their hilltops on the range, awaited news, that he was still the king cowman of Lelargo; and that if anybody wanted any of his range it was a lot cheaper and safer to buy it.

Many men were dead, including some of his own. The crowd that had been rounded up in Mike's saloon were mostly hard-fighting men, down on the Robbins-Strodd-Wiggins payroll at from forty to sixty dollars a month—top wages, those days—and worth it, too. They had broken through doors and windows and had come out shooting, being too proud to lie down unless overweighted with lead.

Many of those that had got out were rounded up, some badly hurt, and were brought back to the saloon—as the nearest thing to a jail-like place—for safe keeping. They lay about on the floor or propped themselves against the wall. T T men squatted in front of them, passing back and forth tobacco and papers, some beer and a little whisky, with water too for such as were hurt and feverish.

As they talked together they seemed like a badly shaken lot of bronco busters after a hard-riding contest. They had been hired to ride and fight for Robbins, Strodd, and Wiggins. Robbins, Strodd, and Wiggins being dead, the fight was now over. Most of them were strangers to the T T men, so there were no personal hard feelings.

Nobody, especially among those who knew him, was much surprised when Mr. Powell, with his right arm in a sling, walked in with solid stride, swept them with hawk-like eyes, and said:

"You that give me your word that you are all through can go. Some breakfast is bein' cooked. Eat it an' ride. You that can't set a horse will be took care of, same as my men."

There was no cheering. Some said, "Thankee, Mr. Powell." . . . "We shore got caught with our pants down!" . . . "Me, I never liked this country nohow. Too easy to get overhet in!"

Powell said to the big saloon keeper: "An' you, Mike. You was a good friend to old George. A good friend is a good man, allus. Old George, he overplayed his hand. But for all of me an' my men, you can set right here an' run this saloon, same as always."

"Thankee, Mr. Powell. But me, I'll pull my freight. Ol' George done me some favors in my time. I sort o' would feel sneakin' to find my business wasn't hurt none when he'd lost out, complete. That there Red o' yourn sure put one over on us. He played it clever. I don't exactly want to put my arms around his neck an' hug 'im—but I ain't got no particular hard feelin's. He done what he was sent to do, an' done her proper! Him an' his matches! But one thing I shore would like to know. Why in hell did he shoot Diego?"

Powell, who seldom smiled, smiled now: "Diego was a-ridin' in for to tell you boys to look out for Red who was here spyin'. Met Red on the road an' thought he was one of you boys—an' spilled the beans! That boy don't look it an' don't act it, but—just ask about him over in Tahzo! I'd give the only good arm I got left for to know who sent in Diego. You wouldn't give me no symptom of information, Mike?"

"No, Mr. Powell, it just happens I can't. Happens, too, I prob'ly wouldn't if I could. But I can't, an' that's flat. If old George had a-listened to me, he wouldn't have listened to Strodd an' Wiggins. But it's all in the cards."

Big Mike gestured as if discarding a poker hand.

When Powell had been gone some little time, Pincher strutted in, with Red not far behind him. There were no powder burns on his clothes. During most of the fight he had been on the *inside* of the corral. He and Buddy both.

"Well, you big slob," he said to Mike, "put one over on you, didn't I? 'Twas me as sent Mr. Powell word o' this here meetin', an' see what we done to them old—"

Mike reached out a big arm to get a hold on Pincher's neck, but Pincher jumped back, pulling at a big gun. He drew it and started backing Mike to the bar. Pincher talked big, told who he was and what he had done, could do, would do.

Red's voice came through the doorway:

"Turn around, you—" The names he got out were fighting names, would have made a jack rabbit sit up and slap a hound dog in the face.

But Pincher knew that voice. He almost dropped the gun. He lowered his arm and turned, fear-struck. Red wasn't grinning. His arms were loose at his side, inviting the man with a drawn gun in hand to make a fight if he wanted. Pincher stared wildly, trembled with the irresolute wish to try it—he, gun in hand, Red's arms loose and hands empty. But Pincher was scared stiff. Buddy had told him a lot about this redhead, the outlaw from Tahzo, who had killed a deputy, shot the sheriff himself, dropped Cliff Hammon, and cleaned out Bundy's there in Mekatone. Buddy hadn't been complimentary; but Pincher got the notion that Red was a killer, like Walt Higgins or old Leon Lenard.

"Drop it or use it!" said Red, moving his hands slowly toward his gun butts.

Pincher whimpered: "I—me—T T men—friends—"

At the word "friends" a look popped into Red's eyes that simply unnerved Pincher. His gun fell to the floor from fingers that trembled.

Instantly the onlookers booed Pincher, who crept off, leaving his gun where it lay.

He passed close by Red at the doorway and went away, hot-eyed and boiling with sour wishes. Pincher had to find his friend Buddy. It seemed to Pincher that he just didn't have any luck at all. He felt himself as good a man as the next, better than most, ready for any old thing; but somehow folks weren't friendly. He felt misunderstood and badly abused.

When Pincher had passed him, Red walked in, stopped before Mike, pointed at Pincher's gun: "Want yourself a nice souv'nir, Mike?"

"I'll have me a souv'nir," said Mike calmly, "every time I look at a burnt match. You done it clever. I hear that little devil Johnny Howard put you through the Basin. I sorta halfway smelt an Injun when you rode in. An' that Diego shootin'—you done it clever. All of it. Asked no questions much, an' wouldn't answer none." Mike nodded with aloof approval. "Most fellers would have overexplained how they come to be here. An' about Diego, too. When you get full-growed, you're goin' to be a mighty good man or a mighty bad one. Most likely bad. From what I hear, you shoot better'n is customary 'mong honest men. But I don't wish you too much bad luck. So listen. Pincher's right smart of a good shot with a rifle. He figgers it's safer. *Savvy*?"

"Yeah, I do. Thanks, Mike." Red put out his hand.

Mike said with steady glance and level tone: "No, no, I can't do that. I'll never lift a hand or say a word 'gainst you for what's happened in this here town. You didn't do nothin' worse—'r half so bad—as was bein' done on both sides. You jus' done it successful. But me, I got sentiments. An' old George Robbins was my friend."

"Old George, he must've been a better man than I been thinkin'!" said Red.

He then went over to the restaurant to have a little talk with Leon Lenard. The old outlaw sat with his leg in splints of pine resting on the seat of a chair before him. There was a pile of ham, flapjacks, potatoes, stewed dried apples, and a big cup of coffee on the table before him. As a usual thing he didn't eat heavily, but this morning, in spite of the hurt leg, he was hungry. Also, though a surly cuss who gave welcome to but few persons that came near him with sociable intentions, this morning he looked up at Red over a forkful of potatoes, smiled a little and said, "Set."

"Gosh, me I couldn't swaller nothin' but coffee. I ain't got over shakin' yet!"

"Um-m-m," said Lenard. "Tother way with me. I don't eat beforehand."

"Leg troublin' you much?"

"Nothin's troublin' me, son." Then he reflected, looked cautiously about. " 'Cept maybe—" He broke off the sentence with a nod that held much meaning.

Red answered with a nod.

"What you learnt?" Lenard asked, laying down

the fork, pausing as he chewed, fixing those gleaming slits of eyes on Red.

"*'Learnt?'* I ain't sure. But I've *heard* a lot, 'specially just before Diego fell off his horse. He was talkin' for his life an' may have lied. He sure wanted to keep me listenin' till he could jump the draw. It was thisaway. . . ."

Now and then as Red went along with his story Lenard took up a forkful and chewed slowly, sometimes looking off into space, sometimes down at his plate, now and then running a hand down along his injured leg and again and again flashing his eyes at Red as if to surprise any secret look that might be on his face. But that was just the old outlaw's habit. This time he had no suspicions of Red. When Red had told it all, Lenard calmly continued to eat.

Red fidgeted, rolled cigarettes and threw them away half smoked, waiting; and at last, unable to wait longer, he asked:

"Well?"

"Well what?"

"I mean what's to be done now, Mr. Lenard?"

Leon Lenard put down his fork and fastened those deadly eyes on Red, held him with a half-minute's look, and at last said softly:

"I'll do it!"

A sort of chill went through Red. He knew it all with only three words spoken. Lenard had passed the sentence of death on Buddy Powell.

Somewhere, somehow, unknown to other men they would meet. A word or two from grim lips to let the miserable wretch know that justice was striking, a shot from a gun that could not miss—and men would say that some of Robbins's, or of Strodd's, or of Wiggins's cowmen had done it. The gentle girl that somehow had got down inside of Leon Lenard's lonely heart and warmed it as with a daughter's love would be avenged. Old Bill Powell would never know the shame that lay hidden in his son's grave.

Red's thoughts swirled in a dizzying protest. For one thing, he knew it was like butting your head against a granite slab to try to make Leon Lenard yield from a decision. For another, he couldn't quite shape up the words to carry the burst of feeling that had seemed to kind of explode within him. For a time he sat dumb, then stuttered hesitatingly. But at last his thoughts laid hold of some of the words he wanted, and they came with blurting vehemence:

"My God, no! That won't be right! The boy they hung—Tom Terry—he's got folks! They curse his name an' hate themselves for havin' blood of his. They'll allus think—I onct was near hung, too—an' I got folks—*Just think if that hanged boy was your son an' you'd never know he wasn't really guilty!* No, Mr. Lenard! No, I tell you! The fellow that done it has got to be hung right out in the open, legal, so folks'll know why. This has to be done honest! Though for Mr. Powell's sake—if it wasn't for Tom Terry's folks— My God, I can't forget the time I was purt-near hung! An' you, you've got to think of what you'd feel if Tom Terry was your son! I'm sorry for Mr. Powell—you know I am! But by the living God, I'll fight to see the right thing done for Tom Terry an' his folks!"

It had the sound of a challenge flung right into Leon Lenard's face.

Lenard put down both knife and fork noise-lessly, without the least click of metal on china. He half turned in his chair, fixing his slit eyes, all agleam with steady light, on Red.

Lenard looked at him and kept on looking, as motionless as if turned to stone with only his eyes alive. The old outlaw had turned his thoughts inward. He brooded. All of his long hard lifetime he had killed when killing seemed needful; and when he killed he felt justice had been done. Red had put his face right up against a new aspect of justice. Lenard was not angry with Red. Much of the old outlaw's contempt of the world and its men was because he knew so few of them spoke up honest and straight, and were downright brave. This boy was.

So Leon Lenard turned over and over in his thought what Red had said. Lenard was stubborn as iron. Always when he said something he meant it, and would back it up. Every impulse he had was against giving in. He didn't like being argued with, and he couldn't be bluffed.

Red knew Lenard was having a fight with himself and sat patient and said nothing. At last Lenard pushed his plate away with his breakfast not half finished. He dropped his look to the floor, studied, said:

"I reckon, all in all, you're right. So have it your way. I know Tom Terry's folks. I hadn't much thought of them before. They are nice folks." He lifted his eyes, eyed Red: "Too damn bad Mr. Powell never had a boy like you!"

Red heaved a great sigh, relieved. He had no feeling of triumph, just relief and admiration for Lenard's reasonableness. And he dodged any reference to Lenard's having given in by saying:

"Aw, hell, whatever good I am, my dad's to blame—I mean tother way round! He just naturally licked the tar outa me any time he ever halfway suspicioned I wasn't doin' right. It wasn't never so much what I done as if I looked sorta like I was goin' to lie about it! Yessir! The fact is, now I just can't be comfortable unless I think I am doin' purt-near right. I feel all sick an' sneakin', sorta measly, if I don't. I got no gumption at all unless I feel I'm doin' like I oughta. It's something I can't help—a sort o' weakness, like. I'm tellin' you the truth!"

Leon Lenard smiled faintly, nodded just a little, and murmured:

"I know. Some day, most likely, you're goin' to be a sheriff. An' a good one. When you are, maybe you'll remember me." The smile trembled like the stirring of ripples, widening. "So I'll tell you something few know. I got me a pardon. Signed by a man who was President some years ago. So some folks think I ain't all bad—which maybe shows how folks can be mistook!"

Again there was silence between them. Lenard shifted his wounded leg a little and sat brooding. After a long time he looked up and asked:

"Just what are you figgerin' on doing about *him?*"

"I don't know—yet. Something, though. Somehow maybe snake him across into Tahzo County, I guess. There's that girl's brother—but he's bad hurt. His friend Wilkins will help. Maybe I won't need no help, me bein' lucky. Once over to Tahzo—there's Valdez. The sheriff was holdin' him when that paymaster was killed. So what Valdez says will be listened to. And when the sheriff of Tahzo gets his hands on that fellow, however it's done, I'm through. My job, it is done."

"Yes?" Lenard asked quietly. "Well, let me tell you something. You saw Bill Powell go into action last night. Let the sheriff of Tahzo put his hands on that boy, an' Bill Powell will come a-roarin'—and there ain't men enough in the whole of Tahzo to stop 'im!"

CHAPTER XIX

SHOTS FROM AMBUSH!

The range war was over and Nelis City was once more quiet. Powell and his men were riding out.

Leon Lenard could not ride easily, but was lifted into his saddle and sat there as erect as ever. His lips were thin, tightly pressed, and no word of pain went through them.

Graves had been dug in the hard sandy slope up behind Nelis City. Chuck, the blacksmith, sweated and grunted, being paid for his work by Mr. Powell. There men that had fought as enemies were laid side by side as if the dead understood that this was the end of some deadly range game that had been played just about like any other game. Those who had lost were not dishonored. Had just cashed in.

Powell had sent after a doctor to take care of those who were badly hurt. The nearest doctor was fifty miles away, but would come—if need be with a rope around his neck the better to show him the way.

Powell was moving his men down out of the Basin country into Nelis Valley—the range that Robbins's men had jumped. But the men there, like soldiers of fortune with their captains dead, would quit, ride off, scatter; and such few as still might want to make a fight of it would not be able to hold the others.

Feuds might drag on, but range wars ended when the leaders died. And Powell's men were out in force, strategically awaiting the outcome of the Nelis City raid which Powell led in person to make sure it was done right.

When Mr. Powell, with his right arm in a sling, was ready to mount, his horse could not be found. After a little inquiry, more than one man spoke up to say that Johnny Howard had been seen riding off on it. As Johnny was always more or less in charge of Mr. Powell's mounts, no one had given it a thought until questions began to be asked as to where the horse was.

Powell swore, half tolerantly. "Harder'n a flea to hold and watch! The little devil's up to something, an' this is not the first time he's stole the best horse!"

So another horse was brought for Mr. Powell and they all rode off, two or three men loping on ahead. Red straggled behind, knee to knee with Leon Lenard, both silent and riding at a walk.

"H'm," Red mused, looking all about. "I ain't seen Pincher. Maybe he's took his pay an' gone. I'd liked for to make him pay back what I loaned him. I sure would, just to help him feel unhappy!"

Buddy Powell rode by his father. The old man was talking with him and again and again had

246

to turn and say with some exasperation, "Keep 'longside of me. I want to talk!"

They went along the road where Red had met Diego. Red looked about with the interest of one revisiting a place where something of importance has happened. A tall elbow of rock stood out ahead.

He touched Lenard's arm and pointed. "Diego. Right there's where I backed him up and listened. He'd-a had to ride over me to get out. He sure had hopes but no luck."

Lenard swept the small box canyon with a critical glance and lifted his eyes toward the wall of broken rock. He nodded. That was all, but he seemed to signify his approval.

A few hundred feet on ahead, at a sharp turn in the road, Buddy Powell's hat suddenly fell off. It was a windless day; his big hat was weighted with a silver-studded band and chin strap, but it had dropped from his head. He swore just as a sort of matter of habit when anything went wrong and got off to pick it up. His father drew rein, waiting.

Buddy picked up his hat and stood dusting it with a lot of care. Another man or two rode on by. Buddy was still fiddling with his hat when Lenard and Red came up. Lenard drew rein, and Red too, merely keeping company.

"How's your leg?" old Powell asked.

"How's your arm?" Lenard snapped back.

"Fine, Leon."

"Same here, Bill."

Old Powell grinned affectionately. He understood that Leon Lenard did not take it kindly to be reminded that he was a cripple of sorts.

Buddy, brushing away at his hat, lifted his eyes furtively toward the upper ledges of the rock. Red, watching closely, saw the look and also a little furtively stared up. There was nothing to see but a high wall ending in an overhanging ledge that some day would surely break as the scattered piles strewn about showed that other slabs of the ledge had crashed.

Buddy started to remount, but, with foot in the stirrup and hand on the horn, shook the saddle and said, "Aw, hell. My cinch is loose. Go on, Dad. I'll catch you."

"Tighten her. I'll wait," Powell told him. Then, with what was very good humor for Powell, asked, "What makes you so quiet, Red?"

"Me? You want some truth? Well, for a fact, I'm sleepy. I ain't had no pleasant dreams any night I been over to Nelis City. An' last night, for instance, a lot of thoughtless folks, they kept me awake, shootin' and carryin' on. Maybe you heard 'em?"

"Ho, well," said Powell, almost playful. "Is that so? Too bad about you."

"Danged if my cinch ain't loose, too!" said Red, rocking in his saddle.

Off he dropped and flung the stirrup over the saddle, having it in mind not to let Buddy Powell kick up any excuse for riding behind him. Red figured that if anything happened, Buddy would just say he had pulled the gun to shoot at a ground squirrel and it went off accidentally. He chattered aimlessly as he worked with the cinch, saying:

"Reckon I was sort o' nerv'us when I pitched on my saddle a while ago. Come on, Blackie, draw in yore belly. Don't swell all up thataway!"

Buddy fidgeted and fumbled with his cinch. Red brazenly was just as slow and fumbling. He meant to stand there all day rather than let Buddy have an excuse to get behind him. Buddy at last had to give up stalling and crawl into his saddle. Red then with deft quick turns whipped the strap through the cinch rings, slapped Blackie on the shoulder and asked: "How's that, huh? You ol' scarecrow o' hair, hide, an' bones!"

Mr. Powell and Buddy rode on together. In turning the bend, Buddy with a furtive glance from under the broad brim of his hat glanced high overhead. He drew his horse down into a slower walk, letting his father get ahead.

Red too looked up again. And old Lenard lifted up an arm, pointing:

"Right up there is Rimrock Roost. That's where ol' Nelis, who give his name to all this here country, used to hide out and plug folks till—"

As if the words had called old Nelis once again

to life, a puff of smoke from high overhead was blown from a rifle's mouth. The sound of the shot bounced with staccato echoes from rock to rock.

Lenard, with his usual presence of mind, drove a spur into the horse and pressed close beneath the shelter of the rocks, followed at once by Powell; then Red noticed that Mr. Powell's hat was gone. Buddy Powell with repeated jab of spurs galloped on ahead, rounding the bend, disappearing.

As soon as Blackie was in the shelter of the rock, Red drew the rifle, jumped from the saddle, and scurried to the other side of the road. He tumbled down behind a rough-edged block of rock just as a bullet thudded near his side. Red lay where he could peer up at the high ledge known as Rimrock Roost. He held the rifle ready, head lowered, half squinting to take aim, but saw nothing.

Powell passed his hand over his forehead. "Some one o' them fellows from last night, Leon. Must've guessed we'd be passin' this way. That was a new hat, too. Well, now she'll have some vents in her."

Lenard did not reply. His glance slid across Powell's face with almost guilty quickness. His guilty feeling was that Powell might be able to read his thought—and he was thinking about the fact that Bud Powell had had a hunch at just what point to make sure of getting well away from his father by reining up, by dropping his hat, by tightening his cinch, then by pulling again into a slow walk.

Lenard called calmly:

"See anything, Red?"

"No, an' if I did I couldn't hit 'im. I ain't much of a hand with one of these damn rifles."

Powell said again, good-humoredly, "Too bad about you!"

"Well, now me, honest, I like for folks that are shootin' my way to stand up clost—then the luckiest man wins!"

"This fellow wasn't shootin' at you," said Powell, just giving information.

Red knew that as well as anybody, but called back:

"Don't be grabbin' all the compliments, Mr. Powell! That there second bullet was mine, personal!" Red took off his hat. "I'll try me a little trick like I was a real Injun fighter." He put the hat over the rifle muzzle and slowly lifted it. His trick didn't work. The man on the Roost had either gone or was too wise to be caught by that old stunt. "Why you reckon he won't take my bait?"

"Most likely," Powell suggested, "he thinks you'll come out in the open if he don't. Have more to shoot at."

"Glad I'm skinny," said Red. "If you an' Mr.

251

Lenard there had been skinnier, maybe you'd been missed, too, last night!"

"I been missed plenty times in my life!" said Lenard, almost irritably.

Two of the Powell riders had heard the shot, had heard Buddy's squawk of alarm as he came up with them. They at once turned back and now came tearing along the road. In a moment they were out of the saddles with rifles in hand and slipped into place from where they could watch.

"Hi, cowboy!" Red called at the man nearest. He felt more free and easy with the T T men since the shake-up last night.

The fellow grinned at him. "You get more shootin' at than near any man I ever seen!"

They lay and watched. Nothing appeared.

Red, with a half-grown idea in mind, asked, "How do you get up there, anyhow?"

Powell explained, "You got to go away round back, an' most of the way climb on foot. Take a couple of hours. Rough as hell's bottom. Hard trail to find. That old murderer Nelis—men would know where he was, but find him? That was different. He could be gone before they was near 'im!"

"This fellow," said one of the men, "he prob'ly lit out, so he'd be gone if we did go up after him. But it's whatever you say, Mr. Powell. Us boys are willin'."

"Be a waste o' time," Powell told them. He

had been shot at too many times to be much concerned. "You boys just stay here a while an' watch. Me an' Leon'll ride on. Hand me up my hat, will you?"

Red, with no particular haste, came from behind his shelter, walked along the road, took up Mr. Powell's hat, eyed the hole in the crown, then dusted the hat, standing in full view of the Roost.

"Is it because you think you've lived long enough?" Powell asked, taking the hat from Red's uplifted hand.

"To shoot at me, he's got to poke himself out a little, ain't he? Well, he knows just as well as I do that two good-lookin' fellows are layin' down here on their bellies squintin' up at him. 'F I was up there under them circumstances, I'd keep outa sight. An' you see, he's just as smart as I am!"

Powell eyed him, then turned and eyed Lenard. The two old range men nodded faintly, each at the other. They didn't smile, but their mouths looked as though they might at any moment.

Then they rode off at a slow walk, hugging the rocks until around the bend.

Red made himself comfortable behind a rock, put his rifle at rest, and waited, not impatiently. Minutes passed. The other two men were alert, peered hard, fingers on triggers, hopeful of a chance. Twenty minutes dragged out; then one said with sudden resolution: "Aw, hell, he's gone," and stood up in full view. The other one said, "If he got a good look at yore ugly face, he cut an' run. I told you, ain't I? It would scare anybody!" He too arose.

They wrangled back and forth amiably, said they were going, asked Red if he wasn't coming along.

"I'll wait a little while longer," Red told them. "But I'll be along after you purty quick."

When they had gone, Red mused: "Now, 'cept that he shot at Mr. Powell instead of me, I'd say that fellow up there—or that was up there—smelt a lot like Pincher. And the way Buddy lost his hat, tightened his cinch, an' kept a-lookin' up yonder—h'm-m-m-m. I can't believe it, yet that wall-eyed pup sure didn't want to stick close to his dad. He must've knowed something was goin' to happen. An' when all's said an' done, what's too bad to believe about Bud Powell, h-m? Just you tell me that, an'—"

Red was peering over the rock as he mused, the rifle held laxly in his hands. He stiffened with a jerk, scrouged down, snuggled the rifle to his shoulder.

The sound of a muffled shot from high overhead came down to him. There was no smoke. Red wasn't sure, but guessed, "Not a rifle." He could not have clearly explained why he thought so when echoes jumped about as they did, but his ears were peculiarly attuned to the difference in sound between a .45 and the crack of a rifle.

He relaxed, lifted his head, stared, making vague imaginative guesses as to the reason for that shot.

Then he swore, moved again to bring up his rifle, for now he plainly saw that somebody was up there on the rocky wall, peering down—just a shadowy dot of hat and face. He asked himself, "But would he have his hat on?" and shook his head even as he looked up at the hat above the face.

The figure arose almost into full view, a small figure with empty hands.

Red swore softly. "Looks something like Johnny Howard—but it ain't! Him shoot at Mr. Powell? Me at my grandmother!"

The figure was near the edge of the rock, standing upright, looking down. No furtiveness there, but the figure seemed expectant, as if waiting to be noticed. Then with hands to mouth the figure sent out a long-drawn, "Yip-ee-eye-oh! Hi, down there! Wake up!"

Echoes caught the sound and tossed it about half mockingly so that, from such a distance, the words did not come clearly; but Red said with conviction:

"That *is* Johnny Howard!"

He jumped up, held the rifle high overhead with one hand, and shouted.

Then Johnny flung his hands about, wig-

255

wagging violently. He put his hands to his mouth and shouted words that were vague and mostly unintelligible, being mangled by the echoes. Some were understandable, and one was, "Wait—" though whether it was a command or part of an explanation Red could not be sure.

But he sat down on a rock, waved his hat, indicating that he was waiting. Something was wrong, big and wrong, yet he could not suspect Johnny, who moved away, disappearing.

Red said to himself, "Am I to set here till he comes? An' if they ain't something wrong, why didn't he show up awhile ago?"

Red stood up restlessly and rubbed at the back of his neck because holding his head far back in a peering strain made it ache.

He heard horses coming on the lope. Red hadn't shown up after they had gone on quite a way, so they turned back anxiously to see what was the matter. They reined up, asking questions.

"Johnny Howard's up there—"

"No!" said Powell, flatly and with anger. Johnny was a favorite.

"Well, sir, he looks like 'im, 'pears to talk like 'im, and—"

"Johnny shoot at me!"

"I ain't crazy! All I said was he's up there, an' he's up to something—'Wait' was about all I could catch clear. Echoes messed up that squeaky kid voice of his. He sure had a lot to say!"

Powell said, taking off his hat and peering up, "Johnny knows this country better'n most of us know the inside of our hat. But how'd he know that somebody'd be up there—an' shoot at me! If he is there, that's why he went!"

"Me an' you are bettin' on the same card! I hadn't thought o' that, but I believe it now."

"Johnny'll sure talk plenty when he gets down!" said one of the men.

Johnny appeared, looked down, waved his arms and shouted. He seemed pleased about something, then he disappeared again. A moment later he came to view, and they could tell that he was dragging something heavy, almost too much for him, to the edge of the rock.

As they stared upwards a man's body was rolled off the ledge, dropped with outflung arms and legs, and crashed out of sight a hundred feet below the ledge. It was still high above them, far beyond any chance to see except by a difficult climb.

The men on the road peered up, not speaking, then looked from one to the other, each with complete understanding. The savage little devil high above on the rimrock, not content with merely killing the man that had shot at Mr. Powell, had flung him from the ledge.

"That's why he took my horse back there in town," said Mr. Powell quietly. "Wanted a gentled one for to climb around back up there.

Though most of the way you have to go on foot. So I been told. I never been up there. Fine boy, Johnny. You stop an' wait for 'im, Red. He likes you fine. He'll be an hour or more comin'. Then catch up. We're goin' on. I want to hear."

Red, left to himself, hummed, sang a little in very low tone, smoked cigarettes, and somehow felt unhappy. The first shot from the rimrock had been at Mr. Powell, and Bud Powell had known it was coming.

"A fellow that would stand in to have his dad shot at—" he said and couldn't think of words suitable to apply to that sort of boy.

In due time there was the clatter of a hard-ridden horse, and Johnny came along the road in a great hurry. He jerked the horse up sharply, not expecting that anybody had waited.

Red eyed him. All sweaty and dirty, with clothes snagged, Johnny looked as though he had been thrown a couple of times.

"Well, feller!" Johnny sang at him shrilly. "Ain't you goin' to come an' kiss me? That there was Pincher!" He flung his arm vaguely toward the rimrock.

"Yeah?"

"Yeah! An' when I heard that rifle o' his'n crack onct, I thought he'd got you sure. Then when he shot again, I thought maybe he didn't get you the first time, but maybe the second—though I didn't think it so hard. Anybody as has to take two shots at you, you red-top ol' hoss straddler! is purt-near liable to miss both times!"

"Yeah?" Red grinned just a little.

"Yeah! Then Pincher heard me comin'. Right up close behind him. He sung out, 'Who's there?' Me, I said, 'Nobody ain't here, Pincher. It's yore 'magination!' Only I kept my mouth shut when I said 'er, so he thought maybe it was his 'magination. He waited. Seemed like a couple o' hours before he'd move. I know that damn ol' rimrock. I usta climb up there just to lay an' look over the country. I was where he had to stay put or come out where I could see 'im. Well, he came, creepin' cautious! I laid back, outa sight— then let him have it! Then I crawled out around an' got to the ledge to see if anybody was down here yet. I thought maybe you was your ghost!"

"Yeah?"

Johnny swore at him with a kind of hurt friendliness. "What's the matter with you? You act suspicious or something! Don't you b'lieve me, Red?"

"I do, kid."

"But you act 'spicious, as if you didn't."

"I am suspicious. Mighty. Y'see, kid, me, I was right out here in plain sight, on Blackie there— an' nobody could make a mistake about Blackie bein' my horse. But 'twasn't me he shot at, Johnny. 'Twas Mr. Powell!"

Johnny opened his mouth and kept it open as

if he had lost his breath. When he spoke it was a whispered gasp: "Hones', Red?"

Silently Red crossed his heart and half raised his hand, palm outward as if taking an oath.

Johnny frowned and blinked, mystified.

"But, Red, I heard 'im—him an' Buddy, out back o' the restaurant—me with an ear to the open window. Pincher was a-cussin' you. Buddy's got it in for you, too. 'Pot him from Rimrock Roost!' Pincher said. 'I'll do it!' 'After that ever'thing will be easy,' said Buddy. I looked for to tell you, Red, but I couldn't find you. An' there was Pincher lightin' out across the valley. So I said, 'Hell, why bother Red? More'n one way to stop 'im.'

"My horse, he had a loose shoe, so I hopped Mr. Powell's. I let Pincher get so far ahead he wouldn't know I was followin'. When we got to the rocks, I climbed out o' the saddle an' took off my boots, an' that was a mistake. I didn't know my feet was so danged soft. But if he'd-a heard me comin' he'd simply have waited on ahead an'— But damn it, Red, he couldn't have shot at Mr. Powell! You are crazy!"

"Maybe, yeah. But me, I'm a loose, half-ganglin' build. Me, on a black horse, allus. Mr. Powell he is thickset, sorta chunky-like. Yet 'twas Mr. Powell's hat as was knocked off. Pincher ain't no such bad shot with a rifle as all that!"

Johnny swore some more and wound up with:

"If I'd knowed he drawed down on Mr. Powell, I—I'd have et him alive! Shootin' was just too damn good!"

"An' what's more," said Red, "Buddy knew who was goin' to be shot at. He was a lot more willin' to get near me here in the bend than to stick close to his dad. Now you just listen. . . ."

When he had heard how Buddy lagged and stopped with furtive upward glances at the ledge, losing his hat, tightening his cinch, pulling the horse down so as to keep well behind his father though told to keep stirrup to stirrup, Johnny sat with face pinched and taut about the lips. He was like a man hard hit by a bullet and trying not to show it.

"I don't un'erstand it, I just don't!" he said over and over, and the words were like a groan that escaped unwillingly.

Red had notions of his own as to why Buddy Powell, the only heir to the big T T outfit, might have some wish to wear his father's boots.

Most likely Buddy had figured it out that if his father were out of the way it would then be easy to send Red scrambling face down into the dust. Buddy would be rich, could have all of the people he didn't like knocked out of their saddles, be himself the big cowman. As for shooting at his father—the chance to have it all blamed on one of Robbins's men was too good to be lost.

They rode on, and when they overtook Mr.

261

Powell the horses were stopped, everybody crowded up close and listened. Buddy from under his hatbrim looked watchful and uneasy.

Johnny explained cleverly, saying he had overheard Pincher talking about Rimrock Roost. "A feller like Pincher wouldn't climb up there just to look at scen'ry! When I seen him ride off, I was suspicious an' tagged along. After I left my horse—"

"Mine!" said Powell, laconic and pleasant.

Johnny grinned wanly. "I knowed you wouldn't care—much! Well, I had to go mighty cautious, 'cause he had all the advantage, bein' up ahead. When I heard his rifle crackin' I most near shed tears. I never suspicioned he'd shoot at anybody but Red here. An' I never meant for to give him a chance to shoot at anybody. I was tickled to think what Pincher was goin' to say when I nosed in around the ledge an' caught 'im belly down up there, waitin'. I sure as hell meant to kill 'im. I wouldn't make that long climb up there jus' for nothin'—not no more!"

"H'm," said Powell. "I don't know just *why* he'd shoot at me, seein' as he does most things for money. This mornin' he seemed to think I wasn't payin' him enough for the news he sent in. Maybe that was his way of gettin' even. Well, then too, the last thing I said to him was that I'd sure skin him alive if he ever so much as poked a gun at Red here. I 'magine that Pincher meant to pump fast an' get both of us, Red. He did put in a second shot at you, didn't he? 'F he'd got us, he'd backtracked an' lit out for rough country. I didn't think he had gumption enough to do a thing like that even from a hideout. So Pincher had a lot more spunk than I ever give him credit for. You can see what my 'pinion of him has been all along. All right, boys, let's be joggin'."

Powell turned and clapped a hand on Johnny's shoulder, patted it, smiled a little. And Johnny looked just about ready to burst with pleasure. It wasn't many men's shoulders that Bill Powell patted with approval.

"You ride 'long up beside me, son," said Powell, mounting. He spoke to Johnny, seemed to have forgotten Buddy who, with a kind of jealous solicitude, put himself on the other side of his father and for once kept stirrup to stirrup.

As they rode along, Red again put himself beside Leon Lenard. The slow walk of Lenard's horse soon left them far behind the others. Lenard's bad leg made it painful to trot or lope, though had there been any good reason for trotting or loping, the grim-lipped old fellow would have driven in his spur and have ridden right along.

Red asked, very casually, quite as if making some trivial conversation:

"Do you figger that you saw everything that

happened as we come along the road back yonder, Mr. Lenard?"

Lenard grunted, vaguely but with emphasis; then, with a kind of grim playfulness: "Yes, Mr. Clark, I sort o' figger I did."

"'Pears like some folks, they have most reliable hunches, Mr. Lenard."

"Bill Powell's a smart man, Red. But he's just plumb blind about Buddy's doin's."

"Now if anything sort o' happened to Buddy, like smallpox or chokin' to death on a chicken bone—anything accidental as cut him off in what folks call his prime—who do you reckon Mr. Powell would sort of adopt and make his heir?"

Lenard took a long time to reply, then nodded as if satisfied with the pondering decision he had made. "I think Bill 'ud most likely sort o' settle his likin' on two fool kids, one bein' Johnny Howard, an' the other'n a ganglin' redhead—"

"You ain't talkin' sense, not to me, nohow!" Red said quickly, not pleased.

"I'm talkin' a lot of sense," Lenard snapped. "You listen to me. You coaxed me into your way of thinkin' this mornin' about how they ought to be a trial an' something done right out in the open, legal. But I know, an' you know, Bud Powell has now got himself the bright notion of havin' his father killed. He wants to be footloose an' to cash in on all the T T holdings, then maybe go off East somewhere an' make a splurge. He's afraid

264

of you. He's afraid of Valdez. He's afraid his father will learn about things and maybe halfway believe. So he's stoppin' at nothin' but tryin' to be cute about it. Now me, I'm goin' to kill 'im. Things is changed. You can just forget all your ideas about Tom Terry's folks! Bill Powell is my folks. I ain't goin' to have him killed!"

"I un'erstand," said Red, "but—"

"Shut up," Lenard told him. "There ain't no 'buts.' Powell likes you an' he's got cause for to like you. You've done square. He's goin' make you one o' his range foremen right off. Won't be no time before you're his manager. You an' Johnny are cut out of the same piece o' leather. Good boys, both of you—though neither ain't quite outgrowed bein' damn fools. But you will. So—"

"Me, I'm over here like a snake in the grass!" said Red. "I'd swaller my gun's muzzle an' pull the trigger before I'd work for a man an' have him like me when he didn't know I had a hand in havin' his son killed! I can't stop you from shootin' Buddy. But I shore can, an' by God I will, waltz right up to Mr. Powell an' tell him all about myself when Buddy's body is brought in!"

Lenard looked hard, asked cautiously, "You would?"

Red said, with meaning and no bluff, "I would."

They walked along in silence a mile or more. Lenard brooded and at last spoke:

"I must be gettin' old an' losin' of my grip. Usual, what I say is the way things are done. But twict today you've made me back down." He swung his head a little as if regretful. "They ain't no doin' anything with a man that thinks he's doin' right—an' makes you think it, too. So have it your way again. Only this is goin' to happen: I ain't goin' to have him hangin' around old Bill an' maybe shoot 'im in the back. I'm goin' to fix it so Buddy is sent off somewheres. Keep your eyes open. That'll give you your chanct to get him!"

CHAPTER XX

RED MISSES HIS BREAKFAST

Late that afternoon Mr. Powell met up with a bunch of his men who had been sent on to the range, with chuck wagons as if to a round-up, to await the outcome of the meeting in Nelis City.

There was much powwowing and gleeful satisfaction. Men were sent riding here and there, carrying orders, and whenever anybody came near Red he was stared at admiringly. According to all reports he had surely lived up to his reputation as a hellbender in a hurry; all of which made him feel a little embarrassed but wasn't displeasing. Any man would have been proud to have the approval of T T riders.

The fight was over. Everybody was joyful. The loose talk was that T T cows would now run from the canyon clear up to Nelis City and get their water out of the town pump.

It was after dark when Powell, who had kept Johnny and Red near him, rode into camp where there was a horse herd, and smoke with the smell of food in it wavered up from beside a chuck wagon. There was plenty of food, blanket rolls, and enough wood within easy distance for a nice fire. Powell, like a good range general, had provided for the easy comfort of his men. He sat about in a most friendly humor, chatting with the men. He was warmed by his victory, warmed by the loyalty of his men. Called it the happiest day of his life, which made Red feel bad because he knew it was likely to be pretty close to the unhappiest day of Powell's long hard-fought up-and-down life.

Red kept an eye on Buddy, which was easy, since Buddy stayed in plain sight, most of the time sitting not far from his father and saying little. Buddy sure did not look pleased, seemed to have something on his mind.

Old Lenard had had to lie down. Tough as he was, the long ride had hurt his leg. He wouldn't say so, and it made him mad to be asked about the wound; so he just became sourer than ever and wanted to be left alone.

Red was quite sure that Buddy would not be able to find anybody among this bunch of men who would fall in with any such plans as had inveigled Pincher. A lot of them were no doubt on the dodge for horse-stealing and worse; but they weren't the kind that shot in the dark or got behind a man's back to let him have it. And since Bud wasn't man enough to do much of anything for himself, it looked to Red as though the night would be peaceable.

It was, though Red slept poorly and had some feverish dreams. Again and again during the night he raised up on an elbow to listen carefully or watch some shadow that moved about.

Red was up with the first gray streak of dawn, and, quite as if at a signal, so were other men, bustling about, jeering sleepily, passing the morning's compliments one to another with playfully insulting words.

Red happened to look around and saw Buddy Powell riding off, and there was nothing to indicate whether Buddy was going a mile or twenty or more. Red said, "H'm-m-m. Me, I need some information." He tossed his roll into the wagon, strolled over to the cook and asked in his most polite manner for a light from the fire.

The cook looked him over, knowing who he was. The cook wasn't used to being treated politely; and being a cook, he glowered, but said, "Help yoreself."

Red took a light, squatted on his heels, inhaled. He said that last night's supper was one of the best he had ever eaten in his life, and that this morning's breakfast smelled as though it was going to be some more of the same.

The cook, being human in spite of his efforts not to act it, grinned in a pleased sort of way. Had any lesser puncher, or man without a reputation, tried to be friendly, the cook would have scorned his advances. Range cooks, for some mysterious reason, mantle themselves with more disdainful pride than Solomon in all his glory.

Red then, in a casual sort of way, pointed toward the vanishing Buddy and asked:

"Wonder where he's makin' for?"

"Mekatone," said the cook. "The Old Man's sendin' him in."

Red mused. Leon Lenard had promised just some such thing as that.

Ten minutes later Red was standing before Bill Powell.

"I'm a lot sorrier than maybe you think, Mr. Powell, but me—I said I'd stick till you won your fight. You won 'er. So this mornin' I guess I'll be ridin'."

Powell meditated reluctantly, but admitted: "I remember. That is right. But you'll come back, Red?"

"I don't quite expect as how I will—though I never rode for a man I liked better!"

"If you got any little problems as I can help in —" Mr. Powell suggested.

Red shook his head, felt very unhappy. "None as I can ask you to help in, Mr. Powell."

Powell wasn't a man to stand and beg any puncher not to leave him. "You know your own business, Red. An' you are a pretty comp'tent fellow. Now if you ever want to come back to the T T, you'll allus be welcome. We got pretty well acquainted in so short a time. An' no man ever lived who before in so short time got the likin' of old Leon."

Red grinned a little, almost blushed, felt pretty low and measly at hearing these nice things from old Bill Powell when he was riding off to try to drag Mr. Powell's son to men who would surely hang him.

"Just let me give you a word of warnin', Red. Look out for that sheriff over at Tahzo. He's tricky. He's got courage. An' he don't let up when he wants to get a man."

"I got me the same notion of 'im," said Red.

"I ain't got money enough left with me for to pay you, Red. Not like I want to pay you. But I'll give you an order. Where you lightin' out for? Back to Mekatone?"

"I'm sort o' headin' that way."

"Why, I just sent word by Buddy in to a couple o' men. Wish I'd known. But you can catch 'im. Ride along together. I'd like for you an' my boy to get well acquainted. I'll give you that order."

Mr. Powell wrote out the order, not for wages, but for one hundred dollars.

Red felt ashamed to take it, but he didn't think it would be right to refuse to let Mr. Powell have the pleasure of being generous and rewarding. So he took the order, thanked Mr. Powell, shook hands. A moment later he tore it into bits and covered the bits with a handful of loose dirt.

He saddled Blackie, got directions, and started off, leaving a disillusioned cook staring at the dust Red kicked up. The cook felt that the world was plumb chock-full of hypocrites: Red had ridden off without even pausing for breakfast.

With a long ride ahead, Red, for all of his impatience, wasn't senseless enough to push a cold horse. He pulled Blackie into a walk every few minutes. Buddy had got a good half-hour's start, which ordinarily wouldn't have been much. It was this time, because Red thought a lot of Blackie and Buddy cared nothing about saving his horse.

About ten o'clock Red reached a line rider's camp. There was nobody at home. He found a badly knocked up horse with the marks of the saddle scarcely dry. The horse, though turned loose, stood dejectedly in the shade of some scrub oak. Another horse or two nosed about, cropping.

One glance and Red understood quite as clearly as if somebody had come out of the adobe hut and explained. Buddy had lashed his horse half to death, caught another mount, and gone on. Red was tempted to set off at once and push hard, but there was the chance that he might not get on Buddy's trail, then Blackie would be worn out and Buddy not caught.

So instead of doing that, Red got off, removed the saddle, watered and fed Blackie and staked him out by a long rope where Blackie could roll in the dust and enjoy his rest. Then Red made himself free with the line rider's provisions and left a scrawled note of thanks, signing his name. After that he cleaned out the skillet, washed the dishes, swept the floor. "I hate messin' with dirty dishes so much," Red told himself, "that I sympathize plum' deep with how the other feller would cuss me if I left 'em for him to do!"

He took some hardtack and a can of tomatoes for his saddle bags and rode on. He was no longer even hopeful of overtaking Buddy. Early that afternoon he made camp because he found some muddy water which was a lot better than none.

He ate half his can of tomatoes and some hardtack. He didn't want to put hobbles on Blackie, because a hobbled horse can get a long, long way off when the feed isn't very good near the camp. There wasn't much to chew on in the circumference of a stake rope, so Red squatted about, holding the rope and leading the horse here and there to whatever was the best feed.

Red made a bed of saddle blankets, with the saddle for a pillow, beside a little fire that he built just to make it seem more homelike; and after pondering and studying things over with the stars in his face, he slept well.

The next morning he finished his can of tomatoes, smoked a cigarette, and called it breakfast. He let Blackie crop again and take a long drink, then rode on.

Late in the afternoon he reached Powell's ranch. Buddy had pulled out a little before noon.

Red ate and rested, or rather let Blackie rest, and meditated.

"Yessir," he said to himself, "it's goin' to take some persuasion for to get him to trot along with me over to Tahzo. If I go to town, the first thing he does when he hears about me bein' there will be to make some funeral arrangements. I know from the doin's at Bundy's that he is quick at that. 'Pears to me like it is needful to get word across to the sheriff. But if I sneak out and start for Tahzo, some meddlesome folks may follow or be met with on the road. I sure need me some ideas."

So Red lay back on the ground with his hands locked under his head, crossed a leg over a knee, and sang soft and low, with much melancholy, as if deeply saddened:

"Oh, her hair was yaller an' her eyes was
    green;
She had her a nose like a butter-bean;
Her voice had the sound of a pig that's hurt,
But she was a lady—'cause she wore a
    skirt,
You danged galoot—oo—oo—toot—toot!

"An', son, you'll be a danged galoot if you ain't careful! Now then, just what would you like to do, h'm? Well, sir, have Mister Sheriff Martin come an' get him. Save yourself all the trouble.

He's got to be got! He's goin' to kill his dad, who is sure one square man. He's just got to be hung. It's the best favor I can do Mr. Powell, though he won't ever think so."

Red hummed and mused some more:

"Bud's been sober for at least three days. He'll most likely stay right in town drinkin' an' carryin' on till maybe Mr. Powell shows up and gets shot in the back through a window. Yessir, all I can do is my damnedest—an' if angels done the same the world would be a lot nicer place. 'Stead o' whangin' a harp they ought to be puttin' poison in some fellers' coffee. That's what I'm goin' to do when I get to be an angel. Right smart chance of me bein' one, too, before I get that nice Buddy Powell over to Tahzo.

"Well, now, s'posin' I wrote me a letter something like, *Dear Sheriff, Come on over an' get him. Most near all the T T fightin' men are out on the range. Yours truly, Red Clark.*

"H'm-m-m-m." Red sat up and scratched his head. "You know, I think I must be a lot smarter'n I look. I got me an idea. He most likely wouldn't come 'cross the county line. Anyhow, the postmaster, he would drop dead if he saw a letter goin' out addressed to the sheriff of Tahzo. I wonder are you as smart as you look?"

Red pondered and at last seemed satisfied. He went into the bunkhouse and found a pencil and pad of paper that were used mostly for making

I.O.U.'s in poker games between paydays. Carefully and laboriously he wrote a brief note.

He poked about and made discreet inquiries regarding some good honest Mexican family that lived somewhere in the general direction of Mekatone.

Red always got on well with Mexicans, probably because he understood and liked them. As a result, he never went among them without being welcomed.

Late in the afternoon he rode down into a little 'dobe colony and stopped before a long low box of a house where strings of red peppers festooned the wall. Yapping dogs, toddling naked youngsters, and a heavy fat woman in a faded, bedraggled loose dress formed a sort of reception committee. Then a sleepy-looking man stirred within the shadows of the house and put his head through a doorway. A couple of half-grown boys appeared from around a corner and grinned doubtfully.

After some talk they began to understand that he had not come to ask meddlesome questions about the beef supply of their neighbors or inquire into the whereabouts of any Mexican who happened to be missing; so they welcomed him in the name of God Who sends all travelers.

Red had much to say and, jingling the money in his pocket, was heard with respect. He spoke Spanish well. Mexicans are good judges of gringo character, so he was liked. The family trooped with him into the house, where he was seated in the only chair that had a back.

That night, in the dark before moonrise, the father and one of his boys rode off; the father to stop in Mekatone, and the boy to push through to Tahzo, carrying a note to Sheriff Martin.

For the next two days Red lay about in the shadows with dogs snuggling close to him, trying to lick his face, and the children, naked as on their first birthday, piling over him. On the afternoon of the third day Red saddled his horse and rode off, carrying in his ears the fat woman's benediction, "God walk with you!" It didn't mean a thing more than the gringo's "So long," but to Red's ears sounded nicer.

He had found out many things that seemed important and encouraging: Buddy Powell was still in town, keeping more sober than usual; Ramsey and Wilkins were also still there; and Sheriff Martin with some of his men would be right up at the county line to await Red's coming from midnight on.

"Right there on the county line is where my labors, they end," said Red, musing as he rode, "if I have the proper amount of luck. An' if I don't have no trouble much to coax that sheriff into believin' he give me this horse—fair an' square." He leaned over, patting the horse's neck. "If he don't give you to me, Blackie, why, we'll lug Bud Powell right back, won't we, h'm?"

It was a little after nine o'clock when Red reached Mekatone. Instead of riding Blackie down Main Street, he moved in cautiously, got as close as he dared to the hotel, and tied the horse to a wagon spoke off in the shadows. If the horse were seen, it was likely that word would be passed that Red had come to town.

He went directly to the T T Hotel, pausing outside the door and peering through into the hall where the office desk was. No one was there. This was not a busy time of the week. He could hear voices in the barroom, but even there only a few of the townsmen seemed half idling away the evening.

Red entered and mounted the stairs, going quickly. But he paused at the top of the stairs with head cocked toward the front room where he had first met Mr. Powell and Leon Lenard. A lot of noisy talking was going on in there. He tried hard and hopefully to recognize Bud Powell's voice, but couldn't be sure. However, he did feel sure that young Powell was there, for the room belonged to his father, and who else would be using it for a noisy time if not Bud and his friends?

Red went on back to the end of the hall and tapped on a door.

Wilkins opened it, looked through, exclaimed a little doubtfully, "Oh, you, h'm? Well, come in. We been talkin' about you. Ain't talked about much but you."

Red went in. Wilkins closed the door, put his back against it, not as if angry but as if a little distrustful and wanting some answers.

Rand, in bed, was leaning on an elbow. Red went up with hand out, and Rand hesitated a moment, then took the hand.

"You're lookin' better," said Red.

"A lot. I'll be up an' around soon. We wrote that letter to my dad, but ain't heard yet."

"How's that, you reckon?" Red asked.

"Maybe nobody's been to town for the mail," said Rand.

"Seems likely," said Wilkins. "What's more, Red, we been thinkin'—just thinkin', understand—that maybe old Lenard was tricky enough to fix it up for you to tell us a cock-an'-bull story about—"

"Now, Wilkie," Rand protested, "I've listened to you, but I can't think—"

"Go on," said Red, not angered. "Say your say, Wilkins."

"Well, ain't it just possible Lenard heard maybe me an' Rand was over here, so for to throw us off the track he had you—"

Red listened, amused but not happy. "Possible, shore. But you wouldn't think so if you knowed Leon Lenard like I do from the last few days. I don't really blame you boys for kickin' up some suspicions about the story I told you. 'F I'd been lyin', don't you think I'd have figgered out somethin' a lot more easier to believe than the yarn about Sheriff Martin pretendin' I escaped from him an' stole his horse? Gosh a'mighty!"

"I hope so," said Wilkins, his doubts weakening under the influence of Red's frank face and honest eyes.

"Mr. Powell, he sort o' made me join up in his fight or said he'd send me back to Tahzo. How comes he didn't grab you for his fight over yonder—like he done me?"

"I said flat I wouldn't go an' leave my pardner here alone. We ain't talked o' nothin' but you ever since you left, an' have been makin' guesses about who could've killed Bessie if not Lenard. Sometimes we just naturally had to wonder if it was facts what you said, so—"

"Well, sir," said Red, "I ain't goin' to get hot under the collar about that. In your boots I guessed I'd done the same—a little. But now you listen clost, Wilkins. I know now who done it, an'—"

"Who?" "Who!" Rand and Wilkins exclaimed together.

"I ain't speakin' his name—yet. I am tellin' you he's got friends. But I am goin' to make a stab to get my hands on him an' start for Tahzo. The sheriff from Tahzo is comin' along the road for to meet me at the county line. I got a nice big opinion of myself, but not enough of one to feel I wouldn't like me some help tonight from a feller of about your size. Will you chip in?"

"Who? Who is it, Red?" Rand gasped, almost getting out of the bed.

"Yes, who?" said Wilkins, leaning forward all tense.

"I told you I'm not sayin'—yet. But I know all the facts. Just you figger out about the last man in town you'd want to grab, then say you'll help me do it."

Rand swore in an agony of helplessness. "I'm weak as a cat an' couldn't set a horse, but just you drag me to 'im an' I'll—" Rand choked with his own anger and could not go on. He shook a fist helplessly, swore in gasps.

Wilkins looked hard at Red, waited, then said in a low voice:

"I don't care who he is—if he is the right one! That's all. I'll stick. Now say who."

"You an' me is goin' to have to do it all, alone. That means we got to be firm, work fast, an' ride hard. If they is any slip-up, why, you an' me will shore as hell be shot—if not hung. Are you willin' to set in?"

Wilkins put out his hand. Red took it. Their fingers closed firmly, and their eyes looked searchingly into each other's face.

"Now get your heads up here close together," said Red. "I'm goin' to talk fast an' not make much noise doin' it. Here goes. . . ."

Rand grew feverish, and his fingers squirmed together. Wilkins leaned forward with steady eyes, and the muscles of his face grew more and more tense, his look firmly resolute.

Red told his story, all of it: of what Leon Lenard had said, and of Diego; he told what Pincher had done, and of how Bud Powell had acted that day under Rimrock Roost.

". . . We don't know, actual, that he done it. But me, I'm stakin' my head bettin' it was him. If we guessed wrong, then the sheriff can turn him loose—an' you an' me, Wilkins, we will light out for the tallest timber in forty states!"

Wilkins spoke in a husky voice. "Me, I believe you, Red. I'll go an' stick. But just one thing— my pardner here. He'll be here when old Bill Powell comes bustin' in. Ever'body knows me an' Rand here are pardners. Old Bill may try to take it out on him when he hears that I—"

Red lifted a hand, silencingly. "I know how you feel about your pardner. An' Bill Powell, he is sure a bad one when he's roused. But he don't jump cripples." Red turned toward the bed. "All you got to say, Rand, is just one thing. You just say to Bill Powell, 'My name, it is Rand. Your son Bud, he killed my sister!' "

"I don't care what he does to me if I know you've got the damned—"

Wilkins stepped up close, forcibly took Rand's hand, said quietly, "Don't you fret none. Take it easy. He'll be got. I know how you feel. Me an' Red here, we'll do it. From what-all folks say, Bill Powell, he is a man!"

With gentle force he pushed Rand back on the bed, turned to Red:

"I'm ready for to start!"

"All right. But first, Wilkins, since you can move around without havin' folks notice you as they would me, go down an' get your hosses. I got mine staked out around the corner 'cross the street in the dark. We'll need two more. You can tie them you bring here in front of the hotel. Mine better not be seen. When you come back up here, bring along a couple o' ropes. I'll be settin' here till you come back. An' you'd better make sure, sort o' casual-like, that Bud is there in that front room."

"I'll hustle!" said Wilkins, strapping on his guns and taking up his hat. Then he went out.

"I ain't got words for to tell you, Red," said Rand, "how I feel that a stranger like you should be doin' all this for my folks!"

"Shucks! You an' Wilkins would do as much for me an' my folks. So we're even!"

CHAPTER XXI

RED TAKES CHARGE
OF BUD POWELL

Wilkins came back in little less than a half-hour. He opened the door quietly, not stepping in, but held up the ropes and said:

"Me, I'm ready. He's in there—like you thought."

Red went by him into the hall. Wilkins said briefly, "Now don't you fret none, pard. She'll be done, right! 'Bye!"

He closed the door and turned, silently offering to be guided by Red and follow him into whatever plan he thought best.

"If we got to work in smoke," Red told him, "then they'll be some smoke. But maybe not. Come along."

They went quietly down the hall and stopped with heads lowered to listen close up to the door of Bud Powell's room. There were cheerfully noisy voices inside and the chittering click of poker chips.

"Here goes!" said Red and pushed open the door. He stepped through with both guns leveled and a sound in his voice that gave more of a warning than the mere words:

284

"Hands up an' off them chairs! Rise up a-reachin'! Keep yore hands empty or yore coffins will be filled!"

Wilkins, with one gun drawn, tossed his coiled ropes to the floor and pulled the other gun. He crouched slightly, his mouth set at an ugly twist. He was ready and wanted to shoot.

Red, with a backward kick of jangling spurred heel, sent the door shut behind him as the six poker players, with much the same sort of grunts and exclamations they would have uttered if suddenly prodded in their bellies, flopped up their hands, with vague bubble of oaths and half-gasp of "Hold-up!"

"My God, he's come!" That was the squawk that came from Bud Powell as he rose right up out of his chair with hands up. Young Powell gave a backward start as if to run, run blindly anywhere, trying to hide.

"Out o' them chairs, I told you! An' don't speak again—nobody! She shore as hell is a hold-up—big 'un!"

At that the men who hadn't arisen promptly came to their feet with backward scrape of chairs. One good look and they knew that these two boys meant business, were set to shoot, especially Wilkins.

Red sized them up in a rapid glance. A flashy lot of gamblers and town sports, crooked and treacherous mess of snakes—cool enough, and not afraid to kill if the chances were on their side. Among them was that gambler Jack who had enticed Red into Bundy's saloon, and his head was still bandaged from the walloping Red's gun barrel had given him.

Red, more than once, had seen his father, the sheriff of Tulluco, put men in the air and take charge of them. Red knew all about how it ought to be done. The important thing was to work fast, not give men a chance to get over their surprise and pull themselves together enough to offer fight.

"All right. Now get over to the wall an' face it! Backs to me! Git!"

A few turned at once, eager to obey; but one or two hesitated, weighing chances. Wilkins's face was set to kill, his look was like a warning. They knew of Red and judged they hadn't misheard. Yet to sort of soothe their own sour pride they made their glances as threatening as they could but turned and moved stiff-legged to the wall, taking their place in the line-up.

"On yore toes!" said Red. "See how high up you can reach! Up! Up higher!"

They rose to their toes, straightened their arms, reaching. The sensation of perhaps being shot in the back for not doing as told made them fearful.

"Now you, Bud Powell," Red commanded, "take two steps backwards, right out here toward me. Come to it!"

Buddy, with legs trembling and arms held high, stepped back just about as if moving in a bad dream, doing something he didn't want to do but couldn't help.

"Now," Red told him, "you march over there to the *end* of the line an' put yore nose agin' the wall again. Hustle!"

Bud walked with shaky steps to the end of the line of men and again faced the wall, reaching high as if prompt willingness might somehow soften Red's feelings.

Red turned, put away a gun. He stooped, picked up first one and then the other rope, shaking each out of its coils with dexterous flips, and laying them on the floor behind the row of men.

He put away the other gun and said:

"Now, Wilkie, keep yore eye peeled. An' at the first flicker, shoot. You galoots at the wall there have had yore last warnin'. Any crooked move of any kind an' you'll be down in hell explaining to Mr. Devil how it happened. That goes!"

Red took up an end of rope and passed a running loop over the neck of the first man in line. Then he looped a half-hitch over the neck of the next one, and the next to him; and so on until he came to the man who stood beside young Powell, where Red fastened a slip knot. He tied the other rope to the end of the one he had been using and went back along the line, making each man in turn drop his hands behind him. Quickly every pair of wrists were bound. Then, with what was left of the rope, Red took a half-hitch about the leg of each man (excepting young Powell) and tied the last with a hard knot. He did it all with the dexterous quickness of a fellow who knew exactly what he wanted to do and exactly how to do it.

"Now me," he told them, "I'd like to stay an' see the show when you hombres start to wiggle loose and choke yoreselfs. You all got necks a rope was meant to fit! But I think me I'll have myself a good head start before you make folks understand what's happened. Come 'long, Bud. You're ridin' with us!"

As he spoke, Red drew the ivory-handled guns from Buddy's holsters and pitched them at the table.

Buddy wheeled in frantic terror, but with hands still up. There was confession even in his denial, for he exclaimed:

"I never put Pincher up to it! No, honest! Don't make me go—I'll do—anything!"

"Shut up yore bellerin'!" said Red and ran his hand inquiringly along Buddy's waist. He felt something lumpy inside the shirt and, reaching, pulled out a knife.

"Huh!" said Red, sending the blade point down into the floor, then with kick of foot against the handle snapped the point. "Why didn't you use your own knife that day!"

"What day?"

"The day you used Tom Terry's!"

Young Powell's voice left him with a groan. Though his face was well tanned it turned the color of a Negro's palm. He staggered back, gasping like a man that is all but drowned. His eyes looked glazed, like those of a hanged man. His hands were still in the air.

Red said, "Now any monkey business outa you—any a-tall!—and you'll be drug feet first on the end of a rope. That goes! We're off. Come along!" With that, he collared Buddy, saying, "Drop your hands!" and marched him across the room.

"On ahead, Wilkie. An' anybody we meet that says 'Boo!'—put him in the air, or drop 'im, whichever you want. An' you, Bud, trot. If you don't, I'll slam you over the head an' tote you on my shoulder!"

A moment after they had shut the door behind them a confusion of sound broke loose in the room where angry, frantic men, entangled in the ropes, stumbled and fell over one another, every man half choking and cracking the neck of another by the ropes which bound all together.

Wilkins, Red, and Buddy Powell clattered down the stairs. Men came out of the saloon inquiringly, their heads lifted, listening to the sounds above.

Red said loudly, pointing back: "They was

289

tryin' to hurt Buddy here. That's why he's so scairt. They need some help up there, maybe!" Significantly, "But if I was you fellers, I wouldn't be in no great shakes of a hurry to give it to 'em. Old Bill Powell, he's liable to hear of yore eagerness to help 'em! Come on, Buddy. You're safe enough now!"

Old Bill Powell's name carried a threat. The men out of the saloon figured that Red was a pretty trusted and well-liked fellow from the way Powell had approved of how he cleaned up at Bundy's, so they gaped overhead and weren't in any hurry to run up and help.

Young Powell was half dragged, half pushed out of the street door. He was lifted bodily into a saddle. "Fall off, an' you die right there! Damn your soul, you know I can shoot straight!" said Red, feeling a little truth and some fear would be good for Buddy.

Red turned to one of the other horses at the rack, took a rope from the saddle, cut it and hobbled Buddy's feet. Then Red quickly cut the cinch straps of the three saddled horses they were leaving behind.

Wilkins, already mounted, held the reins of the horse Buddy was on.

"Lead him round the corner there. That's where my horse is," said Red.

"Red," said Wilkins in quick apology, "I never before in my life wronged a feller more'n you in thinkin' maybe you wasn't on the square. I'd go with a man like you barefoot to hell!"

"Hell nothin'! We're goin' to Tahzo!"

Red bolted across the street to cut the cinch lace of the only saddled horse he hadn't already attended to. He mentally explained to himself:

"I'm doin' these fellers a mighty big favor, 'cause if they can't chase us they won't get shot!"

With the stirrup over the saddle and his head against the horse, Red was cutting the tough leather when he heard a shout, and shots came at him from the upstairs window of the hotel. Bullets splattered about his feet and sang high. The horse grunted and jumped, hit in the side.

Red felt a certain contempt. "You shoot like tinhorns!" he said. "Anybody more'n a table width away—you can't hit 'em!"

Drawing a gun, he stuck his elbow firmly against the point of his hip bone and fanned the hammer, throwing a fusillade of forty-fives at the window, smashing glass, and hoping that a head or two was knocked off. His blood was up. In his heart he knew he was carrying off Buddy Powell to be hanged not merely because he had murdered a girl, but because he had also tried to murder his father. That was something Bill Powell would never know, or believe if he did know. All of which made no difference to Red. Bill Powell had become his friend.

Red scampered around the corner to where

Wilkins waited anxiously, having heard the shots, and had his gun out, ready and eager.

"Just a little noise!" Red sang out, reassuringly.

Red untied Blackie, paused beside Powell's stirrup to say, "You stick close to me. Try to run away—that'll be all right! I can foller. But try to lag—an' I'll kill you! Let's make some dust!"

He hit the saddle, jerked the quirt that he never used off the horn and laid it over the rump of Powell's horse. "Come on, Wilkie!" he shouted.

They were off with much wild yelling and a few far shots following.

Buddy Powell rode as if the devil ran panting after him. He, half crazy with fear, seemed to have the panicky hope that he might outride them. But Blackie laid his head alongside the flank of Powell's horse and kept it there, running easily, even checked from gaining by Red's light touch on the reins from time to time. Wilkins came close behind.

The pound of the hoofs splashed dust and gravel. Red and Wilkins rode with ears cocked and heads turned, watching and listening for pursuers.

After a few minutes Red shouted, "Whoa-up!" but Powell's hobbled feet must have dug at the horse's sides. Red spurred alongside, reached over, snatching the reins, and began pulling down the horse. A hundred yards farther he brought it to a stop; then said:

"Since you ain't wearin' guns, I can't talk like I feel! But next time I say *whoa,* you'd better *whoa, pronto*! Now *whoa!*"

Still holding the reins of both horses, he dismounted, letting Blackie shake himself and breathe.

"Seem to be havin' ever'thing pretty much our own way, Wilkie!" said Red, looping the reins over his forearm and prodding the empty shells from the gun, reloading.

Wilkins, not a talkative fellow, said "Yeah" and got out of his saddle, too, but a minute later impatiently remounted and sat listening. Presently he said, "I think I hear 'em! By God, I do! They're comin'!"

"Here, take your reins again!" Red told Powell, handing them up. "But me, I'm goin' to loosen my rope, an' if you don't *whoa,* I'll lynch you right there in the saddle! That's them comin', all right. But they're away back!"

He hit the saddle and again lashed Powell's horse and off they went. But now cooler ideas had come to young Powell, and he drew a steady pull on the reins, as furtively as he could. Red spurred up neck and neck. He flogged Powell's hands and arms with the quirt, making him yelp.

"Ornery cuss!" Red reflected, but a moment later half grinned to think he was reproaching a man for not doing all he could to help get himself hanged.

Soon Red again sang out, "Whoa!" This time the horse was pulled down. "Don't you know enough," said Red, "not to slow down when you come to an upgrade? Or do you want to knock up this horse so yore friends'll catch us? If they do catch up with us, they'll find you dead. So just remember you'd better do all you can to help get away from 'em. Now get along at a walk!"

"They're comin'—not more'n a mile or less behind!" said Wilkins.

"Don't—don't kill me!" Powell gasped, screwing his head about. "I'll do—oh, do anything!"

"Yeah?" Red demanded. "Then tell me why you killed that girl."

"I—I—I didn't mean to! It was just—accident—happened—then—oh, please, *please* let me go!"

Red, who had listened to his father talking with prisoners, asked encouragingly, "Jus' an accident, h'm? The knife slipped 'r something, maybe?"

"Yes—yes—that's it. I was just pretending—her horse jumped—shied—" He was lying blindly.

"All right," Red told him. "Let's move a little faster. We'll talk some more soon!"

On they went, now fast, now slow, with ears cocked. Red was happy. He knew that hard-ridden horses could not overtake them. Besides, the pursuers would be strung out. He had no idea how many were coming, but he guessed that nearly everybody who could get a saddle and horse must have started. In a chase of this kind all the curious folks joined in. But young Powell's friends would be desperate. For one thing, they were losing the golden-egg goose. For another, they could not help being afraid that Bud Powell would tell everything he knew about the crimes and dishonesty that went on in Lelargo; and that, according to Diego's story, would be a lot.

They had reached a level piece of road and were galloping hard when suddenly Wilkins yelled. There was the crashing thud of a horse lunging into a headlong fall at full gallop. Red looked across his shoulder: Wilkins seemed to be splattered in the middle of the road some fifteen feet beyond where the horse was down.

"Whoa, damn you, whoa!" Red shouted, having instinctively pulled at the reins. But young Powell, with lash of reins and jab of spurs, rode for his life. He too had seen that Wilkins was down. This seemed his chance to get away—as good a chance as he was likely to have. He had no courage, but much fear.

Red swore and drove the spurs into Blackie, who pitched forward with startled bound on bound. Red, loosening the little rope strap at the horn, shook loose his rope. Rapidly he gathered it into coil and loop, made a far swing. Young Powell saw it coming and bent low, leaning down to one side, but the coil dropped over his bent head and jerked stiffly. Powell screeched, thinking death had him, and jerked hard at the reins. Both horses slowed down in stiff-legged jumps, and Red's tongue boiled.

"Come on back here!" Red shouted, holding the rope taut and turning Blackie. "An' don't take that rope off yore neck. You do, I'll kill you! If 'twasn't for wantin' to see you hung proper, I'd do it anyhow!"

Wilkins had got up out of the dust, but he tottered drunkenly. His horse was half up, scrambling and heaving. One leg was broken. The knee of the other was badly knocked. At breakneck speed an ironshod forefoot had turned on a stone that had fallen from the road's bank.

"Poor feller!" said Red. "Done for! Give him a bullet, Wilkie. Quick! Gosh, we've lost time. Then you climb up here behind me. An' they are comin'. Purty close now!"

Wilkins shot the horse, put a foot into the stirrup and scrambled up behind Red, who still kept his noose on Powell's neck. It was necessary to have it there now—there or on the horse— for with Blackie carrying double, Powell stood a chance of being able to outride them. Red was sincere in his intention to shoot before he would let Powell escape; but he did not want to shoot. He wanted to deliver Powell to the sheriff of Tahzo.

In a little while Red said to himself, "Gosh, we

ain't ever goin' to keep from bein' caught up with this way. A couple miles more an'—they must be six or seven of 'em comin' close!"

Red rode on his toes. He called back, "Keep a lookout behind, Wilkie. I got to watch this feller in front, close! An' hold tight. We're goin' to bounce along as best we can. Come to it, Blackie, old son."

Far-off shouts that sounded like yells of triumph reached them vaguely. Red understood. The pursuers had found the dead horse and guessed that somebody was riding double. From now on they would lash and spur the last bit of speed from their horses.

"Closer'n I thought for!" said Wilkins.

"Yeah, but if they get too close, I'm goin' to yank this feller right out of his saddle—him with feet hobbled, too!"

Red urged Blackie on. There was nothing else for it. They must push along as hard as they could. Luck was no longer making things easy. Again and again he had to put the spurs to Blackie. The good old horse was tiring.

Red was thinking that about the only thing left to do was to roll off somewhere, duck behind a rock, and give 'em hell. But that would be a losing fight. Then around a turn in the road they came to Crow's place. Close behind on the road was the *thumpety-thump-thump* of hard-ridden horses.

"This here house was sure built for us, an' me, I got a friend as lives in it!" said Red. With yell and tug of rope he made Powell turn from the road and head in toward Crow's roadhouse.

CHAPTER XXII

RED BREAKS THROUGH

Red drew rein with his horse's nose right up against the closed door of Crow's place.

"Pile off, Wilkie, an' hold this rope, but watch him careful!"

Wilkins slid off, took the rope, pulled in the slack and drew a gun.

Red dismounted and rattled the butt of his revolver on the door. The echoes rattled through the lonely old house. He tried the door. It was a heavy door, heavily bolted. He pounded again, kept on pounding.

From a narrow window overhead a man's harsh voice snarled:

"What d'ye want?"

"Quick, Crow! Powell's here—Buddy Powell! An' men are comin'! You can hear 'em!"

"Eh? What's that? What's up?" The man was trying to peer down in the starlit shadows.

"Are you comin' or not?" Red called.

"Yes, of course. Buddy Powell, ye say? Mr. Powell?"

"Speak up!" Red told Buddy.

"Y-yes!" said young Powell in a small voice, huskily.

"He's in a bad way," Red explained. "You'll be in a worse one if it's known you refused to let us in when—you hear 'em comin', don't you?"

"I'll come!" said Crow.

A moment later a woman's shrill fierce tone could be heard, protesting angrily. Men's voices rose against her. And from the other direction the clattering thump of hoofs drew nearer and nearer. Again Red beat on the door with his gun.

Crow's agitated voice called out, "I'm comin'!"

The bolts scraped, then the heavy door, sagging on its hinges, rasped the floor as it was tugged open. Crow had opened the door. Another man stood by him, holding a lamp.

Red, still holding to the reins, stepped inside. He gave a quick look about, pulled at the reins, clucked, and Blackie started to come into the room.

"Here! Ye can't bring—" Crow began.

Red's gun prodded his belly. "The hell I can't! Up to the wall! Bring him in, Wilkie. Duck low, Buddy—or you're not goin' to be wearin' your head much longer!"

Red marched in behind a leveled gun, leading his horse.

"My God!" a woman squawked from the narrow twisted stairway. Mrs. Crow, standing in the shadows, had recognized Red.

"Don't you drop that lamp!" Red said, pulling the other gun. "If you do I'll drop both you men!

Quick, Wilkie. Take the lamp an' set it down. Only make sure Buddy stays with us!"

"Sure," said Wilkins.

"Tie these fellows up. You fellows won't be hurt a-tall, maybe!" Red told them.

"My God!" said Mrs. Crow again, more quietly, more mystified, coming down a step or two lower, so that, in her long, not clean calico nightgown, with the lank hair hanging about her shoulders, she looked like the ghost of a witch.

Crow seemed a dried-up villainous old man, almost bald, with many teeth gone. He had pinched-in beady eyes and a nose something like the short sharp beak of a mud turtle.

The other man, from whom Wilkins had taken the lamp, putting it on the bar, looked something like Crow; which was not strange, as they were brothers.

As Wilkins got a rope about the hands of the Crow who had held the lamp, Red backed up and with many heaving shoves pushed at the door, getting it shut. Then he shot home the bolt.

"Now get him, quick!" Red urged, indicating the elder Crow, better known as Bill.

The clatter of horses was heard turning in from the road, and a moment later Red blew out the lamp and pushed the horses toward a sheltered corner of the room. Buddy was still on horseback, sitting helplessly with feet hobbled and his head cramped against the ceiling.

Men rode up, struck against the door, called loudly for Crow as if for someone they knew was their friend.

"What is it?" Red shouted.

"You hear fellers ride by?"—"Open up, Crow! Crow!"—"You hear—"

Crow, with hands and feet bound, bellowed: "They're in here!"

Crow had seen that Buddy Powell was a prisoner; saw, too, that Red had tricked him. Being a poor judge of character, it didn't occur to him that Red and Wilkins would risk making a fight even behind the heavy log walls of the house when so outnumbered.

Red shouted at him, "All right, Crow! You've had yore say. An' if yore house, it gets burned down, you're goin' to the devil, ready-roasted!"

Outside there was much calling and wild yelling. One man called to another, and shots were fired to attract those who had not thought to pause but galloped on past the house, not in the least expecting that the men who were carrying off Bud Powell would stop at Crow's.

Men beat on the door as if to break it in. Others called to Crow. Shots splattered through the windows.

"Get over behind the bar, Wilkie. No windows on that side!" said Red.

Mrs. Crow screamed, "Git my menfolks

upstairs! They'll be kilt here! I want 'em upstairs!"

"So you can untie 'em!" said Wilkins.

"She's all right," said Red. "An' they may be hurt. I'll get 'em up. They ain't heavy."

Somebody daringly put a revolver half through a broken window and fired twice. Wilkins shot, and the gun fell inside the window.

"Pretty work!" Red called and began blazing right and left, jumping from one window to another, wanting to make the men outside scatter and take cover.

A moment later he caught up one of the Crows and began dragging him. At the foot of the narrow steps the woman caught hold, helping. She was much stronger than she looked.

Red trusted her, but nevertheless was watchful.

It was very dark in this low attic room. He struck a match. Mrs. Crow, without a word, offered a piece of candle. They left one Crow on the floor, and she went down ahead of Red on the stairs to fetch the other.

The firing outside was rapid, and bullets *pinged* and struck; but the men who were shooting stayed well away from the house. Wilkins did not seem to care about making a big noise, and when he shot it was at something he could see.

The other Crow was taken upstairs. Red examined the lashings of both, tightening the knots. As he did so he noticed that Mrs. Crow stood well away from him, as if wanting to show that he had no reason to be suspicious that she might whang him over the head, unexpectedly.

He glanced up and she cried shrilly, "Don't make me go back down thar! Whar all that shootin' is! Don't make me! I'll be kilt!"

Red sensed that she was giving him a cue. "Yessir, you got to come along," he said. "I want some whisky an' things. You can find 'em in the dark. Get along there. Ahead of me!"

She went, pretending to cower, but at the foot of the stairs said in a savage whisper:

"I c'n shoot as well as any man! But if the menfolks knowed I helped you they'd kill me!"

Red grinned, patted her shoulder:

"Mother, I suspicioned you had some such worthwhile notions! Get your rifle an' I'll get mine. We'll give 'em hell with all the fixin's!"

An hour later, in the smoky darkness, Red prodded Wilkins and poked the whisky bottle out at him again:

"Mother's sure dug out the best for us!"

"I'd rather have water," said Wilkins, groping for the bottle. "But this takes out the smoke taste." He took a swallow and handed back the bottle. "An' we'd sure been in a pickle but for her, Red."

Wilkins turned to peer toward the dim frail-looking figure hunched down behind a keg. She had overturned the keg and rolled it to the end of the bar. Her eyes were quick, and she knew how to use a rifle. What was more, she seemed to like using it.

"Injuns when I was a girl!" she said laconically.

Men had got into the house, into the kitchen where Red, that morning he first came to Crow's house, had eaten breakfast.

They jerked open the door leading to the barroom and sent a sweeping shower of lead through; but a storm of shots poured at them, answering, and they were glad to get the door shut again and pile heavy things against it.

Mrs. Crow was using a thirty-eight-forty. It threw a slug like a man's thumb.

Red chuckled a little as he thought of what the fellows outside must think when they figured that only two fellows, he and Wilkins, were making the fight.

"Must reckon we got about three hands apiece!" he mused.

Red called, "How you makin' out, Bud?" He was answered with a whine and groan. "Yessir, that's plum' right, Bud. 'Tis gettin' sort o' monotonous. Them friends o' yourn are beginnin' to keep away from us an' wait for daylight!"

"Well, I guess it's jus' about all over with me," said Mrs. Crow wearily.

"What's the matter, Mother?" Red called anxiously. "You hit?"

"Naw, I ain't! But I never thought till too late f'r do any good that he'll tell 'im—my menfolks—an' they'll kill me!"

"Buddy here? He won't tell nothin'!" said Red. "Never! Not 'less it's to his friend the devil, who most likely already knows all about this little doin's!"

Somebody from outside began to pour a steady stream of bullets through a broken window just on the chance that they might hit.

"All right," said Red, with satisfaction. "They don't appear to know how close we are huggin' the floor. Buddy's got the safest corner. We have to take good care o' little Buddy—that's the way he's been raised. Only trouble is that, to shoot back, you've got to get out where you can be shot at. Be fine if we had some guns as shot around corners!"

Red rose up at the side of a window and after a moment's peering in the dim starlight let drive with his rifle. "Scairt him, anyhow!"

Shots blazed back at him. Red scrouged down where he could be comfortable and made comments:

"My dad, he allus warned me agin' keepin' bad company. An' just see what associatin' with Buddy has got us into, Wilkie. And we sure as hell ain't gettin' nowhere settin' here! I bet they've sent word back to town for more folks to come. That, I bet, is why they've slacked off.

Now they're just shootin' enough to keep us from sleepin' peaceful. Come daylight, we are goin' to be plum' outa luck!"

Wilkins grimly said nothing.

A few minutes later Red crept closer to him and said, "Listen. One of us—we'll draw straws—has got to make a break. Take Blackie, bust out o' that door, an' ride for the line. The sheriff's there—an' he'll come. He don't want to cross the line, but in a fix like this he'll come. We may not get through, but one of us has got to try. What you say?"

"How far?"

"'Bout five mile, I guess. No ride a-tall, Wilkie."

"You go."

"Let's draw straws."

"You go. They can't bust in here. Not that bunch out there. If more come—better men than these—and if you don't get through—well—well, hell, she'll shore be a good fight! An' I'll take some particklar pains to drop that—" He looked toward young Powell. "He don't get outa here alive unless the sheriff of Tahzo takes him!"

"All right, Wilkie. I'll make a try. So I hereby will, bequeath, donate, and give you my rifle with what cartridges I got left. The which ain't many."

Red crept over to the corner where Blackie was close up against the wall, and, as if he thought

307

bullets were flies, stood stamping and switching his tail.

"Son, you've had a nice long rest." Red tightened the cinches. "I love you, Blackie. Yessir. But you're goin' to call me a liar in about ten minutes!"

Red stood thoughtfully. "Wilkie, they think we're cornered an' goin' to be easy took, come daylight. What some folks think is bad for 'em. Ask Bud there! If you'll just open the door, I'll be on my way. Then slam 'er shut—only she don't slam easy."

Wilkins came to the door and eased back the bolt, which was a long piece of iron half as thick as a man's wrist.

Red squirmed up into the saddle, knocking his head against a beam and swearing. He lay over the saddle, the reins in one hand because he would have to make sure that Blackie turned the right way on the road. He held a gun in the other.

"All right, Wilkie. Now give me a good wide crack. 'Bye, Mother!"

" 'Bye an' God bless ye!" she whispered.

Wilkins gave a backward tug at the door, lifting as he pulled.

Red clucked. Blackie stepped forward with doubtful caution, looked through, hesitated, like any horse when about something unfamiliar.

Red's spurs flicked the horse's flanks gently. The horse stepped through, the spurs struck

hard, and the horse lunged ahead into a gallop.
Men saw what was coming. They bawled their
warning one to another. They blazed away with
hasty guns, rising up the better to shoot.

Red headed Blackie to the east, dropped the
knotted reins, slammed the spurs into the tender
flanks. With both guns out he rode straight for
the men that had risen up at the roadside's bank,
where they had taken shelter. Blackie went like a
devil on hoofs.

Bang—bang—bang! The shots came from
behind Red: that was Wilkins's rifle blazing
from the doorway where he stood, clearing the
way for Red.

Red, low on Blackie's neck, shot as well as he
could, again and again and again. Bullets were
singing in his ears. Men mixed curses with their
yells, for Red seemed charmed.

Of the men in the way ahead, one went down,
crumpling forward with the sudden drop of a man
who has had his feet pulled from under him.

Blackie's nose was forward and his ears were
back, neck straight as an arrow. He drove ahead
with springy bound on bound, and Red's guns
flamed.

A second man dropped knees down to steady
his aim, then fell backwards, dead. His rifle went
off in an aimless shot overhead.

Two seconds later, as Blackie took a high
leap, Red looked down into the face of Gambler

Jack. Jack fired upward as Red straightened in the saddle, rocking back against the cantle and snapping both guns. The hammer of one fell on an empty chamber. The other sent its bullet into the gambler's body. Red had a glimpse of the gambler's astonished face as he died on his feet.

Red's guns were empty, but the road was clear ahead. Fumblingly, he poked his guns at their holsters, then turned his head to see. Men were making for their horses.

"More that come after me, easier it'll be on Wilkie an' the old lady. Gosh! That ol' woman is all steel springs an' wildcat!"

Red lay along Blackie's neck and blessed him.

In a very little while Red looked up the bend of a steep hillside curve and saw horsemen coming toward him. "They can't have got ahead of me—can they? They's a dozen, an' comin'!"

He pulled Blackie into a slow walk, hastily loaded his guns.

When the horsemen were within far voice call, Red rose to his stirrups, cupped a hand to his mouth and yelled:

"Who the hell are you fellers?"

The answer came back clear and firm above the clatter of hoofs:

"Sheriff of Tahzo!"

"Then f'r God's sake hurry!" he yelled at them.

They came on, drawing rein about him, asking questions. But Red flung out his arm:

"On—hell-for-leather! To Crow's place! We had to make a stand, but I broke through to come an' tell you!"

They swept by him, riding hard, with Sheriff Martin's words echoing in his ears:

"We had scouts out. They heard shootin' an' come back. We're on our way!"

"So that's that an' a plenty!" said Red to Blackie. "I ain't goin' to break my neck tryin' to keep up with 'em. 'Cause you've got a fightin' heart ain't no reason for me bein' a fool! Besides, Blackie, they ain't goin' to be no more of a fight!"

Which was true. By the time Red got back to Crow's place the sheriff and his men were ready to leave. There had not been a half-dozen shots fired. The men about the house had broken and run, some taking off on foot.

Buddy Powell sat like a dead man. Never having had in him much of what makes a man, he was now like a bundle of rags, so weak with fear was he.

"All my ride wasted," said Red to Wilkins. "The sheriff had scouts out. Heard shootin'—so the sheriff was a-comin' anyhow. Whatever you look so glum about, Wilkie?"

"They killed 'er, Red!"

"Who killed her!"

"Them Crows. They squirmed loose up there. They had some guns up there, too. First thing

I knowed, I heard her yell—she'd looked up an' seen one of 'em sneakin' down. Gosh! She snapped a slug into him quicker'n I could wink, but the other'n reached down an' cussed her as he shot. I dropped him. Then me, here by myself, I was afraid a chance shot might get me, so I almost purt-near two or three times walked over to give it to Powell, point-blank. 'F I'd waited much longer, I would have. But I heard men comin'—the posse. Took me a look through the window an' saw they was chasin' off the Mekatone bunch.

"Do you an' me make her a little grave, Red? It ain't much, but it's all we can do, now."

CHAPTER XXIII

OLD BILL POWELL
RIDES INTO TAHZO

During the next two days the town of Tahzo swarmed with men, armed men that came riding in down from the hills and off the plains. They filled the streets, packed the saloons, slept on floors and in chairs.

Old Joe Richards, the biggest cowman of Tahzo, came with twenty men at his back. He squatted down in the hotel right across from Sheriff Martin's office. Justice would be done in a just way or Joe Richards and his men meant to fight.

The town hummed with low voices, and hard-eyed men stood about, waiting. Nothing had ever stirred the county half so much. Night and day men sat before the open doors of the sheriff's back office where Bud Powell lay on a cot. He could not have moved his little finger without being seen. All day long and half the night men crowded up to have a staring look at him and to mutter curses.

Somehow, there was no talk of lynching. Men seemed to understand and to respect the grim sheriff's stand for a trial. They felt he had earned the right to have it his own way.

Everything was known. The sheriff had told it all: of how and why he had killed his own deputy and sent Red Clark a fugitive into Lelargo.

Nearly everybody had a dull, sickening feeling somewhere inside of him at learning that Tom Terry had been hanged all in too much of a hurry, being no more guilty than any of them. It appeared as though everybody now remembered that Tom Terry was a good-natured, hard-working boy, full of fun—just the sort they might have known couldn't have done a thing like that.

Tom's mother had been brought to town. Men pulled off their hats and stood grim-faced and helpless when she went by with her head down and a handkerchief held against her face. She leaned on the arm of the tall sheriff, who limped along, taking her over to a friend's house where she was to stay until after the trial.

Red and Wilkins were most uncomfortably stared at and talked to; but they had to stay around for the trial. The weak Buddy fluctuated between confession and denial, now saying one thing, now another. Red was one of those to whom he had, even if a little obliquely, calling it an accident, admitted the murder.

Blackie was now Red's horse. The sheriff had given it to him. Old Joe Richards, from whose herd Blackie came, said he would give the sheriff another and better one.

"Oh, no, you won't!" said Red, half grinning but with an earnest tone. " 'Nother 'n maybe—but you ain't got a better 'n!"

Wild rumors fled from across Lelargo way and disturbed Tahzo. It was said that old Bill Powell had sworn no son of his would ever hang. If true, that meant trouble, for Bill Powell was a man of his word. Men's tongues waggled as if both ends were loose. They were sure old Bill would come and maybe try to rip Tahzo clear to pieces. Hence the armed men.

And late one afternoon Bill Powell did ride in. He came alone, his right arm in a sling. He rode a powerful broad-breasted bay and cantered up the street without a glance to the right or left.

He swung off his horse before the front of the sheriff's long low 'dobe office. He dropped the reins as if flinging them away. He walked in with head up and hawk eyes glaring.

Red was there, but if Powell saw him he carefully pretended not to. He said in a low firm voice to no one in particular:

"I want to see the sheriff."

He pushed up his hat, passed his hand along his forehead, and looked about as if for a chair. Two or three men arose quickly. Powell sat down. He looked straight at nothing while men hurriedly left the room, asking here and there for the sheriff, passing word.

The men about Powell talked in hushed whispers or were mostly silent, eyeing him a little furtively and not without sympathy. He was known as a fighter and he looked it.

In the next room, under heavy guard, his wretched son sat trembling, half hopeful.

The sheriff came, limping hurriedly, and paused inside the door.

"You want to see me, Powell?"

Bill Powell stood up; with head up and a hard glance he said:

"Valdez. I want to talk to him."

The sheriff hesitated, then, turning, said:

"Some of you boys go 'cross the street an' fetch Valdez. He's in Mr. Richards' room."

Men went out, pushing through the crowd that had gathered at the doorway.

Powell threw back his shoulders and, looking straight and hard at Sheriff Martin, said:

"Martin, my paymaster was killed the night of the fourteenth, last. If Valdez done it, then don't that explain why maybe he come runnin' to you an' lied?"

The sheriff said, "Before God, Mr. Powell, Valdez that night was sleepin' in my own bed, with me 'longside of him. Nobody knowed he was in my house but my wife."

Powell set his teeth. The thick jaws bulged. He said nothing. He put up his hand to his hat, tugging at the brim, pulling it a little lower, as if to hide his face from the eyes of men. Then he hooked his thumb in his belt and stood waiting, motionless, as if alone.

Valdez came. He was a young Mexican with bright, frightened eyes. He held his hat before him in both hands and nervously fingered the brim. He came up close to Powell but stood in the timid attitude of one ready to back off.

Powell glared and questioned him sharply. Valdez answered in a low voice, his lips trembled, and he gave the sheriff anxious glances as if wanting to be sure the sheriff approved.

The sheriff said, "The truth, Valdez. Not one word more or less. And all the truth!"

"The truth, *señor*! Before God!"

Men all about the room watched and listened, tensely, almost holding their breath. The slightest scrape of heel or spur was noticeable. It was so quiet that the stamp of horses and the jingle of bridles outside were heard distinctly.

"That's all," said Powell. With flip of hand he waved Valdez away. No man knew what Powell thought. His face was hard-set, and his jaws stood out under the clamp of teeth. "Now I'd like a word or two with my son."

"Right back here," said the sheriff. He turned, limping ahead, leading the way.

Men stirred, clearing their throats, taking slow breaths. They uncertainly looked from one to another and edged along after the sheriff and

Powell, crowding right up close to the door of the small back room.

The sheriff said, "Buddy, yore father's come," then stepped aside, making way for Powell to come and stand close up before his son.

Buddy arose, giving a timid upward glance at his father. His shoulders were hunched as if afraid of a whip's blow on them. His face was distorted with mingling of fear and hope. Always before, his father had managed somehow to get him off, no matter what he had done.

Powell stopped short, with head up. His eyes were hard and straight. He seemed to start a little, as if amazed that this poor weak, trembling wretch before him could be his son. Buddy's lips twitched with a trembling whine as he put out a hand. Powell drew back one step from the half-lifted hand. He said, in a low voice, but every man heard his words:

"No, boy, nobody's ever goin' to hang you— not while I live! But the truth—by God, I'll tear it out of you! Did you do it? Answer me!"

No man breathed or stirred in that ten seconds' pause as Buddy, his face all awry with fear, looked up in an unwilling confession. It was just as though he could not lie under the blazing fierceness of old Powell's eyes. So he nodded a little and haltingly began an explanation:

"I never meant—meant to—but—"

Powell's left hand flickered like a passing

shadow. His gun jumped forward, and the roar of it set startled men back on their heels. The boy half turned in a sidling stagger and dropped, shot through the heart.

Powell looked down for a long moment. Then he thrust his gun with a steady hand into its holster. He turned on his heel, paused, swept the faces of the men before him with a straight glance.

In silence they gave way, respectfully, falling back, making room. No man spoke. Powell passed by them without a word and went on through the outer office, where the parted crowd stood like a guard of veterans that salute in motionless silence.

He went with firm stride through the outer door and into the street. Men all about stood silently, staring as if awed and respectful. He took the reins of his horse, lifted them over the horse's head, reached his left hand to the horn and fitted his foot to the stirrup, then swung up. He pulled his horse about, turned toward Lelargo and rode off, a lonely figure vanishing into the twilight.

Center Point Large Print
600 Brooks Road / PO Box 1
Thorndike, ME 04986-0001 USA

(207) 568-3717

US & Canada:
1 800 929-9108
www.centerpointlargeprint.com